THE PA

KYLE KEYES

PRELUDE

She wanted to take the easy way out at first. She went to see a divorce lawyer whose hollow blue eyes came to life at the name, Hollister. The wavy haired attorney was the junior partner of Dawson, Dunn and Pierce, a highly touted New Jersey law firm. He scrutinized case related facts, heard probable causes and told Helena to forget it. Tapping a cardboard folder that contained her background data while staring at her pointy sweater, he said, "In a blood and guts court battle, I'm afraid your husband's boyish flush will beat your one pair."

She left the Camden City law office on angry heels, and jaywalking through car horns at Broad and Federal, the second Mrs. Rodney Hollister plotted an alternate course to grab the family fortune. The chaotic Labor Day adventure would lead to a Hobbs Creek homicide, destined to go unsolved from 1958 until early in the cyberspace age, when Helena Hollister surfaced in Right Bank, Paris as Anna Ward.

KYLE KEYES

THE PANDARUS FILE

Plots and characters that form this storyline are fictional, as is the weather. Public Domain and fringe area details are true. All storyline names are fictional, and any resemblance to persons living or dead is purely coincidental.

Product name usage is not an endorsement by author, publisher or printing house.

There is no Lower Elk County or Hobbs Creek Township in New Jersey, nor a federal T.A.G.

Data for The Jersey Devil comes from childhood memories of Halloween hear-say.

KYLE KEYES

THE PANDARUS FILE

Dedicated To Tommy

KYLE KEYES

CHAPTER 1

Dateline: Post September 11, 2001

Jeeter Potts shot up from his computer. He rounded the noisy dispatch desk and bumped into a slow-footed patrolman. Potts mumbled an apology and burst through an inner door marked HOBBS CREEK POLICE CHIEF - ADAM QUAYLE.

"Sir!" cried Potts.

George Jeeter Potts was now seventy and working hard to be the world's oldest jitterbug. He had Adam Quayle's vote to be sure. Potts' career as station clerk spanned five decades. He was on his third wife and was pop pop to a dozen rug rats. He wore earphones for pocket music. He drove a gas thirsty antique tag from 1958.

Chief," he said again somewhat softer.

Adam Quayle was on the phone - two phones to be exact. He stood by a picture window that over looked a parking lot of black and whites. As he spoke into his cell phone, he held the desk phone at cord's length. He used a free elbow to brush out a pesky shirt wrinkle. He used a knee bump to straighten the swivel chair inherited from former police chief, William Bo Brennan. Eventually, Quayle acknowledged Potts.

"Yes, Jeeter?"

"Chief."

"What is it, Jeeter?"

"Sir . . .Helena Hollister just surfaced."

Adam Quayle closed the cell phone cover. Slowly, ever so gently, he slid the desk receiver onto the black cradle as a distant voice talked on. His troubled green eyes scanned the incoming facts sheet. He ran a wrinkled hand over his shiny head. Then he let out a low whistle and whispered, "Holy shit."

"That's almost what I said," replied the desk clerk, "What now, Sir?"

"Do we still have files on this case, Jeeter?" asked Quayle.

Several long minutes later, the gimpy station clerk dropped a manila folder onto Adam Quayle's desk. Said Jeeter Potts, "Nothing in the computer, but I dug this up in the archives."

"Why is it filed under "P?" asked Quayle flipping through yellowed pages.

"P is for Pandarus, Sir."

"That's right," said Quayle, "I remember now. Pandarus was the nickname that Lieutenant Thomas assigned to Rodney Hollister . . .Jeeter. have you told anyone else that Mrs. Hollister turned up?"

"No sir."

"Good. Don't. Have somebody bring my car around back. And Jeeter, cancel my appointment with the mayor."

*   *   *   *   *

Adam Quayle strapped on a bulky seat belt and switched on the bubblegum light to get onto Main Street. He drove southeast out of Hobbs Creek until the cedar swamp smell gave way to salt air. He sped past some new high rises and parked under an awning that read: Shady Rest Nursing Home. A desk clerk looked up saying, "Can I help you, Officer?"

"I'm here to see William Brennan," said Adam Quayle.

"Do you need an attendant?" asked the white clad woman.

"Has he been moved?" asked Adam Quayle

"No sir."

"In that case I know the way," said Adam Quayle clutching the facts sheet.

Former Hobbs Creek Police Chief, William Bo Brennan was in the last unit of the West Wing. There were two beds in the room, two TV's, and one small bath. The window curtains were ripped. The olive green carpet smelled slightly like urine. Brennan shared the cubbyhole with an ex fireman named Felix, with no last name. Felix probably had a last name, but couldn't remember it.

"Quayle!" boomed Brennan who had lost most of his great strength to mother time, but little of his resonant voice, "Will you tell this ninny he has to keep his pieces on color!"

The two roommates studied a game board on a coaster table stained with coffee and forbidden cigar ash. Each man would make a move, then spin the red and black checkerboard around to study the opposing player's view point.

"I can see that this is serious stuff," said Adam Quayle.

"We are playing for the championship of the world and every other place," said Bo Brennan.

"He cheats," said Felix shaking hands with Adam Quayle.

"Felix, I do not cheat! " cried Bo Brennan.

"Do to."

"Do not! "

Adam Quayle dropped the facts' sheet onto the game board and stepped back to give Brennan more reading light. The former Hobbs Creek police chief wiped off his bifocals. He grabbed a magnifying glass from a nearby drawer. He stopped scanning at the name Helena Hollister and bellowed, "Holy Smoke! "

"That's almost what I said," replied Adam Quayle.

A stocky female nurse appeared in the doorway. She wore a tight hair bun and carried a long needle. She looked past the visitor and locked eyes with Bo Brennan who gave her his best bobcat growl. The nurse ran off, and Brennan returned to the facts' sheet. He wheezed from disbelief and too many cigars. He packed up the checkers and said, "You win, Felix.. Now, I need to go with this gentleman. We'll be in the dining room. If Maggie comes back with the doctor and that needle, have her give the doctor the shot. ..maybe in a dark part of his anatomy."

Brennan paused in the doorway to ask, "You want anything from the vending machine?"

"A chocolate bar would be nice," beamed Felix.

"You got it," said Bo Brennan.

The cafeteria, kitchen and sitting lounge were grouped together just off the Shady Rest main lobby. There was a library, workout room and hair salon scattered throughout the four wings. The nursing home held the customary three levels of care. Thus, doors were kept locked to prevent certain patients from wandering into the street. Said Brennan to the waiter, "Jason, bring us the dinner menu and put my friend's order on my tab. And Jason, don't give us this morning's coffee."

"You have a new roommate," said Quayle to Brennan, "I assume they moved Emmet up a level?

County detective, Lieutenant Emmet Walker Thomas died September 10, 2001 - one day before Nine Eleven. Thomas was a black man who spent most of his life in the back of the bus. They buried him at County Memorial in the back of the cemetery. He had no living relatives. His service medals went in the grave with the body. Off in the distance, someone fired a rifle. It wasn't the shot heard 'round the world.

"Sorry, we just don't stay in touch do we," said Adam Quayle watching some pond ducks play follow the leader outside the table window, "Shame, Emmet would have liked to been here for this."

"So, how did the French discover that Anna Ward was also Helena Hollister?" asked Bo Brennan tapping the facts sheet, now soiled with spilled cream and spaghetti sauce.

"Fate," replied Adam Quayle, "Details are still coming in, but here's the update version I got from the county, earlier. Two cars collided on a narrow road in Right Bank. Witnesses said a Maserati Gran Turismo swerved to miss the crash and plunged through a guard rail."

The speeding red coupe rolled down a rocky embankment, and somehow landed right side up in waist high water. Rescuers pulled the female driver out through the passenger window. She was in a coma. Her handbag went missing. But, local authorities traced her watch back to a shop on Rue de la Paix. The jeweler came up with the name, Anna Ward. And that name jibed with the license plate trace.

Concluded Adam Quayle, "Now lady luck steps in. Interpol is based right there in Lyon. The hospital submitted her prints to the Judicial Police as a Jane Doe. And presto. Back comes the name, Helena Hollister. Residence: Delaware Township, N.J. USA."

"Paris," muttered Bo Brennan, "Son of a bitch. She went to Paris. No wonder we couldn't find a body in those woods. So what now? "

"Commercial break," joked Adam Quayle.

Six waiters encircled a nearby table and broke into an off-key version of happy birthday. The two lawmen waited for the noise to subside. Then, Adam Quayle donned his rigid trooper hat and slid into his dress blue jacket. He crossed two fingers for luck and said, "The County has already contacted Washington. Now we wait and hope for the International Warrant we need to extradite."

*　　*　　*　　*　　*

Hours later, Special Agent Jeremy Wade stood before a hospital receptionist in the Right Bank section of Paris, France.

"Room number for Mademoiselle Helena Anna Hollister?" he asked in broken French.

"I'm from Cherry Hill New Jersey," grinned the desk girl.

"Oh, I have a distant cousin in Maple Shade," said rookie Jeremy Wade smiling back.

The perky receptionist scanned through her computer listings. All smiles faded as she said, "I'm sorry, sir. Helena Hollister died an hour ago."

CHAPTER 2

August 29, 1958:

"Helena, I'm going to kill you," muttered Rodney groping behind bucket seats for a long leather case that was not there, "And this time I mean it!"

They sat sweltering in the car chain that connects the city to the seashore every summer week end. It was Friday afternoon. Temperatures hovered in the nineties. The charred odor of a recent forest fire filtered through the open windows of their Venetian Red Corvette. A jumpy car horn laced the lazy after noon air. Rodney snapped off the fading rock music coming out of Philly. He glared at his girlish wife dozing against the passenger door and cried, "Tell me you didn't forget my shooting gear. Please tell me that."

No answer came.

He U-turned against an oncoming semi, and screeched to a stop in the stony entrance of a distant farmhouse. The truck's foghorn cursed through a cloud of road dust. Rodney killed the engine and dug through the luggage. His pocky face began to purple as he sputtered, "Son of a bitch, you really did. You forgot to pack the black carrying case. The one with the rawhide strings!"

Still no answer.

Rodney tugged at his knotty red hair. Helena was either asleep, or playing possum. Rodney beat the steering wheel with bony fists. His beady eyes flashed. He failed to clear a puddle that waited outside the car door, causing his black engineer boots to splash mud on a nearby mailbox. He stormed around the Corvette and nearly got clipped by a flatbed hauling sod. He paused at various intervals to pound on the car top and scream, "I notice you didn't forget the suntan lotion. What the hell do you think we are going to the cabin for? A freaking suntan. This is a bow shooting trip. You want a suntan? You get a freaking suntan. I want to shoot bow!"

This was the last straw to a week of drawing the short straw. Rodney's stocks were down in a market recovering from the flu. His takeover bid for a chain of hotdog stands went on hold - his lawyers blamed The Federal Trade Commission. An achy left foot meant his ingrown toenail was bleeding through his sock. Also, thanks to a nudge from his best friend Charlie, Rodney lost a track bet on a nag named Wind Song, who should have been named Winded. Rodney would even the score with Charlie on that one, the next time a waiter paused with the dinner tab.

A distant five-0-clock whistle blew. Rodney turned on the ignition to check the car clock. He cursed. It was too late to turn back. He kicked the front tires, one at a time. He threw a rock at a Burma Shave billboard. The rock missed the small signpost and toppled a peach basket perched on a roadside table. Yelled a farmer from under the lean-to, "I got a good mind to call the cops. Who the hell do you think you are, Rodney R Hollister or somebody!"

Rodney was thee Rodney R Hollister, son of Everett G Hollister who made a World War I fortune by trading stocks and bonds. The elder Hollister also dabbled in real estate, and bartered in black market whiskey. The latter was a risky but lucrative business that Everett alibied away on the old saw, *I want my boy to have the best*. Thus, Rodney reached puberty with few real credits. The bony lad never made a bed, mowed a lawn, or wore a hand-me-down. He swam in a chaperoned lake, and was chauffeured to parochial school by a silver-haired servant named Washington Jefferson, who answered to "Whitey."

Rodney's first car was a glossy black coupe with a tar pitch roof and mechanical brakes. The clutch plate would swell on rainy days, which made the car hard to shift and led to numerous traffic tickets. Everett bought Rodney the car for a graduation present on the road to college. Everett believed Rodney was a gifted child who would probably become a brain surgeon of sorts. Everett told everyone that when a student takes six years to finish high school, it indicates the student is on a higher wave length than other students.

Whatever the case, Rodney never fell victim to hazing, but the car did. It eventually ran out of oil and Everett had to replace the engine.

Those were the daydream years. Rodney left doors open and lights on. He never thought to bring in mail or wind the clock. Once, he took a spin down town for cigarettes while the bathtub filled.

The loose times would end. At thirty-nine, Rodney inherited the Hollister homestead. The three story dwelling was a Victorian classic tucked between two other mansions in wooded Delaware Township, now called Cherry Hill. The house and endless assets went to Rodney when Everett suffered a fatal coronary After which, change was in the air. The now frugal Rodney stopped the buying sprees, and fired the live-in servants. He filled in the backyard pool, and hocked a tarnished ring left behind by a mother he almost remembered. On Rodney's first day in school, she ran off with a piano player from Pittsburgh.

"This is just like you," moaned a winded Rodney collapsing back behind the wheel, "I had everything packed and set out in the foyer. My shooting gear was right on top. All you had to do was drag the shit to the car. And don't give me that crap about the garage being too far from the house. Like the time you were supposed to bring my bag down to the alleys. We lost the playoffs because I had to use a house ball, and the freaking thing wouldn't stay on my thumb. My foot still hurts."

Earlier, the stockholders meeting ran past lunch. Center city began to empty for the long Labor Day weekend. Rodney wanted to beat the Jersey rush over the bridge. He phoned Helena to pack the plastic sports car and pick him up at their Walnut Street office. They could then go straight to the cabin they rented in Lake Powhatan, a resort area in Lower Elk County. The drive was a good two hour ride, even in the off-season.

"I'd like to be there before dark, but I better go talk to this farmer about the peach basket. I think the asshole just took my tag number," said Rodney wiping sweat beads from his high forehead. He tore loose a thin plaid tie from his Adam's apple. He tugged at the suit trousers matted to thick, curly leg hair. His shorts were packed, and he ached for a smoke. He used the horn and a middle finger to cross traffic. He braked in front of the farmer's produce stand and jumped out, ready for battle.

*　　*　　*　　*　　*

On the road again, tar joints thumped beneath droning tires. A loose car jack rattled somewhere in the rear. Helena Hollister squeezed open a pair of empty green eyes, and pushed her long legs against the firewall. She yawned and rooted for sunglasses kept in a large white handbag. Then she asked, "Why do we have a basket of peaches in the car?"

"Never mind," snapped Rodney, "And now that you are awake, what about the paper? I hope you stopped the paper. I do not want papers piling up in the driveway. Thats a real green light for burglars."

"Rodney! There are peaches rolling all over the car!"

"And what about the mail, Helena? I hope you called the post office. And Bertha? I hope you gave Bertha the spare key so she can get in to clean."

"I remembered your prune juice," said Helena dryly.

"Oh funny funny," replied Rodney, "And if you must know, the bastard coerced me into the peaches.

When he found out I was the real deal, he wanted to sue. Can you imagine? A lawsuit over a freaking basket of peaches. The bastard. People today will do anything for money."

Helena stifled a cough and turned on the radio. She used the visor mirror to replenish her faded lipstick. She pulled a thin comb through an ocean of red hair, and stared at the scorched oaks and shrubby pines that whizzed past the window. Hunger sat in as she said, "Keep your eye open for that burger joint. And don't fret about Bertha getting in. I forgot to lock the front door."

Traffic stopped abruptly. Rodney braked just shy of ramming a fishing boat towed by a muddy pickup. He stuck his pointy chin to the windshield, and complained to the prop blade that now hovered over the Corvette's sweeping low hood. "Can you believe this, Mr Boat Motor Prop? Can you believe this woman? She's screwed up my whole vacation and all she can do is smart mouth. Like the time I broke my arm on the ice, and all she could talk about was fingernail polish."

"Actually, I was talking about toe nail polish," said Helena tossing a rotted peach out the window, "I had a busted toe nail and it hurt like a bastard and why are you talking to a boat motor?"

"Because I'm not talking to you," said Rodney who always groaned whenever Helena used what she called "descriptive" words. In Rodney's cuff- link world of tax loopholes and dark business deals, men cursed, not women. Although, Rodney did peek once at the wall comments inside the ladies' room, and that was somewhat an eye opener. He threaded a twisted arm between the bucket seats to recheck the storage area. The car lurched and he jumped on the brake while saying, "Just for the record, I could have bled to death out on that sidewalk."

"And just for police files," replied Helena, "You just clobbered that boat."

"I didn't hit the damn boat," whined Rodney trying to feel between a large suitcase and a box of soda crackers, "I almost hit the boat and I hate buying burgers at tourist traps. They really take the wind out of your wallet."

"Have it your way," belched Helena tossing another peach out the window, "But there's a fresh crack in the front glass, and whoever sold you these peaches must have seen you coming."

Rodney stared at the silver propeller blade that kissed the windshield. He backed up and tapped the bumper to his rear. Snorted Rodney, "This windshield crack is not fresh. This crack is from that parking lot fight with the beer bottles. Which, I might add was initiated by your smart mouth. Do you have to be such a wise ass because you were born in a crap house?"

She was born Helen Ann Wenchel on January 12, 1936 in N. Y. City. She blossomed in the shadows of tar and cement, and slept amid sirens and sewer stink on a street where people still live in fear, and time staggers on. She wore mama-made dresses to school, and ate eggs chopped through shredded wheat for protein. Sometimes, Christmas would show up without a tree, and she learned early on that Mother Goose was just a nursery rhyme.

Her father worked as a rigger down at the docks. When he worked. In lean times, he hustled amateur pool sharks and ran numbers for two-bit hoods. He loved his booze and couldn't drink without getting rowdy. He enjoyed smacking around women, and took on male foes with a hunting knife concealed inside a boot. Some said he could out drink and out fight any man in Brooklyn. One wintry night, Helen watched him go down in a rain of blood one block from their door stoop. It was her thirteenth birthday, and her first venture on high heels. He died before she could wobble over the first snow bank.

Fittingly, they buried him amid a small circle of gin mill cronies, and a prohibition buddy called Snake Eyes, who recounted tail gunner days on a beer wagon. Leaving the weedy cemetery, her mother cried a lot about the high cost of coffins, and Helen commented that one of the pallbearers had a really cute ass.

"It was the blue suitcase," coughed Rodney scanning the road ahead for a food stand, "I had my shooting gear packed out on the blue suitcase. And do you have to smoke that thing right under my nose. You know I'm trying to quit."

At nineteen, Helen packed a suitcase and thumbed a ride to Manhattan. She upgraded her name to Helena and found work in a Times Square night club. Tips were good and she got to listen to songs that would someday be called Do Wop. She met Rodney there. It was New Years. He was freshly divorced and in town to watch the big ball fall. It started by the book. She gave him her best smile, and he left a twenty under his whiskey glass. The next week he showed up in a high school sweater. The third time without the lady friend. After that it was every Friday night. Helena laughed at his empty jokes. She fingered his neck hairs with each trip behind his chair. And while other girls giggled and dubbed him the man with the thin brain and fat wallet, Helena said yes to a wedding ring. They honey mooned in Paris, and then returned to Delaware Township where she soon learned it was Everett and not Rodney, who held the purse strings to the Hollister fortune.

"Could we maybe hurry it up a bit?" asked Helena, "I have to take a piss."

Rodney pulled into the passing lane. The car boasted a four-speed transmission and a new fuel injection system called Ramjet. It was armed with a 283 horsepower engine that could do zero-to-sixty in 6 seconds. It was the elder Hollister's final play toy. He bought the car to stay in the game. Also, he thought the low slung roadrunner matched Helena's hair, and a pair of spiked heels that Rodney scorned as cheap looking. Everett Hollister said the shoes set up Helena's calves nicely, and that Rodney should not be such a bluenose.

"Father was indeed a pervert," said Rodney swerving to miss a gravel truck running a stop sign. A second truck forced the Corvette off the road, and Rodney almost leveled the roadside stand he sought. Still cursing, he returned with two skimpy cheese burgers and one bottle of soda. He tripped on a car rut and stumbled over a weathered railroad tie that defined the parking spot. He managed to grab the paper food bag before it hit the mud. "Sometimes Helena, I think you forget things on purpose."

"I wanted black cherry," said Helena now back from an outdoor privy, holding her nose.

"They only had orange and I think you enjoy picking fights," grumbled Rodney woofing down the meat cake as he talked. "Like last week when you backed over my bicycle. It wasn't even in the driveway for cris'sake. It was on the grass. And then you tried to feed Horace to Charlie's dog."

"I was not trying to feed your precious turtle to Charlie's dog," said Helena prying off the bottle cap with her teeth, "I just wanted the mutt to have something to sniff besides my crotch. And bicycles are for kids. If you want to exercise, you should jog. Or lift weights. Dumbbells maybe. Dumbbells would be a nice touch."

"Oh funny funny," said Rodney wiping off the glass lip to finish the soft drink, "You know I can't lift weights. They throw my back out. And I hate jogging. And now that I'm thinking about it, I had my quiver tied to the handle of the blue suitcase. And I had the bow bag tied to the quiver. Which means you actually had to untie all those knots to get the blue suitcase into the car without the shooting gear. Which means this whole oversight business was no accident, Helena. You pulled this shit on purpose!"

Rodney threw the bottle to the wind and glared at his wife, who studied a fire tower off in some distant trees. He swung into an Esso gas station and almost hit the pump. He shook a fist at Helena and cried, "I know what you are up to. This is your sneaky way to drag me to the beach. Well, it's not going to work. I'm not lying around in the sun until I look like a piece of bacon!"

Rodney stormed off to find an attendant.

Helena ran for a nearby phone.

"Your husband has quite a temper," said a distant male voice.

"He's going back tomorrow for the bow," said Helena.   "

What do I do?" asked the male voice.

"Nothing," snapped Helena, "You do nothing. I'll arrange everything from this end."

"You are the boss," said the male voice.

Helena cracked open the folding booth door and flicked her cigarette toward a rusty metal drum. She peered inside the open bay to watch Rodney coax a pair of greasy overalls from under a crippled station wagon. Quickly, she whispered into the silver handset,

"The pea brain is coming back. I have to go. But you are right. Rodney does have an ugly temper. And we are going to use that temper to hang him."

CHAPTER 3

Darkness fell as the red Corvette rolled under the swinging entrance sign to Lake Powhatan. Two wrought iron gates that sealed off the park were rusted open. A weathered pole marker that read *KEEP OUT* shadowed a third sign that warned trespassers of heavy fines. Weeds flourished everywhere.

Today, the gates are oiled and shiny. Green hedges border a slick macadam entry that leads to a busy guardhouse, awash in flood lights. Resident cars pass through, while visitors are questioned. In 1958, the park had no street lights or sidewalks. Service arteries were dirt roads that often disappeared in heavy rain, and nobody bothered much with chuckholes. Rodney flicked on high beams to weave between log cabins that circled Lake Powhatan like a disorientated wagon train. Mud cakes smacked the car's bottom. A sudden splash caught the windshield.

"I have to take a piss," said Helena.

"You just took a piss," said Rodney.

"Well, I have to piss again," said Helena.

The cabins were mostly one story. Porch in front. Shed outback. Single wall construction. No heat or air.

Some rented, but most served as a second home for those who would escape the rigors of rising taxes, weary work loads and pokey stop lights. The park was indeed a get- a-way, the grounds an oasis of nature. As of this writing the cedar lake still sparkles like bits of cut glass under bright skies. Trees flutter with sparrows and blue jays come spring. Squirrels rob seed from handy bird feeders. If encouraged, a bold mallard will peck your screen door for stale breadcrumbs.

"It's the air I love," chirped Rodney pulling into Cabin Eighteen, "Smell that aroma. No exhaust fumes."

Through July and August, this rustic retreat bustles with lazy fishermen and fast boats. Swimsuits hang from droopy clotheslines. Sporadic night flashes mean some kid's father travels south where Roman Candles can be bought legally at roadside stands. After dinner, card players gather under the lakeside pavilion. And every other Friday night, the local VFW still drums up a square dance. Then by mid-October, the happy waters return to dormancy, as do the island beaches a few miles to the southeast.

"Well, I'm ready to pull the plug," yawned Helena, "I don't play pinochle. You know I hate fiddles and I hope that commode's not stopped up again."

THE PANDARUS FILE

"Helena, you don't have to dance. You can stay on the sidelines and drink cider. Just don't disappear like you did at the pig roast last month," warned Rodney searching a tangle of keys, "I know you weren't in bed. I checked the cabin. And I don't think you went on a hike. Not after dark. Especially around these woods."

The Jersey Pine Barrens skirt Lake Powhatan to the north. This infamous wasteland is rich in folkways and folklore. City dwellers who leave the main road for a shortcut to the ocean, often vanish in these gloomy woods. Much of the 1.3 million acres is uninhabited. And if you stay lost long enough, the countless sandy trails that lead nowhere, begin to dig tiny graves in the mind. Natives say the mafia bury victims here. Whiskey stills outnumber houses. Buckshot often echoes through trees. And, there's this place called Quicksand Pond. But the most colorful yarns tell of the Leeds Devil, a green faced demon delivered to a Mrs. Leeds of Atlantic County's, Estelville,

By the Devil, himself.

One story goes that after bearing a dozen healthy babies, the woman became pregnant by fooling around in the barnyard. Thus, the Devil delivered a deformed creature who would gain notoriety as The

Jersey Devil. Born to be an outcast, the creature grew up in coastal swamp lands, beyond the reach of truant officers and table manners. Various sightings depict the demon as a vampire, a large bird, a kangaroo, a grizzly and a horse with bat wings. Almost every South Jersey native has either seen or heard of the devil. Since the late Eighteen Hundreds, his calling card has been a hoof print left in the sand, and a blue mist that precedes his appearance.

"I've seen the Blue Mist," said Rodney.

"You've seen the Jersey Devil?" asked Helena.

The year was 1928. An uncle took Rodney and three cousins on a Halloween trip to check out a *devil sighting*. It was a great night for apparitions. The moon was full, the air chilly as Rodney recalled. You could taste apprehension woven between wide-eyed giggles. They stole between tombstones until every moving leaf sounded like an invisible footstep. Then, an eerie blue fog suddenly appeared over the lower end of the Winslow Township graveyard.

"So what does this creature actually look like," asked Helena.

"I don't know," said Rodney, "We didn't stick around to find out."

"I have to take a piss," said Helena.

Despite the scary tales, many New Jersey natives paint the devil more saint than sinner, oddly enough. They credit the creature with scaring schoolboys to obey curfew laws, and inducing grownups to walk the straight and narrow as an atonement for Mrs Leeds' carnal misbehavior.

Fact or fiction, Elk County folk believe the devil patrols the Pine Lands, swinging a vengeful hammer of justice, while stomping out forest fires and wiping graffiti off grave markers.

"Well, this really is the last straw," cried Rodney wrapping a pink towel around his angry right hand, "What the hell happened to that key and will you hold the damn light steady!"

"It was your shortcut," said Helena, "We should have been here an hour ago."

The cabin window cracked, but would not shatter. Rodney cursed and threw the towel to the creaky porch floor. He leased the place back in June. It came with two keys. One was on a cardboard tag that read Bayside Real Estate. The other key was out with an agent. At that time, a skinny blonde named Julie swore on a stack of rental agreements, she would mail out that second key as soon as it came in. Somehow, the key never showed up. Muttered Rodney, "Damn real estate people. They should have made us a second key on the spot and will you please hold the damn light steady!"

Helena brushed wrinkles from her white tennis shorts, and picked sand burrs from her nylons. Her back throbbed from the long ride - and the long wait while Rodney picked his way back to the main road. Once inside the cabin, her spiked heels would come off, along with a tight bra with a twisted strap. She slapped at a moth trying to eat the flashlight, and stared bitterly at a fingernail broken in a car search for fresh batteries. Bats and night crawlers were the order of the day.

"Alan and Jayne are in Paris," she said, "They took one of those new jets."

"Alan and Jayne sleep together," said Rodney, "They belong in Paris. The last time we slept together, it was the Japs who surrendered. And if you would dress properly, your feet wouldn't ache. No one wears heels and nylons with shorts. They wear sneakers. Also known as tennis shoes. Canvas cuties."

"Sneakers are for kids," said Helena, "And I'm wearing stockings because my tan has faded. I always cover my legs when they look too white."

Rodney stopped fumbling through the silver ringlets of a black leather key case, and literally turned his pockets inside out. He opened a long bill-fold to again finger the empty slot designed for a spare key. He dropped on knees to check under a smelly doormat while grumbling, "Don't think for a minute you are fooling me about last Wednesday. I called the house four times. Each time, Bertha answered. And we both know she covers for you. First you were shopping. Then you were cleaning the Caddy. That was a hot one. You, who never washes anything but your hair and the bathtub. And the tub only because you are sitting in it."

"I keep the silver polished," said Helena.

"Yes, I've noticed some pieces missing lately," said Rodney fingering a dirty ledge over a metal door that didn't match the cabin. He peeked through a narrow mail slot and said, "I hope you are not screwing around with a neighbor, which would be just like you. I mean, even a dog knows to keep his dirt at a distance. And, I'm sick of hearing about Alan and Jayne. I'm sick of the Merefields, and the Radcliffs. If they want to zoom around the world faster than a speeding bullet, that's their business. I like it here. I like the atmosphere and the tranquility."

Rodney liked the fact that Lake Powhatan was less than two miles from Pykes Pit, a worked-out gravel hole converted to target lanes for gun and bow shooting, which was Rodney's latest whim. He joined the Belly Snake Hunting Lodge a year back. The lodge was a sportsmen club hidden along a dirt road that connected civilization to animal kingdom. Members were mostly seasoned police officers and weekend warriors, who could track faint footprints for hours, and shoot warm-blooded creatures. Most club members could breakdown and clean a rifle, blind-folded. They could gut a fallen buck, and skin a rattler with never a blink. Others did little more than play poker, sample moonshine, and toss darts at a naked calendar girl hung on the dingy back wall.

Rodney gained entry to the Belly Snakes through his best friend, Charley, who was club treasurer and a shareholder. Charley said that shooting deer and rabbits would be good therapy for Rodney's jangled nerves. It would also be a service rendered to the commonwealth. Charlie said that game shooting was an important cog in nature's balance. Without hunters, Charlie said that wart hogs and wildebeests would over run the earth.

Club President Bucky Harris rejected Rodney's first application because Rodney could not *hit a bull in the ass with a ping pong paddle*. Then, weighing the new clubhouse estimate against a sagging treasury report, Harris bit the bullet and voted thumbs up. After which, Rodney bought an assortment of archery items and a double fold pamphlet entitled: The New Jersey Summary Of Hunting And Trapping Laws.

"The Merefields aren't on a plane," said Helena gazing at a toppled canoe kissing the water edge, "They are on a cruise."

"Wunerful," said Rodney, "I hope the boat sinks."

"And Bertha doesn't lie for me," lied Helena.

"Well, she sure doesn't side with me, and I'm the one who pays her," said Rodney.

"Not anymore," replied Helena, "Our new checks now read Either/Or. Which means, I can do bills and sign payroll."

Rodney grimaced. Their new financial agreement really meant that Helena could spend more money. The upside was supposed to be more sex for Rodney. Currently, buy-time was way ahead of play time. He toyed with a fatty cyst maturing under his hairline, as he thought about rousting the entire real estate firm from their cozy TV sets. It was well past closing, and some post work calls would serve them right. Instead, he decided to tackle the lockout, himself.

"And if you're thinking about squirming out of our deal," warned Helena, "You will be back humping a pillow for good."

Rodney scowled. He pocketed the useless key case and studied break-in options. The porch door was the only entrance. Real estate kept the rear door locked from the inside. He thought about jimmying a window, then dismissed the idea. The swollen sashes were tough enough to lift, unlocked. His nose began to run as the flashlight again went dead. He fumbled for a large purple handkerchief to catch the sneezes. Then said, "Maybe we can pry loose some molding. Maybe there's a key hidden along the foundation, or under the crawlspace cover. Damn, I wish those crickets would shut up."

Before bow shooting, Rodney had tried water polo, surf fishing, mountain climbing and skydiving. His dream of soaring through the clouds evaporated at that first *jump* door. The landing site looked like a fly on the moon, which caused his stomach to heave like a rolling sailboat at sea. On Rodney's third tour around the cabin, Helena punched through the window glass and unlocked this lakeside retreat smelling of stale air and lined with fresh cobwebs.

"Sorry, but now I have to take a shit," she said.

Some of the cabins were spacious. This one was not. A sitting room and kitchen made up the front. The back was two bedrooms split by a bath. Blond paneling covered the walls to eliminate paint or paper, and tiled floors meant quick scrub downs. The cabins were built with square nails and round timber. There was little insulation. White romex played hide and seek with cloth covered wiring. Whoever designed this model got their nickel's worth. Beneath each bed were extra storage drawers, and pocket doors opened each room. The main fuse box was concealed in a corner kitchen cabinet, for lack of a garage.

"Now we have lights," said Rodney happily.

"I hope we have something for roaches," said Helena.

Rodney hurried in the luggage and dug out the watch he never wore through back alleys. He set the plastic wall clock via the phone operator, and tested for hot water.

"At least you remembered phone service," he called out while stocking the refrigerator, "And you better move it before Grogan locks up."

"Not to worry," hollered back Helena from the bedroom, "The kitchen won't close unless they get word you are coming."

The master bedroom had one lone bureau that Helena always grabbed, forcing Rodney to stow his packings in the storage drawers. This was a rub that Rodney put up with just to be here. A dangling ceiling bulb spotlighted smudges on the dressing mirror, and pointed out dust balls that rolled along the window ledge. A floor puddle was a damp reminder that the roof leaked. The closet smelled like swamp mud.

Helena held out some skimpy green shorts and a white pullover sweater. You didn't dress up for Grogans Bar & Grille, the Friday night hot spot of Hobbs Creek. The rustic pub catered mostly to a local crowd. Women wore hair buns. Men folk sat around in bib overalls and sucked beer from a bottle. Rodney liked the shrimp and cheap prices. Rodney also liked the fact that Grogans was not a pickup joint, as were many of the island clubs

"A woman needs attention," said Helena talking over Rodney' s complaints, "And don't embarrass me by scrutinizing the check and then asking for the owner."

They were supposed to be on a new page. They called it the *"Big Start Over"* before they left home. New agreements. Fresh goals. It was supposed to be the real reason for this Labor Day getaway, or so a hopeful Rodney thought. Helena would stop flirting with men. Rodney would tone down his temper.

"Okay okay," snorted Rodney, towel draped and shower bound, "Just don't embarrass me by coming home with some guy on a motorcycle. And do you have to chew gum with your mouth open? You know I hate that."

'It wasn't a motorcycle," said Helena, "It was a motor scooter. And I met the guy at the beach, not in a club. If you'd learn your way around the Island, I wouldn't have been stuck for a ride in the first place."

"I was not lost," countered Rodney, "I was bogged down in that stinking shore traffic. Besides, you know my stand on the beach. I hate that sticky feeling. The salt makes my eyes burn, and those little jelly things make my skin crawl. They belong in a jar."

He paused to watch Helena inspect her naked waistline in the closet door mirror. Continued Rodney, "And why do you need a new wardrobe for down here ? All you do is wear bikinis. I just hope you don't screw up and pay the same bill twice. Or, run off with the meter reader, which would be just like you."

He exited the shower blowing water from his watch face. He cursed as moisture bubbled under the glass. He coaxed down a stubborn window shade, and snapped off the clock radio in the midst of Love Me

Tender.

"Hey, I was listening to that," cried Helena.

"I should have listened to my Uncle Dudley," said Rodney, "He was against you from the beginning. Uncle Dudley wanted me to marry someone who inhabited ballrooms, not bar rooms. Someone who enjoys songs like Tea For Two, and knows what knickers are."

"Knickers ! "

"Yes, knickers. Pants that come to the knee where they meet the socks."

"I know what knickers are," said Helena, "And Uncle Dudley is a pervert with a monocle who corners me in the wine cellar whenever possible."

Rodney turned in the narrow doorway and re-gripped the soggy towel that defended his privacy. He lowered his voice to say, "I never told you this . .but that first night I brought you home . . it was father who cornered me in the kitchen, as I complained to James about the wine. And even father said maybe I should think it over. That maybe you were too much like Lucy Lu."

"Who?"

"Lucy Lu. My first wife. Father said you and Lucy Lu had the same points of interests, and that Tiffany might be a better choice for me. You remember

Tiffany."

"The skinny one with the bump on her nose?"

"Yes. Tiffany. And to think I wanted to kill father for saying that. I should have kissed him."

Rodney should have killed him. At fifty-eight, Everett Hollister was still a fox with silver hair, straight legs and lively eyes. His life one long roll in the hay. He never folded on jacks, and unlike Rodney, Everett always dove into deep water. He knocked up his first girl on a Sunday school picnic, in some woods behind Wilson Lake. He bore a second child out of wedlock with a Glouster City barmaid. Dark secrets kept from Rodney and Rodney's mother.

Helena's first turn beneath Everett came in a sailboat just south of Sweetwater, with wind spray from the Malaga River to excite their bare bodies. That torrid event followed by many midnight rendezvous' between the bed sheets in the down stairs guest room. Sometimes, shortly after Rodney had finished with her. And Helena loved it all. For a time, anyway. This soapy melodrama of candid looks and daredevil timing. Woven through the charade that she and Everett played. Each trying to pull an invisible mask off the other. Each putting up a pawn to win a pound.

T'was an affair ignited by a diamond bracelet the elder Hollister surprised Helena with at Christmas. She thanked him with a kiss beneath the mistletoe and some over active tongue play. Eventually, the champagne went flat and Everett bared his teeth. They were dueling over tea, waiting for Rodney to return from a business trip. Everett told her point blank that she was more transparent than cellophane. She could still hear the probate attorney's small cough when he read the phrase that called her a cheap gold digger.

"I guess we never really know our parents," yelled Rodney now back in the shower without the watch, "I never figured father for a reflective sort, and would you throw me in the soap?"

Helena left the shower noise behind and faded into the kitchen. Minutes later, she returned to the bed-side. A crack in the full-length mirror distorted her image. She shifted to recheck her waistline. Satisfied there was no unwanted fat, she began to count. Elbows out, fingers interlocked, she pulled one hand against the other. This was an exercise she believed would keep her breasts firm. She donned a rubber cap, and tilted her sturdy chin to check for necklines. The shower stopped. She was next. She grabbed a bathrobe and hummed a few bars of Love Me Tender, Everett's favorite song. It was the song he loved to dance to, whistle along with. And it was playing the night she plugged in the radio as he soaked, and dropped it into his bath water.

"You will get a big kick out of this," said Rodney standing in the doorway, "Here's our cabin key."

"You found it?"

"In the linen closet. I went for another towel and the key just fell to the floor. What the hell was it doing in the linen closet?"

"That is a funny place for real estate to hide a key," said Helena.

"That's not the strange part," said Rodney holding the key to the light, "This is the key we had. Here's where I spilled coffee on the name tag."

"That is strange," agreed Helena.

"Wield, I would say. And were you just in the kitchen?"

"No," she lied.

"I thought I heard you talking on the phone."

"You must have water in your ears."

CHAPTER 4

Late Friday Night: August 29, 1958

William Bo Brennan took a giant mouthful of cold water. He grimaced and spit the overflow toward a trash bucket that sat near an empty wood stove. An ice cube missed the dented container and hit the top opening of a ready fishing boot. Frowning, Brennan straightened the brassy desk plaque that read POLICE CHIEF, and rocked back in the weary swivel chair that came with the territory. His pale blue eyes swung from Helena Hollister to Elmer Kane.

"So," asked Brennan, "What were you doing on the floor, and what were you doing on top of her?"

Commotion erupted.

The Hobbs Creek Police Station was the front room of Brennan's two-story farmhouse, located at Elm and Main. The bare plaster walls and hardwood floor, coupled with the chief's high blood pressure, could not accommodate a four party debate. Brennan's thick right hand slammed onto a stack of unfinished paper reports. The crossfire of conflicting stories stopped abruptly.

"Now," growled Brennan, "I would like to take this one person at a time."

The other half of the Hobbs Creek police force was a young Jeeter Potts, who fell out of a tree during lunch hour, playing hide and seek with his kid. Potts was in the third barren week of a trial separation, and working hard to restore a rank of husband and father. Climbing a weeping willow was probably not a wise decision. The doctor told Brennan over the phone that Potts had lost his grip on a knobby branch. After which, Brennan chortled to the doctor that Jeeter needed a grip on growing up. Then, the doctor said that Potts would be out until after Labor Day. That meant the burly police chief would have to pull both shifts over the long weekend, and the smile faded.

Brennan refilled the plastic water glass. He tugged at a sticky tee shirt. Humidity packed the late summer air. His uniform hung on a nail next to a black cowboy hat. A gun belt looped the cushioned chair back. He killed the squelch on a noisy walkie talkie, and swatted a fly that touched down on his sandy crew cut. He stared at Elmer Kane and asked, "What were you doing with your pants off?"

"I should have belted him," snorted Rodney who stood nearby glaring at Elmer, "I should have belted both of them!"

A bony black man named Emmet Walker Thomas dozed in a hardwood rocker near the desk, hands folded behind head, feet extended. A white hat covered his sleepy eyes. The large brim rested on one floppy ear that was a mite larger than the other. At Rodney's last outburst, the black man's reading glasses jumped from his tiny nose, over a trim white mustache and caught on his tailored blue slacks. The black man was a county detective - rank of lieutenant. He was on a two-week retreat in Hobbs Creek, because he and Brennan shared a secret fishing hole, unknown to anyone else in the whole wide world. In Brennan's off hours, they would pack beer and sandwiches, and steal away like schoolboys at large. Now, that kettle of fish sat on the back burner until Jeeter Potts returned.

Next to the black man, lay a metal serving tray covered with loose sugar and dried coffee stains. Gray filing cabinets filled a far corner. A homemade gun rack that held two rifles and a twelve gauge accented a protruding deer head.

"I had too much to drink," burped Helena teetering against the inside door that connected the station house to the house proper. Her bra ran uphill. Her skimpy green shorts were on backwards. She held the white pullover in one hand, and grabbed onto Rodney with the other while complaining, "You know I can't drink gin, honey. I drink screwdrivers. Why did you let me drink gin?"

A bald bartender named Henry Porter pointed a broken chair leg at Rodney and wailed, "Before this asshole belts anybody, he's gonna pay for damages."

Elmer Kane filled the room center, head down, hands folded to the front. His 305 pounds quivered like a water filled balloon. A squatty neck disappeared as he cowered. His black oxfords trembled. Elmer was born with a neuromuscular disorder, commonly called Motor Slowness, which led people to believe he was retarded. He was not. Elmer Kane had an average IQ. However, immaturity and blubber made Elmer the township dart board, a heavy cross that brought more embarrassment than body pain. He was the butt of all moron jokes, and Elmer's mother fueled the fire by dressing Elmer in full suit and tie - if only to fetch the paper. His father who was bank president at Hobbs Creek, made a clear point to show warmth, but always referred to Elmer in the third person.

At times the awkward 24 year old fought to throw off this saddle. He could not hold a job, thus he would hand out Bible tracts and deliver phone books in a fruitless effort to carve a niche in society. He also sold benefit tickets to aid those who were truly moronic. But, Elmer's attention span was short and his feet tended to stray after sundown. Squirming, his sheepish eyes rolled, each at a different speed. His mouth foamed as he coined each word. "I knew we were doing a bad thing."

"A bad thing!" echoed Rodney, "I went to the john. Gone five minutes. Maybe ten, tops. I come back and these two are rolling around on the floor, stark naked!"

"We weren't stark naked," said Helena, "Elmer still had his socks on."

The verbal war rekindled and Brennan again rapped the desk for silence. He fumbled through a deep bottom drawer for a bag of mints, already eaten. He had skipped supper in defiance of a new diet prescribed by Doc Hooper, the local medicine man. The menu called for greens, grains and fruits, and lots of them. Thus, Brennan's jovial stomach was not very jolly. Nor was Brennan. He missed an adult western called Trackdown because the station room had no TV. The Phillies were losing a 5 to 3 squeaker to Cincinnati at Crosley Field, the Philadelphia nine being Brennan's team of choice. Grumbling about pop-ups, he shut down the radio and reached for a cigar kept in a balky top drawer. He accidentally yanked off the varnished wood facing and swore softly.

Brennan was the strongest man in Lower Elk County, which is how this backwoods trapper got to be police chief. Tales of Brennan's strength range from a fishy odor to sheer flapdoodle. It's said he once rolled a getaway car upside down with his bare hands. Then used a jack handle to cuff the holdup man to a doorpost. In another incident, he tossed an entire motorcycle gang out of Binkys Liquor Store with no call for back up. Corky Tabor, a connoisseur of wines, whiskey and cough syrup, claims he saw Brennan hand brace a broken timber under the Cedar Gap Bridge while a runaway freight train crossed to safe ground.

Pure or colored, the stories became a spring-board for Brennan's appointment to Top Cop on December 4, 1949. He was given one part-timer to man the radio during rush hours, and some black and white paint for his private car. The pay was meager, but the benefits were good, and it was a short drive to work. Scowling, he dropped two aspirin into the water glass and fumbled with the busted drawer. He stared at the lusty redhead and said, "You have the floor."

"Me ? "

"Yes, you."

Helena pulled the sweater on sideways. She sought out the armholes and tossed her ocean of red hair. She double struck a match and lit a cigarette.

"Sometime tonight," growled Brennan.

"Well, that stripper song was on the jukebox," said Helena blowing smoke through her straight white teeth, "The one you take your clothes off to the music. So, I began taking off my clothes. It's just a teaser act. I did it a few times at a club where I used to work. It gets the old farts hot and bothered and they buy more drinks." She giggled and blew a silly smoke ring toward Elmer Kane. "He sat at the next table over. He got all happy looking and began to take off his clothes. He's kinda cute, so I showed him how to move with the music. I slipped off my heels and stepped out of my shorts. He dropped his shirt and removed his belt."

It turned out to be the show of shows. Most of the pineys who frequented Grogans were strangers to burlesque. There were no movie theaters in Lower Elk County. Fifties' TV was black and white. Listings were PG rated. Thus, all male heads turned to watch Helena while the women pretended not to notice. Then Elmer joined the act and the place went bonkers. Hooting. Howling. Tossing money into the bright spot light for added encouragement.

"We probably got a little carried away," admitted Helena.

"But why were you butt down on the floor," asked Brennan.

"We tripped," said Helena twisting to free a bra strap caught inside the sweater. Her makeup kit was lost in the messy white handbag, and she dumped the contents onto a typewriter stand used by Jeeter Potts. She missed a large ashtray putting out the cigarette. She caught her tongue putting on the lip-stick. She burped and said, "I was showing Elmer how to kick and turn when his feet got tangled with mine. Or maybe my feet got mixed up with his. Or maybe a table leg reached out and grabbed us. I don't know. Any way, we were just dancing."

"Dancing makes me feel good," said Elmer Kane, "I like to dance."

"You were laying on my wife you idiot!" cried Rodney.

Brennan double coughed and poured some stale coffee into a chipped mug that read *Love*. He tested before swallowing. Spit. Discovered the loose cord and grunted. The brown double outlet was worn, which caused a topside plug to work loose at the slightest vibration. Someone had plugged the pot into the topside, and Brennan knew that someone was Jeeter Potts, odds down. Potts worked with his mind out the window, and sometimes had his underwear on backwards. Brennan took a crank call, slammed down the phone and rummaged through the desk clutter for a frayed logbook. He peered at Elmer Kane and asked, "Isn't this the third time this month you have been in here?"

Brennan paused to answer a second wrong number, and then searched on for the missing log book. Behind the phone sat an oil lamp converted to power. Next to the lamp stood a picture of the burly police chief, his wife Molly and their son Chip who was shot down in a Sabre Jet after Korea - or so the papers said. Truthfully, Chip was on a drunk without leave, and got run over by a wayward army tank. The boy's belongings were longed packed away, but there were still wee hours when Brennan would sit bedside and steady Molly's quivering hand. He spotted the log book under the desk and used a boot toe to drag it out. He turned back to Elmer and said, "It says here that on August 2nd, you were caught peeping through Gloria Sweeney's bedroom window. Like to scare the kid right out of her sixteenth birthday. And that upset the family dog who then wet all over the Sweeney's new carpet."

Brennan's thick fingers thumbed over smudgy pages as he read on, "On the tenth, Elmer Kane had Emma Hopkins sweating blue ink when he followed her daughter home from the bus stop. Then he gave the girl a rose that he picked from her father's prize garden, where Elmer managed to jar loose the water hose. Which, was turned on at the faucet, I might add. There's a small note here concerning a dry cleaning bill for draperies because the bay window was open."

Elmer's puffy face went from red to purple. Sweat rings circled his flabby armpits. Although this was Elmer's third station house visit in a month, it was not a three count in all. Elmer's running tally on misdemeanors was closer to a dozen. There was always sex involved. Once, a local store manager caught Elmer masturbating in the men's room. The manager confiscated the girlie pictures and politely asked Elmer to shop elsewhere. Still flushing, Elmer toyed with a skinny black tie, it's gold clasp lost somewhere on the tavern floor. He stared at a deep scratch etched across the duty desk. His right eye roamed freely. There was a bright side to this ordeal. Brennan would take him home in the squad car when the interrogation ended. Asked Elmer happily, "Will I be allowed to turn on the siren again?"

"You people just aren't getting the picture here," said Rodney hedging a look at the burly police chief, "Everybody's taking this a bit too lightly."

"Well, did anybody hit anybody?" asked Bo Brennan.

"Nobody hit anybody," said Helena trying to light a cigarette with the wrong hand, "I can vouch for that."

"But he broke this over a table," cried Henry Porter pointing the busted chair leg at Rodney, "Just picked up a chair and smashed it, like he didn't give two shits for anybody else's property."

Porter owned Grogans Bar & Grille. He tended bar to keep expenses down, and sold real estate on the side. He also did income taxes and was a notary public. A large key ring hung from his belt. A wart marked his ruddy nose that he scratched more from habit than itch. "I can show you how he did it, Bo. He did it just like this!"

Porter smacked the broken spindle against the wood stove. The dozing black man jumped. His bony legs shot out and kicked a nearby fishing pole across the sandy hardwood floor. Bingo came from nowhere and licked invisible salt off the varnished rod. Bingo was a raggedy-ear, house guest en route to the pound. Brennan now loved the animal. Molly complained the dog would eat buttered cat dirt.

"You people are not getting the picture here," reiterated Rodney.

"I don't need a picture," snapped Henry Porter, "I need a payment."

Brennan rocked back to light a black stogy he smoked against good judgment. He returned the cigar box to its hideaway and locked the drawer. He rubbed sore eyes and tugged off the sculptured boots that Molly needled him for buying. Molly said the house was roach free, and Brennan didn't need boots that came to a point. Molly also mentioned that the job jar came before the fishing pole, and perhaps her Brennan was a bit overboard with cowboy shows. After which, Brennan explained to Molly that Gunsmoke was not a cowboy show. The late night giant was classified Adult Western. Then Molly said if a wooden tub was next, or no bath at all, that Mister Chief Of Police would sleep with Bingo. Brennan wiggled his now happy toes and studied the mutilated chair leg. Then he said, "Henry, that looks like one of those high backs I saw down at Luke's fire sale."

Porter winced.

"They were all painted jet black with some missing spokes," remembered Brennan.

Porter shifted from foot to foot.

"I saw the tag on them chairs as I checked out a kitchen stool," said Brennan, "That was just a two dollar chair, Henry."

"Well, it's not really the money," said Porter wrestling the broken spindle away from Bingo, "It's the sting of the thing, Bo. Like when your desk clerk holds a hand over the phone, and refers to me as Ole Cue Ball Head."

"You mean Jeeter Potts?" asked Brennan.

"The same," said Porter.

"I will speak to Jeeter about that," said Brennan, "Now, do you really want me to sit here and fill out a long report over two measly dollars?"

Porter sighed. He tossed the chair leg into the wood stove and wiped his hands on a greasy apron that cut a crevice across his belly. Porter said he didn't really want to press charges. He just didn't like certain people hanging around the bar. He looked at Elmer Kane and muttered, "He almost lives at my place, Bo. Sits there every night. All night. Nursing a beer. One beer. That's all he buys. He's like a stick of furniture. Well, maybe not a stick. Anyway, the sale's over. And with this guy

Hoffa pushing up shipping costs, who knows what a new chair will cost."

"My father says I should not drink too much beer," said Elmer Kane, "Too much beer is bad for me."

"Elmer, zip up your fly," growled Brennan.

"You are nuts," cried Rodney looking like a grenade with the pin pulled, "You are all fruitcakes!"

Just before the phone rang, Bingo came to attention, head up, ears back. He sounded a series of long howls. Simultaneously, Brennan told a female caller that he knew the siren was stuck. That, the whole town knew the siren was stuck. He slammed down the black plastic, handset. He paused for a deep breath. He flipped closed the logbook and addressed the group. He used the frayed cigar as a pointer. "Now this is the way we handle this. Mr. Hollister will pay the plaintiff - that's Mr Porter -the sum of four dollars. Breaking that down: two dollars for a new chair; one dollar for gas; and one dollar for irreparable harm,

"Henry, I want you to take the two dollar back to Carson City, and have Luke give you another chair at the sale price. And Henry, while you're at it, take back that toaster Luke sold me. The one that turns everything black. And don't take any lip from the little weasel,

"And you Elmer," concluded Brennan, "I'm gonna talk with your father, now everybody clear out of here."

Rodney Hollister's pointy chin trembled. His heated neck cords bulged. He glared at Brennan. He glared at Elmer Kane. He glared back at Brennan to holler, "That's it. That's all. You are going to talk to his father!"

"My mother and father are in the Poconos," drawled Elmer, "My mother said that maybe they needed a second honeymoon."

Brennan yelled through the open house door for Molly to summon the howling dog. He slammed down the front window to muffle the high-pitched shrill coming from across the street. The siren sat on the firehouse roof. The noisy alert box would sound for fire, ambulance and air raid. It also served as noon whistle, and blew again at five-o-clock. Brennan dropped back into the swivel chair. Air hissed from a yielding cushion as he grumbled, "Shittin' siren. Been this way for a month. Turns itself on. Turns itself off. If the town fathers don't soon fix it, I'm gonna shoot the damn thing down and skin it."

Elmer's glossy eyes rolled and stopped on Helena. Said Elmer, "She has really smooth skin. I like to touch smooth skin."

And that set off the simmering time bomb.

Rodney grabbed the stove poker and charged Elmer Kane, which brought Brennan around the desk like a fullback running off-tackle. Henry Porter jumped clear. Helena feigned dismay by touching fingers to mouth. Bingo who once ran from a rabbit, disappeared without further coaxing. Rodney stopped just short of striking distance and waved the solid iron rod while shrieking, "This lunatic was trying to fuck my wife!"

Grunting, Brennan wrestled the poker from a battling Rodney and warned, "You don't curse in my house, junior!"

"But he was trying to fuck my wife right on Grogan's dance floor," screamed Rodney, "Right there in front of everybody. And you're talking about busted toasters and broken chair legs. What the hell kind of cop are you!"

Brennan curled the poker into a rigid loop and collared Rodney. Snarling, the burly police chief herded the three men outside. He lifted Rodney over the white porch railing, and dropped him like a fertilizer sack into a flower bed. Barked Brennan, "I do the cursing around here, and you're damn lucky I don't lock your ass up for attempted assault!"

Brennan glowered at Elmer Kane. "And you wait in my car. Don't scratch anything and don't puke on my new seat covers. I'm taking you home as soon as I get my boots on."

Rodney jumped up dusting ruffled feathers. He wiped mud from his britches and threatened Brennan's job as police chief. Then he screeched at Porter, "I'm the one with the complaint here, asshole. You won't look so smug with your liquor license revoked, and I've got the contacts to do it!"

Rodney backed across the shabby lawn and caromed off a concrete birdbath. The shaky top spewed water. He regained balance and thrust an ominous finger at Elmer Kane who cowered behind Bo Brennan. Warned Rodney, "This thing is not over, moron. You better know that. It doesn't end here!"

Meanwhile, Helena seized the chaotic moment to seek out a washroom. She returned stumbling onto the porch and tripped down the steps. Another nose appeared in a window down the street. Next door, Old Man Stoker's bulldog snarled. Helena grabbed Rodney's arm and weaved toward the Corvette. She giggled, "I should have never tried that White Lady. What a sleeper."

"I'll going to kill that bastard," sputtered Rodney disappearing into the car, "If that moron comes near you again, I'll kill the sonofabitch!"

*   *   *   *   *

Brennan was back at the station house for the midnight sports report. Cincinnati's 5 to 3 lead held up when the Redleg's Bob Purkey starved off a Phillies' eighth inning threat. Frowning, Brennan snapped off the small tube radio. He tossed the stale coffee and lit a fresh cigar. He sat down to file the incident report and whistled, "Helena Hollister."

"Do you really think the boy was trying to hump her?" asked the black man from beneath the white hat.

"Who knows," said Bo Brennan, "I'd like to stick the pork to that, myself. I wonder what she sees in a twerp like Hollister?"

"It's the size of his wallet," said Emmet Walker Thomas sitting up and nodding toward the open house door, "And forget it, Bo. She'd probably break your pecker."

Brennan closed the door that led to the inside hallway and returned to the paperwork, grinning. He turned off the two-way and said, "I think *break your back* is the correct terminology and I'm listening."

"Money," explained Walker Thomas, "He's got money and she wants it."

'C'mon Emmet," scoffed Brennan, "He had on work jeans and a shirt I wouldn't wear to put out the trash."

The black man turned down a cot set up on the far wall. He fluffed a lacy pillow from inside the house, and wound a silver watch kept in a hidden pocket. Out of habit, he sat on the floor to remove his black service shoes. He untied the block style lacing, and scratched a leg itch below the right knee where wood joined flesh. He looked up at his long time friend and said, "Bo, those boots Hollister had on cost a hundred dollar. His hairstyle was a scissor-cut. That silver bracelet was worth more than we make in a month. And by the way, that was my fishing boot you was spitting in."

CHAPTER 5

2am. Rodney snored peacefully. Helena lured him to bed by slipping a hand between his legs from the rear. She knew that would arouse him as it always did, no matter how black his mood. Soon, he tore off clothes and dropped window shades. Buried passion resurfaced. Talk of divorce faded. Eventually, the storm passed and left a wake of apathy conducive to sleep.

Quietly, she redressed in the green shorts and white top. She used the dim flashlight and a screwdriver to remove a lattice section that enclosed the porch crawl space. There were no windblown leaves or dead pine cones to crawl through. Helena had brushed them away on that Wednesday she lifted the missing cabin key from Rodney's nightstand.

She surveyed the black hole for coons and snakes. There were none. She bellied into the crawl space to recover a brown gunnysack, stashed well to the rear. She brushed away a fresh cobweb, and undid a stubborn drawstring. The rumpled bag held two plastic tablecloths, tennis shoes and a rubber doggie bone. Helena bought the items at the five and dime store back in Delaware Township. She was careful to burn the receipt because Rodney habitually nosed through the trash.

A nearby hoot owl set off noisy crickets. Helena checked the yard next door to make certain Tom Grundy was not sleeping outside. Tom and Angel Grundy quibbled constantly. When the bickering turned to battle, the ruddy camper salesman would finish the night in a hammock, roped between a porch rail and a weeping willow. When the battle became war, they would pack up for home. No such luck this weekend, Helena noted.

Sudden headlights flooded the area.

Helena froze.

A lost car used the cabin driveway to make a U-turn. Helena breathed easier as taillights faded from view. She scanned the lakefront for any lovers lying loose under the stars. Satisfied there were no prying eyes, she walked to the far property line.

Winds built. Shadows moved. All else was still but for whistling treetops and lake water slapping against sailboats. T'was a good night for apparitions and ghost stories, but not a great night for the task at hand. Helena wished it were darker.

She laced the tennis shoes and clamped the rubber bone between her teeth, the latter a gimmick she used during early lipstick trials and tardy bedtime arrivals. Her mother was a rigid churchgoer who did not hold with dancing, movie going or makeup. She kept a wide belt in the wine cellar, and would drape her wayward daughter over a beer keg kept near a coal bin. Always, Helena would bite onto a mitten, or schoolbook or anything handy. Once, she bit onto an arm attached to her drunken father. Afterward, she stowed away with a neighbor until the troubled waters settled.

The rubber bone in place, Helena pulled the gunnysack over her head for face protection. She took a deep breath. The world smelled like bad onions. Fists clenched, she charged hari-kari. A rather tall oak refused to move and she crashed to the earth, silently screaming - like the day she got caught shop-lifting a perfume bottle. A security alarm sent her tumbling down the escalator in a center city department store. She broke a collarbone, twisted an ankle and awoke staring at a police matron.

Helena groped around the tree and resumed running. Cedars bumped her off course. Pine branches scratched her bare arms. She stubbed a toe on some thing sharp, a testimony the grounds needed work. Heavy underbrush lined the property. Creeping vines grew where nothing else could flourish. The cabin owner was a white collar whiz who accumulated air miles and real estate. He wasn't a gardener.

Briars scraped her bare legs as she ran on. Dead branches snapped beneath her flying feet. Startled toads jumped for safety. She cringed as a wiry fence post gouged her left arm. The cut reopened a faded scar from a subway fight that followed her senior home coming dance. She slept over with a girl friend named Tiki, prior to the cross-town affair. It was a ploy to fool Helena's mother. The episode ended as front-page news, as fate would have it.

Well past midnight, three street gang members cornered Helena and Tiki as they waited for the return subway train. The teenage hoodlums sought handbags and anything else they could grab. Fur Flew. The gang leader slashed Helena's forearm with a switchblade. After which, she splattered his nose with a flying foot kick.

She learned the move from Chico Gonzales Mendez, a backyard friend who hung out with an oriental called Black Belt Lu. Martial Arts was the neighborhood fad at the time. Lu showed the basics to Chico who passed them on to Helena. Chico also taught Helena how to eye-poke, groin kick and sucker punch. She was an able student. Chico said she had natural speed, and to be born with such quickness was a gift.

Helena used the gift to bloody more than a nose. She sparred with the hoodlum as their awaited train neared. Then she sent him sprawling over the tracks to watch the grinding steel wheels sever the legs from the body. The press credited Helena with breaking up a street gang. Tiki spread a different message, "When Helena kicks off the heels, get the hell out of the way."

Nearing gauntlet's end, Helena tripped over a tree root exposed by the elements. She spilled into a gasping roll down the muddy embankment to the waters' edge. A jagged rock raped her solar plexus. She knelt on the gritty sand and wheezed. Air came slowly. She pulled the sack from her head. She choked off a tear and wrapped the bloody arm with her white pull over. The lake was choppy. Gathering storm clouds began to block the moon. She smiled weakly. The predicted rain would fall by daybreak. Rain that would justify the umbrella she needed to bring this plot together.

She hobbled to the car. She placed the plastic table covers over the seat and floor area. The covers would catch any tell tale mud or blood. She eased out the driveway. The cabins were put in backward. The front overlooked the water. The rear faced the road. She drove a safe distance from the bedroom windows before flicking on the headlights. She paused to light a cigarette. Then she sped to the emergency clinic where a desk clerk would document date, time and Helena's battered condition.

CHAPTER 6

Dateline: Post Sept 11, 2001

"Do we have a secure connection?" asked Police Chief, Adam Quayle from his red desktop phone.

"As secure as scramble gets," replied special agent, Jeremy Wade talking over road traffic, "If your phone's not bugged, we are good to go."

Adam Quayle laughed. "This is Hobbs Creek. Most of our residents have trouble setting a mouse trap. I want to thank you guys for jumping in here."

"Don't thank us," said the federal agent, "Thank the US Marshall Service. When they heard the name Hollister, they started pulling strings at every level. I just happened to be over here when this thing broke."

"Brief me," requested Adam Quayle.

"Currently, I'm in Rive Droite driving west," said the special agent dodging traffic on Champs-Elysees Avenue.

"I don't speak French," said Quayle, "Where are you in English?"

"Right Bank, Paris," replied Jeremy Wade, "I finally got the subject's current address. We had a problem there. Interpol had nothing under the name,

Anna Ward, and the jeweler's records were flawed. Evidently, our subject lied about everything including name, age and residence."

"Do we have a warrant to get in?" asked Adam Quayle.

"Sir, sometimes it's easier to get forgiveness than permission in this business."

"Yes," smiled the current Hobbs Creek, Police Chief, "It's that way here, sometimes. Anyway, keep me posted."

CHAPTER 7

Saturday, August 30, 1958

Rodney woke up awake as always. He shaved, showered and patched the open window with a card board cutout, before the kettle came to boil. He unpacked the remaining luggage, then ran a daylight check in his jockey shorts, for the shooting gear that still wasn't there.

Also missing were the dustpan and brush. He handpicked glass fragments from the front room floor and gingerly dropped them into a brown bag under the sink. Smaller bits lurked everywhere. Rodney grabbed a rigid broom from the hall closet and mumbled his way out the screen door. "Damn that Quigley. But for him, I'd have packed the car myself."

One of Rodney's smaller enterprises was an electro plating works that nickel-coated TV stands, and then finished them off in bronze or silver. Rodney wanted to pump up the company's assets by going public with the ailing business. He would then quietly seek a buyout bid from a larger plant near Allentown, Pa. He needed some backup to present his plan to a group of potential investors. Thus, he asked his book keeper, Martin Quigley to stand in for a contract lawyer who could not make the meeting. Martin typed up the prospectus and could decipher the wording as well as any attorney. Also, Martin was not one to jibber jabber.

Normally.

Somewhere between the filing cabinet and conference room, the mellow, be speckled clerk must have hit the sauce. Heels together, thumbs hooked to vest pockets, he dominated the meeting with a speech on the merits of mergers. Not only did he put the hammer before the nail, he tipped Rodney's hand to boot.

Things got worse. By the time Martin ran out of air, it was too late to deal with the flat that Rodney found waiting on the Caddy. The spare was road ready, but Rodney didn't know a lug wrench from a screw driver. Thus, he was down to one option: call Helena.

Wincing, Rodney swept the last broken window bits under a doormat. He twisted the red cap off an instant coffee jar. He washed out one dusty mug and yelled into the cabin bedroom, "Your java will be ready before you are!"

Helena yawned from a cozy pillow, "What time is it ? "

THE PANDARUS FILE

It was 8:45 am. Skies were overcast, tide water angry. The bedside radio issued warnings to anxious fishermen and avid boaters along the coastline. Helena hid beneath a fuzzy pink blanket despite the muggy morning air. Red blotches spotted her bruised body. Bandage wrapped her right ankle. A neck muscle throbbed. Her ribs ached. She watched a spider inch up the closet door and shivered. She pulled down a snappy paper shade and called back, "Did you have to open all the windows?"

The kitchen faucet leaked and Rodney dialed real estate to lodge a complaint. He got a wrong number and entered the bedroom in search of reading glasses - a jabbing reminder that his eyes were a true forty. Said Rodney while rooting through drawers, "You don't have any blood, that's your trouble and why are you always screwing around with morons and misfits?"

"I won't pursue that," replied Helena giving Rodney a hard look.

"Oh funny funny."

"And you were not in the john any five minutes," she said, "You were gone a good half hour and I got bored."

"I had diarrhea," said Rodney.

"You always get the shits when we come down here," replied Helena, "Which is another good reason to stay home."

"Its the water," said Rodney slamming back sticky drawers. He looked at the chattering radio. "What did he say about rain?"

"I wasn't listening," said Helena, "And your glasses are in the car with your good umbrella."

Rodney muttered that he hated to drive on slippery roads. He searched the refrigerator for the Vitamin C tablets and said, "You should try some of this goats milk. Much better for you than coffee."

He stared at the ceiling tiles, stained from a mid-winter pipe break and thought of Bertha. He squeezed the kitchen phone between an ear and his shoulder to check his watch. Bertha would be cleaning toilet bowls. Bertha always scoured the bathrooms on Saturday morning. He snapped his fingers and began to whistle *I'm A Yankee Doodle Dandy.*

Rodney and the stocky spinster seldom spoke, but she would bring down the shooting gear. For pay. Bertha did most anything for money. Even homework. More than once, a young Rodney swapped his allowance for math answers. And on one occasion, she wrote his back-to-school essay on camp events. That was the summer he punched a milk drum for being empty, and broke his writing hand.

Bertha was not a servant per se. Everett Hollister first hired Bertha in 1927 for deep cleaning. Her hours were 8 to 6 twice a week. At which times she would do a designated area of the six-bedroom mansion. Twelve years later, she stomped off over a pay raise dispute with the elder Hollister, who begged her back after Pearl Harbor as jobs began to outnumber applicants. Everett bitched that the new factories soaked up women like sanitation pads, and said it was a man's lot to bring home the staples. Eventually, he ran out of clean corners and upgraded his pay scale.

Bertha also sold soft pretzels at the Benjamin Franklin Bridge exit, and delivered groceries for tips throughout the Collingswood area. Her familiar red and white headscarf was a fixture in the Friday night bank line, and clothesline talk swore she was secretly a millionaire. Or maybe even richer. Rodney rechecked the time and dialed again. The cabin had a second bed-room. Bertha could even stay over if she wished. He would even reimburse her for the gas. There was no answer at the house and he called out, "Are you sure you gave Bertha that key?"

"I gave Bertha the week off," said Helena.

"You what!"

"She wanted to spend the holiday with her sister in New York State."

"Helena," whined Rodney, "Bertha lost her key and you were to give her your key and you said you did that."

"I lied," said Helena, dryly.

Rodney groaned and shoved a rickety coffee table across the narrow living room. Jaded magazines slid to the floor, toppling the broom, which crashed over an empty flowerpot perched in the picture window. Cursing, Rodney began doing sit-ups.

"Sorry," called in Helena.

"Monotoso," wheezed Rodney doing knee bends and toe touchies. Winded, he tucked into a yoga position, arms folded, legs crossed. He stared into space and again whispered, "Monotoso."

Rodney bought a book on mind games and how to roll the dice for health, wealth and happiness. The book said to choose a study word. Rodney picked Monotoso, mostly because Monotoso reminded Rodney of monotony. The exercise was not terribly exciting. He would sit and star through space while honing in on Monotoso, simultaneously blocking out all else. The book claimed this was a mental drill to sharpen concentration for whatever cartel waited down the road. Missed glass bits nicked Rodney's bottom and he rolled over to do ten push-ups. He collapsed at seven and glowered toward the bedroom. "Since when do you give Bertha time off. Bertha always comes to me for a leave of absence."

He squeezed in a quick second shower and re dressed. He toyed with the car keys by the bedside.

"I thought maybe you would go along," he mumbled, "Just for the ride?"

Helena burrowed deeper into the fuzzy pink blanket. She wedged between pillows. Her muffled voice said, "I left my clam diggers in the downstairs bath, if you think of it. The white ones."

"Your clam diggers?"

"Clam diggers. Pants cut off at the calves. Used for wading in shallow water. Often made of cotton."

"I know what clam diggers are," growled Rodney, "And the next time Bertha wants a week off, check with me first."

*   *   *   *   *

Helena watched Rodney back out the driveway and swing toward the main gate. He would be gone two hours each way. Maybe longer, depending on traffic and road conditions. She bathed and put on her face. There was time for a second coffee. She stood half-naked before the picture window, it's deep ledge now dirtied from the broken flowerpot. Random raindrops pecked the lake. Two black bathing caps headed for shore. Farther out, a boater madly pulled the cord on a balky outboard. She lit a cigarette and blew a smoke ring for the local weathermen. This was one time they were right on the money.

Her pants suit waited in the closet, wedged between dresses. The sleeves and long trousers would cover bruises. Then later that evening while Rodney was still up, she would stay in pajamas and pretend to read.

She inched the clumsy sleeper bed from the living room wall, and knelt in a triangle of dust balls and dried up crickets. She brushed aside a fresh crossword book and some eraser bits. The sofa bed was a bulky red relic once used by six children as a trampoline. Stuffing and springs stuck out the back. Helena pulled an arrow from a gaping hole. The feathers were white and blue. The shaft was aluminum.

Rodney bought his shooting gear at a popular sporting goods outlet just south of Camden. Helena could not chance being identified by the owner who lived in Delaware Township. Thus, she drove into Philly to buy this duplicate. She peeled away the price tab, and picked away the glue with a long fingernail. It was imperative the arrow match those in Rodney's quiver.

The umbrella hid among some spare blankets in the utility closet. It was long and black, like those that bloom on Wall Street. She slipped the arrow into the umbrella and closed the snap. She fingered the phone, impatiently. "I'm in Cabin Eighteen and tell the driver I'll be on the lookout. He needn't lay on the horn and wake all the neighbors."

She hung up and dialed again.

"Martin? Helena. .I'm fine, let's cut the small talk. First thing Tuesday morning, I want ten thousand dollars transferred into the checking account."

She stood at the kitchen counter with her coffee. She spilled sugar onto the green Formica. "I don't care how you cover it up. That's your problem. Forge Rodney's name if you have to."

She tasted and spit. Cold. She cursed and dumped the rosy mug into the tarnished sink with a splash. "Martin, you'll do as you are told. I still have the motel receipt. You're the one who signed for the room. And you were dumb enough to produce your driver's license. . I know it was just a one-night stand, but you were not getting it for free. . don't whine at me you little wimp. It's not my fault you couldn't get a hard on. And don't think about carrying tales to Rodney." She squeezed the phone. "I have that motel receipt in a envelope addressed to your wife. All it needs is a stamp. And maybe you'll get to the mailbox first, or maybe you won't. It's no skin off my ass."

She lit a cigarette and blew smoke through her straight white teeth as she said, "I thought you would see things my way."

*   *   *   *   *

Sheets of purple rain blasted through the pines as Helena climbed into Barney Kibble's mud caked, station wagon. Barney was the sole taxi service for Hobbs Creek and Lake Powhatan. Barney could usually be found at Mayo's Pike Side Esso, because the coke machine spit out free sodas with a good kick on the coin return. Also, the phone service was cheap. When a taxi call came in, Old Man Mayo would crawl from beneath a car, wipe away grease and answer the waiting room phone. Then the beleaguered gas station owner would walk the message out. Barney was not allowed inside because Mayo claimed that Barney had fleas.

"I hope this thing's safe," mumbled Helena re-hooking a rope that kept the back door closed.

"I'll be 82 years old the day after tomorrow," beamed Barney. Thick glasses magnified his tawny eyeballs. A tiny wire ran from the glasses to one ear. He placed his thumbs behind wide suspenders that criss-crossed a dirty tee shirt, let the elastic snap, and adjusted a red feather that stuck from his hatband. The cab had no meter. He jotted down mileage on a yellow pad. He almost backed into the lake, turning around.

"Shouldn't you have the windshield wipers on?" asked Helena.

"Wipers don't work," said Barney driving around in the backyard, "Blades are missing."

Nobody knows how Barney got a cab license. He learned to drive from a manual. Put in gear. Press gas. Let out clutch. The station wagon was on it's third rear. Before driving cab, Barney painted houses. The ladder hooks were still bolted to the wagon roof. The original factory red was now sixteen shades of brown mix, left over from each job. Barney never washed the wagon. He just painted over the grime. An *I Like Ike* sticker highlighted the rusty bumper. Black smoke poured from the tailpipe.

"Never felt better in my life," said Barney stealing peeks at Helena through the rear view mirror. Barney's hayride days were over, but his oats were still hard. On

Saturday nights he would transport the local widows to bingo, free of charge.

"I think you just went through a stop sign," said Helena.

The road from Lake Powhatan to Hobbs Creek cuts across Route 91, runs three miles southwest and butts into Main Street. Billboards advertise seashore spots. If the wind is right, you can smell the bay. The entire trek takes place within a twelve, square-mile strip that is charted off as Hobbs Creek Township. During the short journey an earthy metamorphose takes place. Oaks and pines give way to swamp cedars. Thorny stalks change to cattail sprouts. Moss to mud. Hunting takes a back seat to fishing, and many a meandering seagull is heard overhead. Helena cranked up a stubborn rear window. She slid around on plastic blue seat covers and cried over muffler noise, "I'm really in no hurry!"

"Worry?" echoed Barney sliding onto Main Street, "No need to worry. I drive these wet roads all the time."

The End Is Near sign and a rolling junkyard greeted westbound motorists to Hobbs Creek in 1958, followed by weathered storefronts and a pair of tangled sneakers that still hang from phone lines behind the grade school. The town did need a facelift. Many side walk blocks were hump-backed or missing. Every other cross street was gravel or pothole bumpy.

"That's Jim Bobs Hardware Store," pointed out Barney, "And next to that is Marty Corson's fuel oil trucks. He's putting the coal people out of business. And that has lots of folks upset."

Continued Barney, "Down on the next block we're getting a new movie house, and that's gonna be real exciting!"

"Yes, that will be exciting," said Helena, "And I think you just ran over some kind of small animal."

It was the movie theater that had Hobbs Creek upset. The neon lit building was going up between the church and the church parsonage. Pastor James W. Rodgers was outraged. Rodgers told the zoning board that a movie theater did not belong next to a house of worship. The zoning board told Rodgers the lot was now recorded commercial, which tied their hands if the new foundation lay within required distances of property lines.

Originally, the lot belonged to Deacon Edward Myers who vowed to will the property to the church. Myers died. After which, the deed somehow wound up with Pinky Thorton, a nephew to the mayor on the wife's side. At the time, Pinky was greatly impressed with the wide screen cinemas that pumped up a sagging film industry. Bucking local liturgy, Pinky argued that Hobbs Creek needed something to pump up it's own backwater atmosphere. He checked into costs, scaled down initial daydreams, and tackled construction. The foundation was in, walls up. He was saving money for the roof. Rodgers said the boy could do better things with the money than build a den of iniquity for the devil. Today, the front half of the flattop building is a rental store called PJ's Video.

"That's the firehouse on the left," pointed out Barney running the light at Elm and Main, "I'm a member, myself. Don't get paid though. It's all volunteer. We used to have two trucks. Lost one up by the ravine. We was fighting this field fire, and the wind shifted back on us just as our engines quit."

"I think that was Millies," said Helena.

"Yeah, it was thrilling alright. 'Course we all jumped down and tried to foot stomp it out. But once the flames hit that gas tank - BOOM! That sucker went up like a Roman rocket."

"Millies!" cried Helena, "You went too far. You just passed the place!"

Barney made a U-turn and his foot never touched the brake. Millies Meat Market was a curbside store with no parking lot. Customers either walked or parked in the street. Barney parked on the sidewalk and beamed, "Want me to wait?"

"Uh . no. .I have a ride back," said Helena emerging into the rain. She tucked the umbrella tightly under one arm and ran for the entrance door.

CHAPTER 8

Dateline: Post 911

"Talk to me," said Adam Quayle.

"I'm in the condo," replied agent Jeremy Wade looking over a wrought iron railing at the Seine River, "Some cleaning lady let me in. But I might have a problem. She's a bit doubtful that I'm Anna Ward's third cousin from Marseille. I might need to work on my French."

"It's easier to get forgiveness than permission," said Adam Quayle suppressing a slight smile.

Helena's Paris condo was the third floor of an ominous stone building that faced the Left Bank. Below, excursion boats carried excited tourists eager to see the Eiffel Tower, Notre Dame Cathedral and Les Invalides, which is Napoleon's burial site. Inside the condo, Helena used marble and mirrors as decor. The windows were stained glass. The bare wood floor held a herringbone pattern. Ornate crown molding bordered the high ceilings, and a drafty fireplace dwelt in a white brick wall that connected the dining area to the living room.

THE PANDARUS FILE

"There's nothing here to help you much," said Jeremy Wade surveying the paperwork clutter that now littered the two-bedroom condo, "I did come up with one thing. The lady owns a string of condos and time-shares around the world. Lisbon, Hamburg, London, Spain, etc."

"Any sign of a roommate?" asked the Hobbs Creek police chief.

"Not a trace."

"Damn," said Adam Quayle tapping a nervous pencil on the idle desktop back in Hobbs Creek, "In that case we need to examine those other residencies. We need something to connect Helena Hollister to some body. And right now I'll take anybody."

A long pause followed. Then the rookie agent said, "I have to go through channels, Sir. Now that the fugitive is dead, the Marshall Service has dropped the case. I'm not sure where the Department Of Justice stands on this."

"Are we talking money?" asked Quayle.

"Expense account." said Wade who was a field agent for the newly formed T.A.G. - Tracking Agency Global. The team territory covered all U.N. sanctioned countries. Wade's primary duty was to collar fugitives outside the reach of conventional agencies. T.A.G. was also committed to local law enforcement, as well as federal and foreign.

Another pause. Then Adam Quayle said, "Let me call the county. Commissioner Lewis is a corner stone over there, and he's got a contact in Arlington. Maybe we can keep this thing going."

"It's worth a try," agreed Jeremy Wade, "Have Lewis contact William Wolfe. We need your Pandarus File added to our main agenda to justify the receipts."

"T.A.G," mused Adam Quayle, "We played that game as kids."

"Yes," replied Jeremy Wade with a laugh, "And I'm still **it**."

CHAPTER 9

Sunday 5am, August 31, 1958

Elmer tiptoed down the tunnel hallway of the Kane Mansion. All was dark. Nothing still. A sudden thunder clap jolted Elmer awake. Timber groans and promised events that lie ahead, kept him awake. His bare belly churned in a queasy roll, as he paused before a Roman statue that stood at the stair top.

"I don't like summer storms," quivered Elmer, "Summer storms make lightning."

Julius Caesar did not reply, but continued to stare down at the French provincial living room.

Elmer let go of the polished guard rail to grab his pajama bottoms that shrunk in the wash, and would no longer button. Elmer had thought about sleeping in the raw, but discarded the idea. He wanted no reminder of that Grogans' escapade and his public exposure.

The guest room door was ajar. He need not test the lock. He switched on the hallway light and squinted. His eyes adjusted. He peeked through the door opening and sighed relief. Aunt Sarah slept. The bed area was dark, but he could just make out her petticoat and girdle draped over the Queen Anne chair back.

Aunt Sarah was John Kane's sister from Norris town, Pennsylvania. She lived on a railroad pension from her late husband who worked as a switchman. Maybe it was the '58 recession, or just a sign of the times, but it was Aunt Sarah's budget that seemed to get side tracked. And quite often. So, Elmer's parents John and Martha periodically ran a care package upstate, coupled with a blank check to cover mortgage and utility bills. In return, Aunt Sarah reluctantly baby sat Elmer when needed. And it was a token thank you at best. Mostly, she sipped through un prescribed heart medicine, and napped on the Florida room sofa with the TV talking. She palmed her languidness on the muggy Jersey air. However, Martha Kane chided that a sink loaded with dirty dishes couldn't stir her heavy ankled sister-in-law.

Elmer secretly despised Aunt Sarah, who gave way to temper fits over the pettiest things. She swung a nasty backhand and would strike without warning. Sometimes at objects. Mostly at Elmer. Never in front of John and Martha. Elmer often wanted to retaliate, but didn't. He was born of mellow substance, and bred to respect elders. Thus, he held his tongue and when Aunt Sarah was near, he walked softer than a farm boy gathering eggs among flighty leghorns.

THE PANDARUS FILE

Sudden lightning lit the guest room. Elmer spotted Aunt Sarah's travel clock waiting to sound off. She always took two aspirins before retiring, and wound the brass timer knobs. Elmer eased through the dark doorway. Finger to mouth, he said *hush* to a noisy hinge squeak. He spread his arms for balance and stole across the heavy pile rug. Silently, he pushed off the alarm button.

Wind blew open the balcony doors back in Elmer's room. White lace curtains danced wildly. Rain water from the porch deck washed under Elmer's bare feet. Frowning, he made another trip down the dark hallway. This is bad, he whispered to Julius Caesar who stayed his post and said nothing. Elmer returned with an armload of towels and methodically wiped up the mess. At least this would please his mother who was very fussy about her hardwood floors. Martha Kane was super meticulous about all things that required cleaning. She was just as squeamish over anything that crawled, except maybe babies. And Elmer could not swear to that. After breeding Elmer, the Kane's didn't go for two.

Elmer left the soggy towels on the floor, and draped a wet throw rug over a knotty pine toy chest. The sky continued to flash like a huge neon sign. Elmer counted off time on his fingers. The seconds between each jagged bolt and the following thunder clap grew longer. This told Elmer the storm was moving on. Relieved, he said *boo* to the sinister tree shadows that stalked the fairyland wallpaper. Then, he locked the balcony doors for reassurance, and closed the heavy blue drapes for good measure. His parents would be back Tuesday, and that was another storm brewing. They would meet with Chief Brennan, after which Elmer would be grounded for at least a week after sordid details of the barroom fracas came out.

"It's good the shade did not break," said Elmer while righting a toppled floor lamp, "I would really be in trouble if the shade broke."

Julius Caesar remained silent, as did the upstairs phone located in the master bedroom. Elmer concurred with the marble statue, and together they agreed that a *watched phone* is much like a *watched pot.*

Elmer left his imaginary friend and peered out a rear dormer. Black clouds dissipated, but angry winds hung on. The metal chicken perched on the garage roof spun crazily. Newspapers danced wildly across the massive back yard. Elmer watched two twisted ropes slap at the manor's reigning oak. The frayed twine once held his boyhood swing. And while the urge remained, the red plank seat was gone. As were the days of birthday surprises and hidden Easter eggs. A time when Elmer was a cradled object, free from diets and chores and lectures.

A garbage can spewed trash over the asphalt driveway. An empty soup can rolled into the hedge line and disappeared from view. Elmer looked from the litter to the sky. Given a wish, he would return to that tinsel time, when Santa was real, and gifts tagged *Elmer* cluttered the house. Kinfolk gathered around a buttered turkey, flanked by cranberry sauce and gravy topped spuds. Jokes flowed like wine at a Polish wake.

He crept to the master bedroom and dragged back a blue satin comforter he borrowed when left alone. It was silky soft and smelled of perfume. It also tasted like aftershave lotion. And if Elmer had a second magic bean, he would step into his father's brown and white wingtips. He would don his father's solid gold key chain and leather driving gloves. He would slip behind the wheel of the silver Mercedes and become - **John Kane**.

The two pillars in Elmer's life were his father and a tutor named Amy Wells. Lower Elk County had no special educational facilities. Hence, John Kane paid the slender township teacher to work with Elmer after hours. Amy was fresh from college and talked a lot about purpose in life and meaningful relationships. Her long legs could stir the dead in any man. Her voice reminded Martha Kane of cotton candy.

Amy loved travel, couldn't handle snow, and called out sick with something at least twice a month. Yet, she was the driving force that got Elmer through the eighth grade, the finish line for his formal education. High school diploma hopes faded when Amy moved on and Elmer vomited all over the bus. He suffered extensive dizzy spells at the Mt Loyal School and often returned home wheezing with a blotchy face rash. After conferring with four specialists who came up dry, the elder Kane conceded that Elmer's most worldly venture would be a trip to the mailbox.

"I liked Miss Wells," said Elmer to Julius Caesar, "I wish she had never slapped my father. That made my father angry."

Like Aunt Sarah, John possessed the renowned Kane temper, an ugly heirloom passed down through generations. John also sported a roving eye and some frisky fingers, which is how he got slapped in the first place.

The melee was not all John's fault. A sneaky winter storm dumped heavy snow on Hobbs Creek back in late March. Amy needed a ride home and John Kane came to the rescue. Somehow, they wound up parked behind the schoolhouse in a snow bank. One kiss led to another. Amy's bra and panties came off. And that's about where the bubble burst. John had his weenie halfway up Amy when Jeeter Potts shone a flashlight through the car window.

Clothes went back on real fast.

John tried to beg off with a hundred dollar bill, but to no avail. Jeeter filed the report, anyway. Soon, word got back to Martha Kane, and feathers flew. Martha beat on John's chest and slapped Amy. John slapped Martha for slapping Amy, who in turn slapped John for slapping Martha.

"I was really frightened," Elmer confided to Julius Caesar, "Everybody was slapping every body. I ran and hid. After Miss Wells left, my mother and father didn't talk for days. Then last week they decided to go on a second honeymoon."

Unlike Aunt Sarah, money was more important to John Kane than fantasy. He was not about to swap his bankroll for a roll in the hay. The money had not come that easy. John rose from a milking stool to bank president, during a decade that saw losers leap from Wall Street windows, and winners stuff greenbacks into mattresses. John ran the football for Mt Loyal High, and graduated valedictorian. His wide smile and rugged looks snagged Martha Grayson, homecoming queen and daughter of the ailing Eli Grayson, who founded the Hobbs Creek National Bank. John's confidant manner kept the doors open through the Great Stampede, while a string of timely land deals branded him *The Baron.*

In 1931, John repossessed Bunky Howards debt ridden Feed & Grain Outlet. John converted the one-acre plot to Kanes Kastle, also dubbed The House That John Built. The acquisition soon became a county focal point. The stone front mansion decorated Hobbs Creek like a diamond in a woodpile. Numerous porches and massive shrubbery embraced the three- story building. A horseshoe driveway shaped the front lawn. Wrought iron gates guarded each entrance. An in-ground pool sparkled on the south side, and tennis courts lay behind the garage. In 1932, Martha became pregnant. In the spring of 1933, fate balanced the scales of justice when the blessed event turned out to be Elmer.

"The radio predicted the rain would end by daybreak," said Elmer crawling from beneath the soft comforter. He rolled over a rubber boot getting out of bed. He searched a top bureau drawer for his watch. He lumbered to his parent's room and parked next to the phone. A jumpy second hand circled a rodent's smile on his watch. Said Elmer, "I hope there will not be too many puddles. I do not want to be standing in puddles."

The call came promptly at seven-thirty.

Elmer grabbed the phone before the shrilling ring awoke Aunt Sarah. He listened hard. Happily hung up. He showered and quickly brushed two front teeth that overpowered the others. On a routine day, Elmer would plug in the electric razor and shave facial areas of peach fuzz. He would read from the encyclopedia, string colored beads and circle Fishers Pond on his 24" girl's bicycle. After breakfast, he would roll each vowel over his laggard tongue to help eliminate his monotone speech.

But, this was no longer a routine day.

He wet down his straight sandy hair, and moved a craggy part from side to center, John Kane fashion. This was a radio day look, and a style Elmer hoped might add years to his callow appearance. A second mirror advised otherwise. Frowning, Elmer moved the part back to the side and broke a nose pimple. Pockmarks and pimples plagued the Fifties generation including Elmer. His mother suggested he abstain from candy bars, chocolate cake and sugar. His father just yawned.

Elmer's next fork in the road was what to wear. His round eyes rolled, each at a different speed. He scratched his ruddy backside through boxer shorts as starched and ironed as any shirt. His deep closet was stocked full of special cut clothes, extra large. He picked out a gray suit and red plaid tie. Gray and plaid would add a mature touch. He snitched a chocolate popsicle from the basement freezer and left the house.

It was a short walk to the deserted schoolyard. Streets were empty, stores closed. Here and there, a kitchen light flashed onto the wet pavement. Distant rumbles rang up the storm's end, leaving silence but for Elmer's footsteps. Breathing heavily, he squeezed into the waiting red Corvette.

"I remembered where to meet you," he said proudly, "And I remembered the time."

CHAPTER 10

An empty oil drum and rusty bulldozer welcome visitors to Pykes Pit. Sometimes, fallen tree limbs or a nosy pine snake will block the winding entrance road. Heavy foliage delays the dawn. Dense fog lingers in low areas.

Helena drove warily, ready for addled deer that might take aim at oncoming head-lights. Elmer sat with clasped hands between knees. Chocolate splatters crept down his bulging shirt. His maroon dress hat buffed the black roof liner. His right shoelace was missing. He peeked at Helena's skimpy white shorts and said, "I'm glad that Mr. Hollister is no longer mad at me. I don't want anybody to be mad at me."

"As I told you earlier," said Helena, "There is nothing to fear. Rodney's bark is worse than his bite."

Elmer grinned and replied, "I know what that means. We once had a dog named Tiny. At least she was tiny when my father brought her home. Then she grew into a big dog and would bark at everybody. But, she would never bite anybody. Tiny would not even bite a mailman."

Elmer giggled at his own punch line, a family adage repeated often when the Kane's swapped pet stories with house guests. Helena turned up the radio. Elmer tediously unfolded a wrinkled hanky and wiped down his plaid tie.

"I didn't know if I should wear a tie," he said, "Will a tie get in the way?"

"You can keep your tie on," said Helena.

"I have to be careful with a tie," explained Elmer, "My tie has a ten-den-cy to get caught in things. One time it got caught in the elevator doors when we visited Phil-a-del-phia."

"Really," said Helena.

"My father calls Philadelphia the city of brotherly love, because everyone uses everyone else's hubcaps. We went there so I could see the crack in the Lib-bert-ty Bell. Then my mother saw this sale on electric mixers and talked my father into buying one. It took a long time. My father wanted to check brand names and war-rant-ties. My father says you only get what you pay for. My mother said we would go another time to see Independence Hall, and that I should not feel put out."

"I think you just put us in neutral," said Helena pushing a chubby arm off the gearshift lever.

THE PANDARUS FILE

The car bucked. Elmer's hat pancaked into the roof. Sudden road ruts sent his voice staccato as he continued talking. "We don't have a cook because my father says a woman should prepare her own meals. Then when we got home my mother mixed up some cake batter and my tie got caught in the blades."

"Well," said Helena popping the clutch, "You certainly stuck your neck out that day."

"My mother screamed and tried to pull me free," said Elmer, "But my father just reached over the counter and pulled the plug. My father is like that. He always knows how to handle a crisis. Especially one that might be harmful."

"What a guy!" quipped Helena, "And with money, too. But somehow I don't think he will save the last dance for me."

Elmer peeked at Helena's bouncing breasts. He could almost see her nipples. The word dance made Elmer recall that brief moment his bare body covered Helena's naked body at Grogans Bar And Grille. He blushed. It was anything but two ships passing in the night. However, it did spawn nude fantasies and prick Elmer's conscience. It also pointed out the true depth of his *motor slowness.* When Rodney returned from the rest room, he first wielded the two-dollar chair at Elmer.

Poking. Jabbing. Like a prodding cowhand igniting a mellow rodeo bull. The crowd held a collective breath. Elmer's eyes rolled. Then, as the verbal jockeying turned physical, Helena's left foot sent Rodney crashing to the floor, pins over pine needles. The crowd cheered. Rodney cursed. Elmer grinned. Rodney jumped up and swung the chair again with blind vengeance. The crowd booed. Elmer cringed. And at that point Henry Porter returned from the kitchen to witness an outsider break a spindle over a pub table. Then, Porter called the police.

"I never even saw your foot move," said Elmer trying to get his shirt buttons to line up, "You can move fast. I have trouble moving fast. My mother says it does not matter. My mother says it takes a sure horse for a long race. But my father says I'm the track's biggest long shot, except once when I dropped the cookie jar."

Helena stared at the rotund 24 year old. She swerved to miss a rock and fishtailed off the road. Back in control, she lit a cigarette and changed radio stations as she said, "You are sweet Elmer. You really are a lamb. But sometimes it's less painful if we don't look back. Besides, Rodney would not have harmed you anyway. He was just blowing off steam. Rodney would not even bite a mailman."

Elmer Kane giggled.

Pykes Pit lies roughly two miles northeast of Lake Powhatan, and some fifty yards inside a weaving Lower Elk Township border. To the southwest run the Atlantic City power lines that feed civilization to the desolate pine lands. To the northwest stretches the Elk County Game Forest, a forty square-mile tract that provides free camping, fishing and hunting. The tract joins the Pine Barrens. Rabbit and deer are abundant. Random rifle shots can be heard year 'round, despite a New Jersey State gaming timetable. Often, a folded doe gets quickly crammed into a ready car trunk. Occasionally, a poacher gets collared by Jesse Joe Jacks, county game warden.

Helena bounced the low-slung car over a one wagon bridge and through a cluster of white birches. Angry gravel chunks smacked the under carriage. Scrub branches lashed the windshield. She skirted a wide puddle and paused on a clearing that sloped upward toward a hidden cliff. She looked around and said, "Well, this is it.

"Looks like a great place," said Elmer.

A white sandy path climbs the clearing, runs the southeast ridge of the crater, and gradually descends to the basin floor. Legend says a man named Leroy Pykes, brought a chest of gold coins here one summer night, when the pit area was yet woodland. Pykes and a cohort, Billy Rice stumbled onto the coins while robbing a sleepy train en route from Atlantic City to points north. They lifted wallets and watches. They took a young virgin hostage, and tossed a rebellious conductor to the wind. They then invaded the baggage car to find the metal-lined box stowed beneath a pile of canvas mail sacks. The chest had been loaded aboard by a beachcomber who dug up the booty along the Brigantine coastline - buried there by the infamous Black Beard back in the Seventeen Hundreds.

Stopping the train, Pykes stood guard while Rice went for a cart to transport the treasure back to their lair. Each rail car teemed with bobbing faces. Thus, Pykes did not notice a fleet-footed brakeman slip away to flag down a county sheriff already in the saddle. The horse and the cart arrived together, from opposite directions.

A gunfight broke out.

Pykes killed the lawman, and hitched the cart to his horse. Rice took a shoulder bullet from an onboard detective waiting for an open shot. Pykes returned the volley, and the railroad guard fled to get rein-forcements. Before a posse could form, the bandits vanished into the pine lands where Pykes finished off Rice for his share of the gold, and raped the girl whose name was not made public record. Pykes then setup camp and began counting coins.

Blue mist filled the air the story goes, when a terrified boy puffed into town and told of unearthly sounds coming from the campsite. The young hobo said the screams were human, but the growls sounded animal. Authorities returned to find nothing but a bloody finger, pulsating amid some eerie hoof prints, etched in trampled soil. Natives believe the Jersey Devil made the prints. Natives say the devil slew Pykes, rescued the distraught maiden, and buried the gold.

Somebody bought the story.

Shortly thereafter, a hole appeared at the campsite. Then a second hole appeared, and a third. At the onset of the post-war building boom, a contractor named Lucas O'Leary brought in a front-end loader and finished the job up brown. Endless loads of foundation dirt rolled out to the meadow lands for a housing development called Bayside Glen. The digging left a cavity big enough to bury the national debt. The gold never turned up, nor did the rest of Pykes.

Today, the rusty slopes are impregnated with tire tracks from trail bikes. Smelly trash and want-me-nots litter the sticky basin floor. *No Dumping* signs are everywhere, and trespassers are stiffly fined if caught. In 1958, mutilated targets plastered the pit walls, targets fired on by tournament sportsmen and local police officers seeking gun qualification. A red phone hung from a pole at the path entrance. A metal bulletin board posted range hours, which everyone ignored. Helena parked next to a battered green pickup that looked like a rolling junkyard. White paint scrawled across the tailgate read **Abel Johnson - Odd Jobs**. The right rear tire needed air. The radiator leaked green water.

There were no other vehicles.

"I dropped Rodney off earlier," said Helena, "He likes to start everything at the crack of dawn. He would have coffee with a rooster, but neither of them drink coffee."

Elmer giggled.

Helena killed the engine and lit a cigarette. All fell quiet but for rustling leaves and a hovering black crow. Off to the far right, an emerging sun began the day's journey. Soon, jagged light rays would phase out the pale moon.

"I always get up early too," said Elmer, "Early to rise, makes me healthy, wealthy and wise."

Helena stashed her handbag behind the arm rest. She paused outside the car door to undo her top blouse button. She said, "See, you and Rodney have something in common already."

Elmer Kane wiggled up from the low bucket seat. He wore a happy face. "I will like learning how to shoot the bow and arrow."

Helena took one last drag and foot-screwed the smoking cylinder into the damp ground. Then she took Elmer firmly by a meaty arm, and led him up the path.

CHAPTER 11

Rodney Hollister stood between puddles on the deep basin floor. Despite sticky morning air, he wore high-cuff jeans and a flannel, hunting shirt. This favorite garb made him feel woodsy and shoot straighter. The outfit also hid his bony limbs.

He sucked on a blister that formed on his left thumb. The heated lump still grew. Soon it would burst. He knew that. And, his first aid kit was back in the cabin. Grumbling, he frowned at the clay caked to his wrinkled boots. The early morning rain came with a chaser. Rodney had left the pit to seek shelter among nearby pine and oaks. Consequently, brown needles and dried leaves now stuck from his wrap-around, headgear.

He looked up. One dark cloud remained, but winds had calmed. He snapped a shooting glove onto his right hand, the left arm guard already in place. His target was a straw wheel pinned by steel anchors and twine to the steep northeast wall. Paper rings covered the straw. A crinkled bulls eye smiled from the hub.

"Damn," he cried as the shot missed the mark.

Things got worse.

THE PANDARUS FILE

Three of Rodney's next four shots missed the entire target. One left the pit completely. His frown deepened. The only clear areas were the pit and the parking lot. All else was nasty under brush. Thus, that wayward arrow could stay lost for all Rodney cared.

He drew another shaft from his belt quiver. The pit contoured like a giant peanut shell, which caused shooting distances to vary from 75 to 250 ft. The footage was ideal for archery and short-range weapons. Most local bow shooters shot from 75 to 100 ft. Rodney used the 75 foot lane. Rodney liked the short middle lane because it was easier to hit the target. Also, it was a quicker walk to retrieve the arrows. Not that he was lazy, just impatient. And that was a character flaw Rodney needed to eliminate to become a better marksman. Thus, he hurried down here at daybreak to practice patience. He wanted to focus on each shot, and not rush. He would use thought instead of rhythm, and this technique would improve his marksmanship - or so Rodney believed.

He threaded the next arrow through the clicker, a timing device mounted on the bow to gauge arm pull. Rodney didn't clutch the bow. Rather, he wedged the rubber grip between thumb and forefinger. He then pulled back the nock as he raised the bow to fire. He used a bow sight and cheekbone for aim. The bow would jump forward after each shot, while a black wrist strap kept the bow from falling.

Rodney copied this shooting style from Mark Williams, the Belly Snakes' top marksman in KD tournaments open to rival clubs. Rodney liked Mark because Mark welcomed Rodney to the Belly Snakes with a warm smile and handshake, while others slithered away. It was also Mark who taught Rodney how to string a bow without suffering backlash to the testicles.

"Damn," whined Rodney lowering the bow. He turned to Abel Johnson who callously pounded a ringing pipe into the silent basin floor. Asked Rodney, "What the hell are you doing?"

The Hobbs Creek handyman stopped beating on the hollow upright. He yanked a dirty bandana from his clammy forehead, and slowly wiped sweat beads from a hairy chest and wide neck. He used the rag to blow his nose. He wore construction boots and khaki's you could pee on, and no one would know. He leaned on a weary sledgehammer and spit, "You didn't see the bulletin board out front?"

"I saw some tin nailed to a tree," said Rodney.

THE PANDARUS FILE

"Then I reckon you can't read," said Johnson, "The sign says that shootin' hours are from 8:30am to dusk."

"Actually, the sign reads from ate-thirdy til dust," said Rodney, "Which makes me question who posted it."

"I got through my three R's," said Johnson checking a tarnished pocket watch, "Right now it's 8:15. Give or take a few seconds. That's 15 minutes before the range is officially open."

Johnson did light carpentry, plumbing, tile, window glazing, etc. He could replace a bad wall switch, but shied away from main fuse boxes and double line current. He had six jobs started and none finished because he spent ebb tide hours checking crab traps off the Bay Street Bridge. His right eye was brown, the left one green glass. When you talked to Johnson close-up, it was hard to keep focused on the good eye.

"So maybe you should be out checking crab traps right now," suggested Rodney.

"Right now I need to be a gittin this safety fence up," growled Johnson spitting tobacco juice into a nearby puddle, "The mayor's giving me a nice bonus for working the holiday, and that tells me this job must be prit-tee important."

Rodney looked at fence pipes connected by heavy link chain that drooped like an icy phone wire. The work order called for the skimpy barrier to run parallel to the 200' long firing line. Johnson elected to space the uprights three yards apart. He would plunge a foot or so with a post hole digger, and then beat the six foot uprights down to three feet showing. This would secure the pipes without cementing the base. Spec's called for the cement, but the pit had no water tap, and Johnson refused to transport the concrete needed to mount twenty-three uprights.

"Don't look important to me," said Rodney staring at the half finished project, "I think this township just likes to waste money."

The safety chain was to keep all non-shooters well behind the firing line. Back in early July, Mayor Willard Green's son and a playmate horsed around with a shotgun in the basin. The 12 gauge accidentally went off and wounded Willard Jr who got a free ride to County General Hospital. It was the fifth shooting mishap in three years, and rekindled an old debate over the status of Pykes Pit. A heated Mayor Green said the ill-fated gravel pit was jinxed and should be filled in. Opposing Green was Chief Bo Brennan who claimed the facility performed a valuable service to the community.

Green said he didn't think so. Brennan reminded His Honor that voters stood behind the Right To Bear Arms movement, and Green began to back down. After which, Brennan showed up at the next township meeting with some rifle club members to fire one last volley.

The verbal melee went on past midnight. It ended with decisions to build the safety fence and install the emergency phone. Costs would be split between Township and the local rifle association. Other business was not recorded because Township Clerk, Betsy Sue Connors ran for the bathroom to fix a female problem.

"So," spit Johnson, "Now you know why this job is so damn important."

"I'm sorry about the mayor's kid," grunted Rodney, "But I just can't concentrate with you back there pounding your nuts off."

"Maybe so maybe not," said Johnson, "But at least I got a pair to pound off."

"And what's that supposed to mean," snapped Rodney turning to face the Hobbs Creek handy man.

"You're a shootin' at the target the wimmin use," said Johnson, "That's what it means. We put that lane in here just for the ladies and juniors. Concentration a'int your problem, anyway."

Rodney's face showed some interest.

"Shot group is your problem," said Johnson.

"And what's wrong with my shot group?"

"You don't have any. And another thing junior, that headgear you're wearing is for gun. Bow shooters don't wear ear protection."

"Oh funny funny," said Rodney, "And I think you just spit down your leg."

"If you was any kind of a bowman," drawled Johnson, "You'd git three or four arrows in a bunch."

Rodney gave up trying to out stare a glass eye. He squinted at the circling crow as he raised the bow to fire. He gave up that notion, also. He turned back down range. His thumb blister popped as he grumbled, "I don't suppose you would have a band aid? "

Johnson uncorked a brown jug that now held water, and washed out his left eye. He popped the green marble back into place and wet down his neck and shoulders. He soaked his savage brown hair and said through a mouthful of fresh tobacco, "Any fella that hunches up as close as you do, oughta cut the bulls-eye right outta that dime store target. And if you wuz really worth your salt, you could split an arrow with an arrow."

Rodney lowered the bow. He relaxed the string and rotated on one heel to keep his anchor spot. He glared at Johnson and said, "Your parents were related weren't they."

Grunting, Johnson withdrew the pipe from the hole to dig out a pesky rock. He dropped the gritty mass to the basin floor and swung the sledgehammer. Powder dust flew as he said, "Had a fella down here last year that could do it. Stood right at this very spot and watched him. Not just once, either. Must have made that shot three or four times. Best damn shooting I ever seen."

Rodney spit, mocking Abel Johnson.

"Suit yourself," said the Hobbs Creek handyman, "But I'll lay you a whiskey bottle against a beer keg that you can't do it."

CHAPTER 12

Helena reached the rocky ridge top first. She paused by the phone station while Elmer caught his breath. She whispered as they continued on, "Don't make any noise, it breaks Rodney's concentration."

Elmer grinned and tried to tiptoe. His lace-less shoe flopped at the heel like a happy beach sandal. He teetered toward the crater edge, arms spread for balance. His tie spun loose in the topside wind. His maroon dress hat went sailing.

"Try to stay on the path," snapped Helena grabbing the hat with one hand and Elmer with the other, "I don't want you kicking loose stones into the pit."

The wind shifted. Elmer covered his mouth and pinched his ruddy nose, which began to itch. He whispered, "I'm allergic to wet gravel. The smell of wet gravel always makes me sneeze."

"Sh-sh-sh," said Helena.

"And I get dizzy if I look down too long. I always get dizzy when I look far down."

"Shh-shh-shh," said Helena.

"Sh-sh-sh," said Elmer.

THE PANDARUS FILE

A guardrail ran between the path and pit edge. Like the safety fence, the guardrail was also made of pipe and chain, and also installed by Abel Johnson. On this particular job, Johnson had figured short on materials. Hence, the chain stopped several yards shy of where the path turned down to the basin floor. The second upright from the end was directly to Rodney's back. It was raised two inches, which left the base a shiny marker.

"Maybe I should have worn my snow cap," said Elmer, "Mr. Hollister has his ears covered up."

"Sh-sh-sh," said Helena stopping at the pipe with the shiny marker.

"My snow cap has flaps that pull down over the ears," said Elmer, "My mother says my snow cap makes me look like an airplane pilot. My father says -

"Shhh-Shhh-shhh," commanded Helena.

"Sh-Sh-Sh," echoed Elmer.

Below, Rodney faced the target on Lane Fourteen. He stood with back against the world. Sick of listening to this rube with rotted teeth. Tired of watching sunlight ricochet off a glass eye, that looked nowhere and sneered at everything. He sucked on the thumb blister, now bleeding. He toyed with the idea of splitting an arrow with an arrow. As stated, Mark

Williams was the best shot in the Belly Snake Hunting Club. Mark could group arrows so tight that feathers touched feathers. And that was deemed expert marksmanship. However, not even Mark Williams could split an arrow with an arrow.

There was a man who could. Rodney saw him perform the feat on a TV show. The man hit the bulls-eye, then followed up with a second shot. The camera went slow motion to highlight the steel point shatter the nock of the first arrow.

Incredible!

But true.

Believe it or not.

Rodney's black eyes kindled. He licked a forefinger to check wind direction. The waking sun was a tad to his right, a nuisance but not a problem. He moved the bow off the blister and spit, this time to clear his throat. He accepted the challenge without facing the challenger. "You're on wise ass, and the whiskey better be a brand name. I don't want any of that homemade shit."

Rodney knew the trick was to believe. He needed to form a mental video of making the shot, beforehand. Use total concentration. The bow, arrow and body would become one. He readied his stance and honed in on the bulls-eye.

Don't flinch as you release the string.

Rodney could hear Mark's voice echo from afar.

Don't drop your arm, and hold onto your sight picture. You must stay locked onto the sight picture even after the shot is gone, to achieve real follow-through.

Abel Johnson sneered and jibed, "You gonna shoot or just stand there and stare into space?"

"That one," replied Rodney as the two figures stopped on the overhead path to his rear, "The one in the outside ring. It's nice and straight. That's the arrow I'm going to split."

Helena stooped to tie a sneaker lace. The sudden move caused Elmer to stop and turn. And that put Rodney and Elmer, back to back.

Helena boldly unbuttoned her blouse. Balancing on one knee, she saucily removed her bra and tossed it at Elmer's feet. Her chalky breasts tumbled into view as Rodney raised the bow to the target downrange. He drew the trigger string to rest against his cheekbone.

Helena winked at Elmer. She tossed her ocean of red hair. Her breasts moved like rippling water.

Elmer's face flushed. He began to sweat profusely. He stood very, very still.

KYLE KEYES

Rodney's fingers opened.
The arrow left in a howling whisper.

CHAPTER 13

Elmer Kane never heard the thunder or felt the lightning. He didn't spin or cry out, not even a stagger. He simply hung, suspended in the raw morning air. His fingers froze and mouth drooped. His doleful eyes rolled, each at a different speed for one last time. Then he collapsed, cut down from an invisible rope by a phantom clever.

The crow sounded the death bugle. Blasting caws caromed off the eerie pit walls like gunfire bottled in a hollow chamber. His black wings quickened, fanning the down currents as he flew in crazy circles.

Helena's screams followed. Piercing. Freezing muscles. Chilling the senses.

Now silence. So deep, it planted the seeds for a nightmare.

Rodney spun to peer at the ridge top. He saw nobody. He stared at Abel Johnson blowing his nose. The bandana was about spent. Johnson buried it alongside the upright that was now back in the hole. The digger and hammer lay in the mud, nearby..

"What the hell is going on," cried Rodney.

Johnson spit.

More screams.

Johnson picked up the grimy hammer and returned to work. He began to whistle, ignoring the pleas for help coming from the path above.

Rodney dropped the bow. He scrambled up the steep embankment, the nightmare building. His pulse raced, touching off a thousand tiny sirens, and pulling the pin on rational behavior. His feet ran off the path. Loose gravel kicked to the basin floor. Panting and clawing, he came over the top on all fours, just short of the guard chain.

The earth stopped.

"Oh shit," Rodney moaned.

Elmer Kane lay belly down across the upper path, his head twisted sickly to one side. An arrow pierced his throat, the silver point protruded from his mouth. Blood gushed onto the sandy walkway like red ink washing over a blotter. The body bucked in spasms, but Elmer's head held steady as though pinned by the arrow. The initial flow subsided. Now, blood trickled down the backside of the shaft, and dripped off the blue feathers into the dirt.

The torso died.

Rodney puked.

THE PANDARUS FILE

The earth shifted from stop to go. Fresh nausea swept through Rodney's body, robbing air, scrambling orientation, and testing cohesion. He puked again and rolled onto his back. The sky shuddered. He covered his eyes with an open palm. Chimes from Abel Johnson's hammer became a rope to grasp, a beacon through the fog. Rodney braced for another look at Elmer Kane and again muttered *oh shit*. He looked at Helena who appeared to be in shock.

The hammer stopped.

Rodney crawled to the cliff edge and looked toward the gelid handyman, now working a new hole. Sunlight gleamed off the metal jaws each time the digger came up. Wailed Rodney spitting dirt and vomit, "We need some help up here!"

"Up here," cried the echo.

Abel Johnson selected the next upright from a clutter of mucky pipes. He dropped it into the fresh hole at Lane 15 and stomped dirt around the base. He looked like an Indian doing a war dance.

Rodney groaned. *Crazy,* he would think later. The man was definitely a loony, like Solly Simpkins who walked the back streets of Delaware Township, saluting bread trucks and telephone poles.

An ant crawled over Rodney's fingers, sticky from wet clay and rejected breakfast. A regiment followed. They were precise in movement and left red swellings as they bit. Cursing, Rodney rolled back under the guard chain and sat up to tuck in a floppy shirttail. He looked around for his ear covers, which suddenly seemed very important and should not have been. He gained strength from his own voice as he muttered, "I think it was the goat's milk that made me sick. Or maybe the marmalade. Maybe I should not mix butter with marmalade."

Helena fastened bra snaps and blouse buttons in hidden intervals. Questions began to surface as Rodney regained his pins. To evade answering, she placed a hand over mouth and slowly sank back to her knees. She kept her head turned from the fallen body. She emitted a few whimpers and faked a spell of dizziness

"I'll get somebody," said Rodney moving on watery legs, "I'll go for help."

She gestured him off with mumbled phrases that meant she was all right. Her peripheral vision saw the crow break circle and soar through the pine tops. When Rodney was also out of sight, she lit a cigarette. It had been a great shot. She blew a final smoke ring out over the canyon. A perfect shot, she thought, well worth the ten thousand dollars she agreed to pay.

The car left. She heard the rear wheels spin over the parking lot gravel. And the ringing sounds coming from the basin floor meant that Abel Johnson still toiled, installing the safety chain to prevent further fatalities at Pykes Pit. She smiled at such irony as she pulled a small, perforated disc from her handbag. She stepped over the body and hurried to the phone station at the head of the path.

She unscrewed the mouthpiece from the handset. She inserted the disc and replaced the cap.

"This is Helena Hollister," she said into the emergency receiver, "My husband just shot and killed Elmer Kane."

CHAPTER 14

"I'll kill the bitch!" cried Rodney Hollister.

"Just answer the question, Suh," said Walker Thomas, "Your middle name is Roland?"

"So help me I'll kill the bitch."

"Is that with one or two L's?" asked the black county detective.

"My given name is Rodney Rowand. That's with two big R's, and one little W."

"And your home address is 112 Hanover Turn, Delaware Township?"

"I'll kill that lying bitch!"

"According to your wife's statement, you fired the arrow that caused the untimely demise of one Elmer Lewis Kane."

"Untimely demise? How would you like me to demise your sorry black ass. I was aiming downrange. I was shooting downrange. I never saw the moron. I didn't even know he was there."

"But you left the crime scene," said Walker Thomas flatly, "Chief Brennan chased you north bound doing a hundred mile an hour. Fortunately for us you ran out of gas."

"What," cried Rodney beating his hand cuffed wrists along the chair-back, "Who the hell said I ran out of gas. That over-sized ape you call a police chief cornered me down a dead-end trail with a fallen tree. And if he ruined my undercarriage, I'm gonna sue this township for car damages."

"But you did leave the scene of a crime?"

"I was going for help," said Rodney, "Then suddenly, I remembered the bruises."

The county detective rested a busy pencil. He tilted back in the squeaky swivel chair and raised his silver eyebrows to form a question mark.

"My wife wore slacks and sweater when she dropped me off at the pit," explained Rodney, "When she returned with the moron, she wore shorts and sneakers. That's what started me to think. Helena never wears sneakers. She hates sneakers. She claims they make her feet sweat. She either wears heels or goes barefoot."

"Would you come to the point, Suh."

"The bruises!" exclaimed Rodney, "She was covered with bruises. And one of her ankles was wrapped. I can't remember which one."

"It's the right ankle, Suh."

"Have you been eyeballing my wife!"

"Suh, please sit down."

"It was a setup, stupid. A stupid setup. She hid the bruises from me. But, she wanted all the world to see the bruises later."

"Suh, I think you just broke Bo's coffee cup."

Rodney snorted and went on to fill in the missing pieces of Helenas well planned frame-up. He now understood the sudden flat tire, the forgotten gear, and the missing cabin key that resurfaced. Concluded Rodney, "It all came together when I hit the main road. That's why I panicked. That's why I ran."

"You sideswiped three cars," said Walker Thomas, "You upset Pop Owens fruit stand. You rammed a news truck, which sent paper sheets skyward like convention balloons. There's a magazine section still under Bo's wiper blades. Not to mention, you drove right through Ellie Mae Jenkins' backyard clothesline."

"Some idiot in a taxi cab ran me off the road," muttered Rodney, "And when I get my hands on Helena, I'll choke the truth out of her!"

"You were a bit early for bow shooting," said Walker Thomas, "What were you doing out there at that hour?"

"Digging for gold," said Rodney.

"What was Elmer Kane doing at the range?"

asked the county detective.

Rodney shrugged.

"No idea?"

"Why don't you ask Elmer," said Rodney.

"This is your wife's statement, Mr. Hollister," said the black man tapping a legal form on the duty desk, "Elmer Kane was at the range because of that Friday night fracas at Grogans Bar & Grille. He wanted to apologize. Set things right. At least that's what it says here."

"I'll kill the bitch."

"Mister Hollister, you are being charged with homicide. It would be in your best interest to cooperate."

"You can't hold me."

"You get one phone call," informed the county detective, "You might want to use that call to get a lawyer."

"A lawyer!" screeched Rodney, "Your sorry ass is gonna need the lawyer. For incompetence. I don't need a lawyer. I have a witness. The handyman. The guy putting up the safety barrier."

"Suh, please sit down before you jump into the overhead fan."

"Johnson!" cried Rodney as he recalled the name on the battered pickup truck, "Johnson's Odd Jobs or something like that. The handyman. He stood right behind me. He can tell you I was firing at the straw target!"

CHAPTER 15

"Your name is Abel Johnson?"

"You know my name, Bo."

"Just answer the question yes or no, Abel. Your name is Abel Johnson?"

"Yes - Sir."

"And you were born February 19th in the year of the big blizzard. Could you be a bit more precise?"

"It was a snow blizzard."

"Yes. . .now it says here. . .*the woman and Elmer Kane walked hand in hand along the rige*. .Who the hell took this statement anyway?"

"Jeeter Potts."

"And he did the spelling?"

"I helped him with it."

"That's what I figured.. Just why would Helena Hollister hold hands with Elmer Kane?"

"Probably so the dumb bastard wouldn't fall off the edge."

"Spit on my floor again Abel, and you're going to fall off that chair. Now, when Lieutenant Thomas and the ambulance got to the range, they found you working on the safety chain. There was a dead boy on the pathway, and you was sinking pipe. You want to explain that, Abel."

"I was putting up chain, Bo. You can't put up chain without sinking pipe."

"That's not what I'm getting at Abel and you know it."

"So what was I suppose to do Bo, tie a turn-e-kit around the kid's neck?"

"You could have gone topside. Maybe calmed down the woman. Made the phone call for her, maybe. In case you didn't notice, she was plenty hysterical."

"Shaw, Bo. What city folk do a'int none of our business, and Elmer Kane a'int my lookout. You know me and John Kane don't see eye to eye. Ever since I installed that fence gate fer him. He bitched the damn thing swung out instead of in. Which he claims made the door scratch in his Mur-say-dees. Held back part of my money, too. Cheap bastard. And that's the last job I do fer him. Anyways, I had to git that safety chain up. You know the mayor's bin on my ass about that."

"All right, let's put that aside," said the Hobbs Creek Police Chief, "When did Rodney Hollister first see his wife and Elmer Kane up on the ridge?"

"Right after I did."

"Did they call down?"

"I don't recollect."

"So, how did Hollister know they were there?"

"Falling stones caught his ear, I think."

"Then what happened?" asked Bo Brennan.

"He got all funny looking. Hollister, I mean. He threw down his headgear and started *bleeping* this and *bleeping* that. I thought the devil himself set upon him. Blew up like the time some trucker backed into Mayo's gas pump."

"And that's when he loaded his bow ?"

"Yes Sir," replied Abel Johnson.

"And he wasn't firing downrange ?"

"No Sir."

"Why was Elmer Kane facing the other way?"

"He weren't."

"He wasn't ?" questioned Bo Brennan.

"That's what I just said."

"Then Abel, how did Elmer get turned around so the shot came through the back of his neck ?"

"I think the woman pulled him," said Abel Johnson after a lengthy pause, "Yeah, that's how it happened, Bo. When Hollister turned the bow upward, the woman tried to pull Kane out of the line of fire. That's what spun the kid around. That's why the arrow entered from the back instead of the front. I don't know if this will help, Bo. But you can tell Martha Kane that the kid didn't suffer. He just went down like a startled buck caught off-season."

"I'm sure she will find that very comforting," grunted Bo Brennan shoving a large yellow pad across a card table that doubled as a desk when needed, "And you eye-witnessed Rodney Hollister fire the shot that killed Elmer Lewis Kane?"

"Yes Sir," replied the Hobbs Creek handy man.

"You may sign your statement, Abel."

CHAPTER 16

Bo Brennan waded through the sea of scratch pads and microphones docked on his station house porch. He waved off a question barrage, and turned his towering back on a pushy TV camera. Growling, he slammed the door on a cub reporter, wetting his pants to tell the world who he was and where he was coming from. Vintage William Bo Brennan.

Labor Day: September 1, 1958.

"Damn news hounds," muttered the burly police chief sailing his cowboy hat toward a wall peg, "How many times do I have to tell 'em. When I find out more, they will find out more. And not a second sooner, unless they want to conduct this investigation them selves."

Elmer Kane was already cold but his story just beginning to heat up. The Pykes Pit murder reached the wire services, late. Facts were fuzzy. Then the name Rodney Rowand Hollister surfaced. Suddenly, all eyes swung to Hobbs Creek.

"I think the city papers are just upset because the locals stole their thunder on this one," said Walker Thomas from the rocker.

"Yeah, and half that thunder is noise and no rain," said Bo Brennan. Air hissed from a yielding cushion as he dropped into the squeaky swivel chair. He slapped the county paper onto an empty ink blotter and asked, "Who cleaned off my desk ? "

"I ditched the beer cans," yawned Walker Thomas showing perfect teeth too white for his age. The far wall cot was already made, the brown Army blanket taunt enough to bounce a quarter. The black man's fingernails were clean and clipped, as was his mustache. He pushed a snappy hat brim to the back of his silver hair, and stretched away some morning stiffness as he added, "Before Molly came down this morning and you got yourself grounded."

"Is that right," said Bo Brennan.

"Not that we is getting any fishing in now any way," said Walker Thomas.

"I wasn't worried about Molly," said Bo Brennan.

The black man looked dubious.

"Well I wasn't," said Brennan, "I was thinking about Old Lady Gerty."

"Clothesline Gerty?"

Brennan nodded. "The same. Right out there on the porch with the rest of them. And you know what we always say. A dog that brings a tail in, takes a tail out."

THE PANDARUS FILE

"I don't member us saying that," said Walker Thomas searching pockets and peering beneath the rocker.

"And Emmet, I hope you're not gonna go and make more out of this killing than what meets the eye. Like the time Elroy Harkins shot himself in the head, and you thought it was murder because he held the gun his left hand."

"Well, it could have been murder."

"Emmet," cried Brennan, "The man was left-handed for chris'sake and if you are looking for your tobacco pouch, you are sitting on it."

As the black man leaned forward, Bo Brennan rocked backward complaining about swollen feet. A busy Molly Brennan came to the rescue. She yanked off the stubborn boots, muttered that men are helpless, and went back to mopping everybody's mud from the hallway. Brennan wiggled toes and lit a stogie. His mood grew lighter as the air grew darker. Coughing, he playfully smacked the bony hand reaching for the newspaper. Warned Brennan, "Not 'til I get Molly's crossword out of there. I get cut off if I lose Molly's puzzle."

"You is kidding," kidded the black man.

"Scouts honor," whispered Brennan holding up three fingers, "And it's no nooky for a whole month if I lose the food section."

All smiles faded as Adam Quayle marched from the annex room and stopped at Brennan's duty desk. Quayle was three weeks graduated from Lower Elks Police Academy, amid a gush of accolades: first in search and seizures; tops in target shooting; highest grades. He stood at attention, a fresh badge pinned to his tailored shirt, teeth gleaming like the black oxfords clamped heel to heel. His eager eyes looked troubled as he spoke through the cigar smoke drifting toward the ceiling fan, "Sir, I believe we have a violation of civil rights, here."

Adam Quayle is of course the current Hobbs Creek Police Chief. He was appointed top cop at Bo Brennan's 1977 retirement party. Quayle directs two dozen squad cars and six dispatchers, from a plush office in the new municipal building that now corners Elm and Main. His hair is gone, teeth capped. He plays Thursday night poker with City Council, and works hand in glove with Special Agent, Jeremy Wade. This was Adam Quayle's first day as a cop.

"Sir, I believe it's against regulations to chain a prisoner to a sewerage pipe," he said.

Bo Brennan stared at Adam Quayle. "Is that right."

"Yes Sir. . .I believe it is."

Somebody kicked an empty can outside the station window. A tender voice shrieked *all free*. This, followed by fertile feet that thundered over raw earth as school kids savored summer's end. Noise that broke the deadlock stare. Brennan buried his cigar in a fresh ashtray and slapped the desktop, rising. He glowered at the rookie officer, and ignored the verbal protests coming from the annex, that doubled as the Hobbs Creek Jail.

The annex was once a side porch to the white, clapboard farmhouse. As township grew, the porch was enclosed. Windows were barred, a steel door installed. This make shift prison held a fold-up table and two rail-back chairs. A naked mattress sprawled on the floor. Nicknamed the *holding tank*, the room mostly bedded down Corky Tabor, who liked to get drunk and weave down Main Street in nothing but a raincoat. More serious offenders were fastened to a stack pipe that came from an overhead bathroom. Bo Brennan lowered the desk window and lumbered to the coffee pot. He grumbled to Walker Thomas, "Who the hell we got in there, anyway?"

"Rodney Rowand Hollister," whistled the black man reading from the paper, "Major investor in a half dozen expanding companies. Has a seat on the stock exchange. Is said to be somewhat eccentric. Also, Hollister has money in some Texas oil wells, a string of root beer stands and a football team."

"Well, I just hope it's not the Eagles," said Brennan who was a big fan of the Philadelphia based team.

Walker Thomas closed the paper and touched a match to a new briarwood pipe. As the flame finally took hold he said, "So that accounts for the shoes and sports car. And if this weren't a holiday, we'd likely be up to our tackle boxes in lawyers."

"The prisoner is entitled to a phone call," said Adam Quayle.

"He got a phone call," replied Brennan.

"Nobody answered," added Walker Thomas.

The house TV suddenly went silent. A hallway light flickered and went out. Brennan fingered his sandy hair, and surveyed the noisy overhead fan still running. He gazed at the fishing poles stacked against the coat rack and muttered, "Well, I know where I'd like to chain Hollister. I'd like to tie his baggy ass to those two dogs the Commies are sending up."

THE PANDARUS FILE

"Belyanka and Peostraya," chipped in Walker Thomas peering over reading glasses.

"Who?" asked Brennan.

"The two dogs," said Adam Quayle, "And you are too late for blast off, Sir. They sent the dogs up Wednesday and got them back Friday night. The 281 mile trip was successful and Tass reported the animals to be in *fine shape* when they emerged from the space capsule. I try to stay abreast of world events, Sir."

"Marvelous," muttered Brennan testing the coffee. He spit and cursed. Now he realized why the television and hallway lamp went dead. It wasn't because space programs invaded the heavens, or that Armageddon lurked around the corner. Cold coffee splashed onto an area rug as he tripped over Bingo and yelled through the house door, "Molly! That thunderstorm isn't due until tonight. Will you stop pulling the plugs on everything. And see if my teeth are on the sink."

Before the coffee got hot, Mayor Willard J. Green showed up in black swimming trunks and beach sandals. His fat eyes boiled. His porky face glowed from sun and anger. He shoved the morning paper under Brennan's nose, and fingered the headline that read: DELAWARE TOWNSHIP TYCOON ARRESTED IN

PINELANDS MURDER. Screamed the mayor, "I want that freaking pit closed!"

"The pit is closed," said Brennan pushing newsmen and nosy spectators back outside, "Closed it myself right after the shooting. And also, I got a guard posted. Nobody goes in. Nobody comes out."

"I don't mean just closed for investigation," cried Willard Green, "I mean closed period. For good. For ever!"

Bingo perked up at the smell of an intruder. The shaggy-haired dog waited for first volleys to sub side, then trotted over to lick sand from the mayor's bandy legs. The Greens owned a beach house not far from the Island shopping plaza. Earlier, Willard kicked along the oceanfront when wife Edie returned with milk, cigarettes and the word on Elmer Kane. News that broke vacation tranquility and caused the mayor to fore go scrambled eggs and grits, cooked down yonder style.

Green shied away from Bingo, and battled with the last button on a flowered shirt that strained to cover his round belly. He pointed toward the porch. His hand shook. Saliva shot from a space between two front teeth as he cried, "I'm working to make Hobbs Creek the place to be, and you're giving the town another black eye. Well, this was your last stand, Custer!"

Hobbs Creek had four councilmen. Wiley Brooks and Sam Burns, who wanted the pit closed. Joe Hicks and Harry Oberfest, who opted to keep the pit open. Green only voted to break a tie. Given three shooting mishaps in three years, the shot-gun incident was not the first time Brennan persuaded Green to switch sides and keep the range operational. In 1956, Hoagie Dwyer shot himself in the foot with an empty thirty-eight. (Blame was placed on Dwyer) After which, Wiley's brother had a rifle blowup in his face. The pit was exonerated in the latter incident, when Brennan found evidence of a cleaning patch left in the barrel.

"But not this time," sputtered Green, "And no more hogwash that a bullet spent is a voter saved. Come tomorrow night, you and your rowdy friends can kiss your little wild west show goodbye."

"I would remind His Honor that Pykes Pit is still private property," said Brennan taking another shot at keeping the range open, "It doesn't really belong to township."

"Half of it does," snapped Green, "And let me remind you that council holds the power to condemn property and close it down."

Nobody knew for sure who owned Pykes Pit, or where the true boundary lines ran. The contractor Lucas O'Leary thought he held clear title until he tried to sell the property. At which time a fresh title search turned up another file that deeded the south end to Hobbs Creek Township.

"O'Leary is lucky I wasn't mayor at the time," said Green, "I would have made the bastard fill in that dump before he skipped out of here."

"Sir," said Adam Quayle, "It's me, Adam Quayle. It's good to see you again, Sir."

"And sooner or later I must face John Kane," continued Green, "And I dread that already."

Much of Green's vision for Hobbs Creek focused on John Kane's money and financial contacts. A new housing developement called Wellington Woods was already in Phase Five, and when completed, the one thousand acre plot would triple Township's voting registration. Many of the newcomers wore business suits to work. They drove fast, carried heavy insurance policies and ran more red lights than Barney Kibble. They talked a lot about sand traps and wedge shots. Also, they paid what Green thought to be high real estate taxes with little or no squawking. They truly were a new generation.

There was a dark side.

The lot owners from Phase One formed a civic club, turned political. These newcomers attended all meetings, some times to the last member. They challenged every motion Green put on the floor. Their latest wrinkle was a call for new government that would include an administrator, plus a master plan for Hobbs Creek. And this proposal kept Willard Green awake at night.

In 1958, the Hobbs Creek assembly room was the firehouse, second story floor. Political battles took place there every first Tuesday of the month. On busy nights it was wise to wear earplugs. A banner that read **Hobbs Creek, Site For The Sixties** stretched across the stair-top. A township map covered a 4x8' platform that spanned two saw horses. When Green wasn't petting dogs or kissing babies, he kept busy gluing cardboard cutouts onto the plywood layout.

Green's master plan for Hobbs Creek included four more residential developments, city sewerage, three Little League parks, two shopping malls, a real municipal building and a high school. The bi-annual elections were two months away. The choice for an administrator would be on the ballot. However, Willard Green intended to keep the current Mayor-Council form of government. And to do that, he would need support from John Kane.

"Sir," said Quayle, "It's me, Adam Quayle."

"So, is he back?" asked Green trying to stare down Bo Brennan.

"Is who back?" asked the burly police chief.

"John Kane."

"He and Martha got in late last night," said Brennan, "They hit bridge traffic getting across the Delaware."

"And?"

"And what?"

"Dammit Brennan," snarled Green, "Don't play word games with me."

Bo Brennan hung up from a wrong number. His pale blue eyes swung back to the mayor. Brennan did not vote for Willard the first trip around. He would not vote for Willard this time. They both knew that. Brennan would vote for a John Kane type who bore a solid head and held a steady eye. But the esteemed banker resolved early on, to avoid politics and stay with finance. Kane claimed that *backwater* politicians were just wallflowers groping for the spotlight. Kane also said that a self-made man didn't need public approval. Brennan on the other hand didn't know what drove a politician, nor did he care. He did know where Willard's goat was tied.

"I'm waiting," said Green.

Brennan burped louder than necessary and leisurely tilted back in the noisy swivel chair. He rocked slowly, hands folded behind head. He took another newspaper call and dropped the black receiver onto the plastic cradle. He touched a fresh match to his stale stogie before going into detail. His wire had reached the Kane's shortly after the shooting. They were at a mountain resort with round beds, good food and fun things to do. It was a second honeymoon, a happy time. That's what John and Martha told Elmer as they left. Actually, it was a chance to regroup, pickup broken pieces, mend busted fences. Ironically, John Kane was at the indoor archery range when he read Brennan's telegram. Three words. *Emergency Come Home*.

"I filled them in after they got here," said the top cop, "Martha took it pretty hard. We sat her down in the kitchen while Molly got some whiskey in her. Fortunately, they couldn't view the body right away. Lieutenant Thomas here sent it over to the county."

Green backed away from the desk and batted cigar smoke with a hand wave. He checked his watch and picked at sand bits caked under a thumbnail. He finally asked, "And John Kane, how did John take it?"

"Could have been worse," said Brennan giving Green the answer Green really sought, "John broke into the Tank Room and I pulled him off Hollister. But, I didn't have to pull all that hard. And that surprised me. I always thought John bonded with Elmer, not Martha. Just goes to show you."

"Your Honor," said Adam Quayle trying to shake hands with Willard Green, "I think we have an infraction of justice here, Sir."

Green looked from Brennan to Quayle and asked, "Who are you?"

"Adam Quayle, Sir. You took my job papers."

"Oh yes, Quaid. . the new officer."

"Quayle, Sir."

Back in April, Green convinced Council to beef up the police force for better patrol of their budding township. Quayle and two other hopefuls took a civil service exam in Green's basement office. Quayle won the job with high score of 92. His GI Joe haircut helped. Afterward, Quayle went through two more interviews and eight weeks of academy training. Boot camp over, he now had long hair, sideburns and a mustache. Explained Quayle, "I thought it would add a touch of authority, Sir. The mustache, I mean."

"What infraction of justice ? " demanded Green.

"With the prisoner, Sir. I believe we have violated the Eighth Amendment, here."

Willard Green's heavy eye brows rose. He was not familiar with The Eighth Amendment. Green favored The First Amendment that guarantees free speech. Frowning, he shifted weight. His shoulder blades burned from too much sun. Also, his lower right molar ached. He rechecked the time. Edie would have lunch ready shortly, and he wanted to squeeze in two fast calls before leaving for the Island. He pushed back the ruffled hair that horseshoed his shiny pate and asked, "Could you come to the point, Quinn?"

"It's about Mr. Hollister," said Adam Quayle, "He should not be tied up with a goats chain."

"Hollister?"

"Yes Sir."

"The Hollister that killed the Kane boy?" asked Green for confirmation, "The one in the paper?"

"Yes Sir,"

Willard Green asked Bo Brennan, "Did you know that Judge Lucas rents the beach house two doors down from me?"

"I didn't know that sir, your most royal highness sir," coughed Brennan.

"Well he does," said Green, "The big place on stilts overlooking the water and you can curb your smart tongue. Anyway, Luke is due back at the county seat, tomorrow. So, we're up for one last clambake later today. After that, we will probably pay our respects to the Kanes. And I can promise you this, Wyatt Earp. Between Town Council and a court injunction from Luke, I'll seal up that damn pit until I get the private portion condemned. And I mean so tight, you won't break in there with a letter opener."

"I think he means bottle opener," said Adam Quayle buying off Bingo with coffee cake.

"He probably means can opener," mumbled Bo Brennan, "And if that mutt throws up on Molly's clean floor, it's on your head."

Green turned back to Adam Quayle and said, As for Hollister young man, I will personally make sure there's no bail. This is one murdering bastard that's not walking away scott free. I don't give a shit how much influence his old man has."

"His father is dead, Sir."

"Whatever."

*   *   *   *   *

Supper was over when the envelope arrived from Mt Loyal Detective Headquarters, down to a bantam crew because of the long holiday weekend. Brennan dropped the dishtowel and yelled for Molly to take over. He let the courier out the kitchen door. Brennan examined the paper contents. Scowling, he strode past a quiet dispatch desk and into the annex room. He slapped the latest facts' sheet onto the card table and said, "Lab report. Shows no prints. Not a one. Just your wife's."

They say that fear follows anger.

Maybe so.

Rodney Hollister winced at the news, and released the shiny chain that gripped one ankle. The spark left his black eyes, replaced by a somber question mark. His stew bowl sat upside down on the seedy mattress. A tin cup lodged beneath a cast iron radiator under the side window. Both items tossed by a storm now subsided. He began to whimper, then stopped. He rolled from his yogi position and yelped from a twisted knee. He had been trying to snap the goat chain by using his study word *Monotoso,* to summon forth a burst of super-natural strength. Thus far, the chain seemed unruffled. One silver loop appeared to yawn. He slowly arose and faced the burly police chief. Said Rodney, "That's impossible, my prints had to be on that phone."

"No prints," repeated Brennan.

"You must be wrong," said Rodney, "Some of Helena's prints could have covered my prints, but not entirely. Not print for print."

"Also, I checked out the footprints," said Bo Brennan, "Easy enough to tell apart. You wear a ten. Johnson wears a size thirteen. Plus, he walks flat-footed. His boot heels go down to the pit floor, up and down the chain line, and nowhere else. I also checked around the perimeter top. If anybody lurked above, they didn't leave footprints."

Rodney stopped massaging sore legs and stiff neck muscles as fresh panic grew in his gut. He turned back to Brennan and muttered, "Well, you must have found puke. I threw up all over the place."

Brennan shook his head, no.

"Then they cleaned it up," said Rodney.

"They?"

My wife and that kookaboo Johnson."

"You're not listening," said Brennan, "Johnson never left the basin floor."

The edge returned to Rodney's voice. "You don't know that. He could have left the pit a dozen times, then returned to work as he heard the sirens."

"Johnson only left the pit once," repeated the burly police chief, "The boot prints tell us that. And the boot prints tell us when he left the pit. He left the pit only after we got there. We know that because some of his footsteps covered the Lieutenant's on the way out. Fact is this. All the prints hold water with Johnson's story. It's your bucket that has the holes."

Brennan's pale blue eyes stared at Rodney Hollister. "Also, I can't dig up any evidence that links Abel with your wife. Not one eyewitness who has seen them together. Not even a rumor. And they sure don't lace up the same shoes. She doesn't hunt or fish, and he don't dance."

"Well, I've seen that guy before," said Rodney breaking eye contact, "I just can't remember where. And there could have been a third person. Maybe someone hid in that heavy underbrush where foot prints would not show."

"Maybe."

"Maybe he fired the shot over my head. Maybe it came from the far topside. I wasn't looking up."

"Maybe it was Robin Hood," said Brennan.

"Oh funny funny," cried Rodney, "There was another arrow! I lost it warming up. It went completely out of the pit. Someone must have found that arrow.

They found it and used it to kill that moron and frame me!"

"I found that arrow," said Brennan, "It was stuck in a tree overlooking Lane 14. Currently, it's over at the county seat with the rest of your shooting gear."

Sudden thunder shook the station house. Lightning lit the humid sky. Each jagged bolt showcased the Steel Pier ad, hand painted across Stokers News Agency. Brennan slammed down a swollen window sash. He paused to study the flashing girl on a white horse that dove into water. He straddled the nearest chair and said, "So Junior, this is where we are. We got a total of eleven arrows counting the death shaft. But that don't help us none because you a'int sure how many arrows you took to the range,

"We got a coroner's report that says the death shot came from the basin floor," continued Brennan, "This is based on spinal alignment, body position and angle of the shaft. You held the only bow down there, didn't you ? By your own testimony, Johnson clutched a sledge hammer and a post hole digger. Neither of which work real good with an arrow,

"You claim you tried to call this office before you left the range. Before you decided to run. But, the phone was out of order. Yet, your wife called right after you drove off, and the phone worked fine. And now we got this finger print report," concluded Brennan tapping the tabletop, "Your wife's prints are all over the phone, but we can't find any of yours."

Brennan returned the latest facts' sheet to the envelope. He pushed the chair back under the table and flatly said, "There will be a man here in the morning to transport you to Mt Loyal. You can try your phone call again from there... I think you should know this. The mayor might be a windbag, but John Kane and Judge Lucas ride around in the same golf buggy. So, whoever your lawyer might be, he better be a damn good one."

Brennan paused to fuss with the lock down key, which needed graphite. He refolded the paper within the envelope. He stared at his cold cigar and mumbled, "Anything I can get you ? "

"Maybe a cigarette," said Rodney weakly.

"I'll get you a pack of smokes junior," said Bo Brennan, "And I'll also get you a bill for kicking that hole in my wall."

CHAPTER 17

Emmet Walker Thomas inched across the basin floor, heel to toe, toe to heel. Fishing clothes on hold, he was suited for work: bright pink shirt; thin white tie; fluorescent green suit. He clutched a red notebook in a wrinkled hand. A yellow lead pencil stuck from a floppy ear.

"Well, if we git another storm," said Bo Brennan appearing on the overhead path, "I know where we can find a rainbow."

The black man dismissed the tort and grabbed his satin dress hat caught in a sudden down draft. A clothesline rope stretched across the basin floor. Walker Thomas wanted to mark off the distance from the firing line to the target on Lane 14. Occasionally, his wooden leg would miss the mark and he would jot down a notation, then backtrack a step.

"You should have told me Pykes Pit," yelled down Brennan, "I'd have driven you out here."

The black man waved off the belated offer and kept counting. He did his best traveling by foot, and his best thinking. Sometimes, he had to blink to check on his whereabouts. He was born April 1, 1898, the day the first recorded car sale took place in Cleveland Ohio. The car cost one thousand dollars and could do ten miles an hour. Ironically, Walker Thomas would never get a driver's license.

He grew up in a Georgia plantation run on black labor and white money. As cars began to pass horses, he marched to Uncle Sam's cadence at Fort Benning Ga. The nation geared for World War I. Walker Thomas learned to fire a Spring field, peel potatoes and stoke coal stoves. He said *morning* instead of *good morning* because the drill sergeant would decide if it was good or not.

Boot camp rules were rigid. Many a raw recruit went AWOL. But, Walker Thomas was happy with the free staples, uniforms and dental work. He withstood the weary walks up Sandhill, the lonesome guard duty and the tedious wait for a Main Post tooth brush. Upon earning a First Stripe, he even considered an Army career, a notion short-lived. The following summer he shipped out for France. And on October 29, 1918, Walker Thomas was part of the American Expeditionary Force that defeated Germany's attack on the Argonne Forest. He returned home with the Distinguished Service Cross, and down to one leg.

KYLE KEYES

Weary of picking peppers for peanuts, Walker Thomas wanted to be a cop. His mother beamed. His father frowned. Bibb County, Georgia was anything but the Promised Land for a skinny Negro boy with little education and no friends in the right places.

Undaunted, a rosy-eyed Walker packed his dreams and hopped a north bound freight. Warily, he click-clacked past Ku Klux Klan members who relit fiery crosses from Stone Mountain to West Virgina. After a tour of blowing with the wind, Walker rolled into Philly with the shakes and shivers, bunched in the dark end of a breezy boxcar. He wore both shirts and had three socks on one frozen foot.

Snowballs and street gangs became the new frontier, each day a dilemma. He would stare at his reflection in giant store windows, and wonder which busy street might be his main drag. Nights were a series of catnaps on a park bench, or under a market awning. Often, a beat cop evicted Walker, as would frigid winds that whispered, *move or move no more*. He almost returned home. Instead, he crossed the Delaware into Camden, NJ, and found shelter with a distant cousin who lived on the city outskirts.

His new roost was a skinny three story, row-home sandwiched between two other drafty buildings adjacent to a junkyard. Cardboard patched the busted windows. Brown shingles littered the ground. Even the grass looked dirty. Walker drew a basement cot amid a line of cots that stretched across the gravel floor. The sizable family made bedrooms a premium. Walker was used to that. He wasn't at ease with the choppy talk or fast pace. Also, nobody put honey on anything. After dark, the back door squeaked a lot. And every Fathers Day, guesswork got a little sticky.

Walker became educated via his younger cousin's textbooks. Walker also learned that Yankee freedom was not the milk and molasses rumored throughout the south. Wages weren't that great and help-wanted ads read like a job jar. Disappointed, he settled for washing dishes at a local diner.

In 1933, a married Walker Thomas moved his family to Mt Loyal, where he came under the wing of Big Jim McDaniel, a newly promoted police chief. McDaniel was fair to a fault, and became the catalyst for Walker's rise from nobody to the county's first black lawman.

The two men met after a daring daylight, bank robbery. T'was the bleakest of times. Banks folded. Businesses failed. The nation stood in a soup line waiting for Franklin D. Roosevelt to find answers. Walker

Thomas stood on the courtroom steps waiting for shoeshine customers. Just before three, an armed roadster screeched to a halt at an open Savings & Loan across the street. Minutes later, a pregnant cashier was gunned down while filling money sacks. The first officer to arrive asked for witnesses and Walker Thomas stepped forward. He gave detailed descriptions of three holdup men and their weapons. Walker also caught their tag number, which had been caked with mud and turned upside down.

The callus daylight killing brought loud public outcry. The story grabbed national headlines from depression woes. After the gunmen were collared, Jim McDaniel gave Walker Thomas the "New Deal" with eight weeks *On The Job* training as a cop. Six years later, the black man from Georgia with the contagious grin and hitchy walk, transferred to Mt Loyal Detective Division of Lower Elk County.

"Emmet, if you are finished reminiscing, I got the fishing poles in the car," called Brennan from overhead.

The canyon echoed back, *car- car- car.*

Walker Thomas teetered to the bulls-eye and entered a final number on the red scratch pad. He turned and looked at a pipe sticking up in the path. The pipe was one of the fence posts left behind by Abel

Johnson. Walker had the upright positioned at the point where Elmer Kane was killed. A second rope wrapped the pipe and hung over the cliff edge. The black man's gaze followed the white cord to the basin floor as he asked Brennan, "Would you say that's a right angle?"

Bo Brennan looked puzzled.

"The wall and the pit floor," said Walker Thomas, "Look at where the rope is coiled. Would you say that forms a right angle?"

Brennan stepped over the guard chain and put a hand on one knee. The burly police chief shied away from rooftops and airports, not to mention roller coasters and extension ladders. He removed his cowboy hat and peered down replying, "Don't look like a right angle to me."

"Me neither," agreed the black man, "That Friday night in the station house, when you brought in Elmer Kane and the Hollister's. Supposedly, Missus Hollister had too much to drink?"

"That's the way it looked."

"And Elmer Kane had been drinking?"

"He had no more than his normal is what Porter told me later," replied Brennan.

"But it was Rodney Hollister who had the dilated pupils," said Walker Thomas, "Didn't that strike you as funny?"

"I hadn't noticed," growled Bo Brennan.

Walker Thomas coiled up the first rope and hooked the roll over his shoulder. He wiped mud from a coat sleeve and said, "If that was a right angle, we could use the square of the hypotenuse which is equal to the sum of the square of the legs. We could then determine aerial distance by using ground footage. But, it's not a right angle, so we go the long route."

Bo Brennan groaned.

Basin clay scented the early morning air. Wildlife rattled the pines. It was Tuesday, September 2, 1958. Rodney Hollister side stepped microphones and flash bulbs en route to the county seat. Jeeter Potts returned to desk duty. Molly awoke feeling lenient, and the catfish were biting down at the cove. Said Brennan, "This thing's cut and dried, Emmet. There's nothing here to investigate."

"I'm not investigating," fibbed the black man, "I'm probing."

"I thought Davis wanted to head up this case," said Brennan referring to a New York City law officer who relocated to Lower Elk County, "Because of the notoriety and all."

"Commissioner Davis is back at headquarters," replied Walker Thomas, "Both him and the captain say this case is cut and dried."

"Bulldog Davis," mused Brennan aloud, "The man cracked so many murder cases, they wanted to turn his life into a TV show."

Walker Thomas grabbed the rope that dangled from the steep entrance wall and stretched the make shift tape to the firing line for Lane 14. He marked the twisted strands, then curled the cord into a lasso and tossed it to the top. Joining Brennan on the upper path, Walker slid the knotted end down the upright and unrolled the cord along the ground.

"If I'm right about this," said the county detective stepping off the distance, "It's gonna make my day and it is an honor to have Bulldog on our team, you're right about that."

"Does Molly know you got her best clothes rope out here?" asked Brennan.

"I'll put it back in the shed," said Walker Thomas reaching the rope's end. He jotted down a number, compared notations and smacked his bony hands together. Both measurements were the same. The footage from the firing line to the target, matched the distance from the firing line to the point where Elmer Kane was killed.

"They're both 75 foot," cried an elated Walker Thomas.

Bo Brennan stared at the empty blue sky. He sighed, shifted weight and glared at the black man. "For chris'sake Emmet, I could have told you that just eye - balling the damn thing."

"But I wanted to confirm the exact distances and here's another coincidence," said Thomas moving to the second chain post from the end, "I saw this when the stretcher crew loaded the body onto the meat wagon. This upright has a shiny base. It almost looks like a marker. And this post just happens to be directly between Lane 14 and the spot where the body fell."

"Meaning what?" asked Bo Brennan.

"I don't know," said Walker Thomas rubbing his mustache, "I'm not sure."

"The fishing poles are in the car," mumbled Brennan.

The black man removed an envelope from his coat pocket. He opened a police report and donned his reading glasses. Condensed, the Teletype read: *Rodney Hollister - Oct 1930 - Misdemeanor -Hollister threw book through classroom window when he blew up at teacher. Shattered glass fell on principal who stood below. Hollister suspended. Principal hospitalized.*

July 1948: Neighborhood kids ran over Hollister mailbox. Rodney fired shotgun at car's wind- shield. Hit blackbirds atop overhead power lines.

Sept 1953: Hollister received parking ticket at faulty meter. In retaliation, Hollister ran over meter, sideswiped school bus, split open fire hydrant.

"And this in just last year," said Walker Thomas looking up, "Hollister and a neighbor fought over a tree dividing their property line. To end the argument, Hollister cut down the tree, which fell into the neighbor's house. The trunk crushed a porch roof, injured three imported plants and caused what the neighbor maintains as extensive mental anguish. The case is due in court day after tomorrow."

"Well, that puts the last nail in the coffin," said Brennan, "Now the D.A.'s got everything he needs but a signed confession."

Walker Thomas folded the report into a pocket and peered over tiny glasses to say, "You know what gets me about this guy, Bo? He never hits anybody. That's been a nagging at me from the start. Hollister hits objects. He hits objects with objects, like when he hit the stove with the chair leg. But he never hits people."

Brennan pushed a dubious hand through his sandy hair. He watched a jumpy squirrel dart across the overhead phone line. He opened some licorice stowed in a shirt pocket, and peeled cellophane off the black sticks. "Emmet, are you making it that Hollister didn't kill Kane. . .that maybe Abel killed Kane?"

Replied a grinning Walker Thomas, "I think Cane killed Abel is how it went."

"Well, I know how one thing went," said Brennan licking sticky fingers, "I know Hollister beat the shit out of his wife. Her statement says her cuts and bruises came after that tavern fracas. She claims Hollister punched her solar plexus and chased her through the back lot into the water. And I checked on that. Talked to Doc Hooper, myself. He was ward doctor that night she showed up at County general. Hooper says the cuts and bruises are consistent with her assault story, and that her garments were torn and bloody."

*   *   *   *   *

The two lawmen pitched horseshoes as Jeeter Potts brought out the message. The fragile desk clerk eased the screen door closed and hobbled across the white farmhouse, back porch. He stopped at the bottom step to straighten his horn-rimmed glasses and readjust the padded crutch jammed beneath one arm. He whispered with chin tilted over neck brace, "You got a phone call, Chief."

"Sh-sh," said Walker Thomas for silence.

Bo Brennan lined up for a final shot at a rusty stake that stood between the tractor shed and Molly's vegetable garden. All fell silent. Brennan's best pitch was a professional *one and a quarter* turn that floated some ten feet high, and traveled a perfect 40 foot to the pin. Brennan often worked on the toss with great enthusiasm. The pitch beat most picnic shooters who threw a variety of flips and spinners. He frowned. Today was not a good day. His timing was off. He made a mental adjustment and stepped forward. Just at the release point, Potts caught the corner of Brennan's eye, and the shoe rolled wildly through Molly' s tomato patch.

"What's the score?" asked Potts handing Brennan some scratchy notes scrawled on blue memo paper.

Brennan frowned at the damaged tomato stake and glanced at the empty kitchen window. Walker Thomas stifled a grin and studied some faded print on the shoe he held.

"Twenty-twenty," growled Brennan biting on the soggy stogie, "And what the hell kind of message is this, Potts?"

"It's a call back message, Chief."

"Call back! It looks more like pig latin."

Potts flushed and said, "I had to use shorthand. The guy talks real fast and stammers at the same time. Anyway, I said you'd ring back. The number's on the other side."

"Bo, you want me to hold up?" asked Walker Thomas.

"Just take your shot," said Brennan still glaring at the desk clerk, "And Potts. . if I lose this game, you clean the coffee pot for the next seven days."

Walker Thomas braced his wooden leg against the stake. He rubbed his hands together. He spit on the shoe. His hat and coat dressed a beanpole in the nearby garden. His twisted tie dangled from his rear pocket like a white tail on a dark horse. He swung the shoe once and waited for the wind to stop. His skinny posterior wiggled. He swung the shoe again. On the third swing, he set the shoe down and rolled up his shirtsleeves.

"Is anything riding on this game?" asked Jeeter Potts.

They were playing for all the money in the world, or one dollar. Whichever came first.

"Will you take the damn shot," growled Brennan.

The shoe flipped skyward. High enough, but short. It bounced off a rock, sailed through some crab grass and went into a kamikaze roll. Just before dying, it wobbled into the pit and lassoed the horseshoe pin. Walker Thomas threw up his arms, triumphantly. An unseen neighbor applauded. The noon whistle blew. Bingo howled.

"Damn," said Brennan fading toward the house. Still grumbling, he returned with an icy five-pack and some chips mixed with pretzels. The two men sat on a redwood table next to a rusty barbecue grille. The picnic benches were long rotted away. The grille was a cut-off oil drum lined with coal. Brennan motioned Potts back to work, popped two beers and handed the snacks to Walker Thomas. Explained Brennan, "That phone call was Bucky Harris returning our earlier call. Haven't talked to Bucky in years. It was me and him that brought down that bear I got inside."

"The one you made into a rug?" asked the black man, "The one Molly keeps dragging down to the basement?"

"I told you this story, huh?"

"The time you was returning to the cabin with nothing but a rabbit rifle and some squirrel shot?"

KYLE KEYES

"It wasn't a rabbit rifle," growled Brennan.

A smiling Walker Thomas munched on a chip and asked, "So, what did Harris have to say about Hollister?"

"It was my thirty-aught-six," reiterated the burly police chief, "And we weren't really after bear. We were tracking deer. Bucky took an early shot and winged this eight-pointer. Course, once you wound them, you gotta find 'em. You know that."

"I thought it was a six-pointer," called a voice from the porch. Brennan glared toward the station house and Jeeter Potts tripped over his crutch getting back inside.

"Anyways," said Brennan rubbing some dirt through sticky fingers, "We gave the thing a little run-out time, then we started to track. And what a chase. Two or three hours. Zigging, zagging. All the time headed for the river. Then as the prints got real fresh we came around this bluff, and here's a bear. Bigger than life. He stood on the cliff just at the waters' edge. You had to be there, Emmet. He weren't no farther away than that horseshoe pin. And he wasn't black. He was brown. And it's the brown ones that test your gravel. They will chew up a man and never stop to spit out his watch or car keys."

174

"I don't own a car," said Walker Thomas.

"Stare him down was my first idea and that's what I did," continued Brennan, "Froze him with a look while I got my rifle in position. Then I aimed for right here. This is where you gotta hit 'em. Right here in the rib cage. This is the kill zone. And wham! Got him with one shot. And when you gun for brown bear, that first shot better count. You go wounding a brown bear and you are in some deep shit."

Unwinding, Brennan sat back down to a cold beer going flat beneath the overhead sun. Then he added, "I think Bucky took a shot too, but missed."

Brennan's shot missed, high to the right. And Harris only nicked the bear in the leg. The startled animal toppled off the cliff, free fell some 'hundred feet and crashed into a floating timber log.

Walker Thomas coughed politely. Bingo yawned and returned to his lookout post under a wheelbarrow, now turned planter. Bo Brennan eyed the crumpled snack bag and studied an ant platoon swarming over a fallen potato chip. He lit a fresh cigar and buried the match with a boot heel. He stared straight on as he said, "Harris claims Hollister has buck fever. Harris says it was a mistake to let Hollister join the Belly Snakes, because Hollister was clearly out of his element."

"Buck fever?" queried the black man.

"Kill shy," explained Brennan, "Someone who has buck fever, might subconsciously aim to miss. Harris claims that Hollister never bagged anything in three outings but a head cold."

"Buck fever," mused Walker Thomas.

Brennan flipped a beer can to Walker Thomas who missed a hook shot into the trash bucket. Bingo bounded over and sniffed the sweaty container. Said Brennan, "Course that don't mean much since this was a crime of passion, but Bucky Harris did confirm that Hollister is a lousy marksman. "

Walker Thomas nodded and continued to polish off pretzels.

"But then we already knew that," said Brennan

"We suspected that," corrected the black man.

Brennan retied the tomato stakes and hung the horseshoes on a twenty-penny nail inside the tool shed door. He turned off the outside faucet and rolled up the garden hose. Lumbering back to the picnic table, he paused to kick dirt on the feasting ants. He stared at Walker Thomas and asked, "So, where's all this going, Emmet?"

"Well, we figgered Hollister was not an expert shot because there were no arrows in the bulls-eye," said Walker Thomas rubbing beer foam from his mustache, "Granted that Johnson was right behind him with a sledge hammer. Still, most of Hollister's shafts just about made the target."

The county detective slowly drummed his hands together, fist into palm. He watched two lazy clouds part company, and waited for a noisy piper cub to outrun a chicken hawk. Then he said, "I guess the point is this. If I wanted to stage that murder and frame Rodney Hollister, I would need to convince a jury that Hollister could make that shot. In which case, I'd damn well make sure those two shooting distances was identical."

"Which they were," said Bo Brennan.

"Which they was," echoed Walker Thomas.

*   *   *   *   *

Just before supper a bus rammed a scrap iron truck at Route 91 and Seashore Road. As New Jersey State Police unraveled the mess, detoured motorists stacked up at Hobbs Creek's moody traffic light. The two Elk County lawmen listened to the frustrated car horns over some steamy chicken parts. Molly was down the street at Millies Meat Market.

"I didn't need pepper," said Walker Thomas between mouthfuls. He stopped eating to place his satin hat under the padded chrome chair. He wiped his greasy lips with a real napkin and sprinkled salt on an oily salad. "And that death arrow, that bothers me. No prints. Where were the prints?"

"Where in the hell are my teeth now," said Brennan gnawing raw toast, while giving the butter a doleful look. Rising, he slapped the glass tabletop, marched through the dim corridor that split the house center, and yelled for Potts to go outside and push the button on the traffic light. Back in the kitchen, Brennan checked the bonus pressure cooker that came with the electric range. He peeked through a window curtain and said to Walker Thomas, "When it gets here, the pepper is a token gift from Molly, and Hollister was wearing a glove, remember? Also, the shaft did go through gristle and everything was pretty much covered with mud and blood."

"I thought we might find one smudged print," said the black man wiping his bowl clean with soft bread, "Good soup. You want to call it even?"

"Call what even?" asked Brennan.

"This meal against that dollar you owe me."

"Emmet, that last shoe was a foul!"

"It went on."

"It hit six foot in front of the freaking box for

chris'sake!" cried Brennan.

Walker Thomas dropped an ice cube into his coffee and added enough sugar to kill the caffeine taste. He stirred with a pinky while saying, "When I ran the NCIC (records check) on Hollister, I also ran one on Missus Hollister and we don't play horseshoes with a box,

"From 1949 to 1953, Helen Anna Wenchel was in and out of three reformatories for various nickel and dime offenses. Some not so penny-ante. Eventually, an uncle from New Jersey had her examined at a Trenton diagnostic center, where she checked out as homicidal. Maybe. Tests results were inconclusive."

"I'm not surprised," said the burly police chief talking over a noisy cuckoo clock, "They probably had her read ink blots. That's how they test you now-a-days for sanity. I had a nephew visit one of those clinics. You look at smudgy impressions and think of something. Like a cow, or a cloud. Maybe two dogs humping. Frankly, spilled ink makes me think of spilled ink."

Walker Thomas suppressed a grin and handed Brennan a second set of phone notes. Said Thomas, "That's the Rorschach Test you are talking about, Bo. Swiss psychiatrist Hermann Rorschach devised it. Rorschach believed there is a thematic content in the associations stimulated by inkblots. Test validity has yet to be determined. But, it does aid the psychologist in obtaining diagnostic pictures of mentally disordered people. And, it's not really new. The Rorschach Test dates back to the turn of the century."

"I'm sorry I brought it up," said Brennan while pushing back the facts' sheet, "And there's no kay in uncle."   "

No kay?"

"No **k**."

"Sounds like there is," said Walker Thomas.

"Well there a'int and we can't haul the lady in here because she flunked an ink spot test."

"No we can't," agreed Walker Thomas, "But it doesn't say here that she flunked an ink spot test. You said that. This says she helped three boys gang rape a neighborhood girl because - according to the police matron - *Helen wanted to see how that sex thing worked.* That was in 1950. Missus Hollister was four-teen. Two years later, she took part in a liquor store robbery where the owner got a knife planted in his chest. Charges were dropped because the man died before identifying any suspects."

"Plants," muttered Brennan grabbing a pitcher that overflowed under the sink faucet. Molly's indoor garden filled the kitchen's deep bay window. It took Brennan's long arms to reach three ferns that hung from ceiling pots. He leaned over a tall palm and frowned as water dripped onto a braided area rug. "I'll give you this much, Emmet. I didn't buy her crying act, either. Too much grief and not enough tears rolling down that pretty face."

Brennan fished scissors from the kitchen junk drawer. He pulled a potted spat from an open corner and gingerly clipped away withered points from the forest green leaves. Continued Brennan, "And she never came here to visit Hollister, not even once. That was as strange as Johnson's odd demeanor."

"That watering was to be done this morning, Bo Brennan," scolded Molly bursting in the back door, "And I saw those two vines you damaged out back. We didn't get that many good tomatoes this year, and I see your cigar resolution didn't last long."

The black man ate quietly and faded into the station annex. Walker's bout with marriage came in 1925, the year he washed dishes at the Camden road-side diner. He swapped rings with an Inez Jackson who cleaned bedpans at a Pennsylvania medical post. Walker went to the army center for adjustments to his artificial leg. He made more visits than necessary and eventually she proposed. He asked, *are you sure?* She replied, *very sure.* Then he winked and kidded that she couldn't cut the cake beneath the sheets.

Proving she could, they bore two children, Lisa and Alexander who grew up in the shanty that Walker rented opposite the Mt Loyal Baptist Church. Lisa bore six kids and retired as a Newark City, school teacher. Alexander welded pipe in a Union City sweat shop, after a rocky stint with the US Marine Corp.

In 1952, Inez took sick. Early signs indicated cancer. Later tests revealed malignant tumors in the stomach and large intestine. A surgical roller coaster followed. It stopped one sunny March day with Walker slumped on a waiting room couch, savoring her funny little smile, and the snowbirds that still show up now and then to check the idle feeder. Just after dark a long white frock jarred Walker fully awake. Whispered the doctor, "Mr. Thomas, she's gone."

She left him with a dish-laded sink, some curtains made from printed feedbags and a lot of empty corners. After the funeral, Lisa and Alexander returned to their nooks and crannies, and Walker Thomas moved into the loft over a Mount Loyal City garage. This upper floor was the "A" formation of a cinder block building owned by an Ivan Borancski, who did brakes and front end alignments on older model cars. Borancski steered away from four-barrel carburetors and automatic transmissions because they were *too tricky.* He was smart enough to offset real estate taxes with rent money. An access ladder hung from a ceiling hole, and Borancski would lease the airy loft to anyone who could climb the rickety steps.

Walker hung the curtains and bought a nine inch TV to watch *I Love Lucy.* On rainy days he setup a faded chessboard and played *one* against *nobody.* Later, as ballads turned to rock and roll, Walker migrated to a new housing project on the city limits. He moved in with a divorcee named Kitty Green to share expenses, and turned the page on yesterday's song.

Bo Brennan entered the room and slapped four quarters on the duty desk. He poured his after-dinner coffee and growled, "Next time we play with foul lines."

The black man's steady eyes locked with Bo Brennan's baby blues. Asked Walker Thomas, "Just what was it you found odd about Johnson's testimony?"

"You have to know Johnson," explained the burly police chief, "He's a funny duck. Most times he won't give you the sweat off his bandana. Yet, when I grilled him on the Elmer Kane killing, Abel just up and spit out everything. A bit too quick, I thought. Almost like he had the details rehearsed."

"Maybe he did," suggested Walker Thomas.

"Maybe," replied Brennan over a parting shoulder, "And maybe not. One sure thing. I'm going fishing tomorrow. You can join me, or you can stay parked up this dead end."

Car horns continued to plunder the evening air. Walker Thomas peered through the front window at Jeeter Potts, who used his crutch to wave heated motorists through the balky red light. Stoker's bulldog growled. Drivers issued each other the middle finger. The black man pulled his duty pipe from a shirt pocket, where he often stored the hard bowl. Sometimes still lit. More than once, smoldering ash burned through to his tee shirt. At which times, he would smack his chest to ease the sting, and then go on pondering.

He dipped the pipe into his black leather pouch. He used a forefinger to push tobacco into the charred bowl. He fired up the tiny boiler and eased back into the noisy swivel chair. Then he sat for a long spell and stared at the silent desk phone.

CHAPTER 18

"I don't see your problem with the phone call," said Helena inviting the two lawmen into the lakeside cabin.

It was high noon, September 3, 1958. In near-by Atlantic City, 52 beauties from 46 States, Canada, Alaska, Hawaii and 3 cities, primped for a Saturday night saunter down the Convention Hall walkway. Outside the cabin window, the Grundy twins fought over a card board crown that emulated the one worn by Miss America. Helena pulled the towel from her freshly showered hair and shook. Naked body parts flashed as a flimsy housecoat opened and closed. She asked, "Would you like a screwdriver with some deep brown toast?"

"No thank you," said Walker Thomas clearing his throat while looking elsewhere.

"No thank you," echoed Bo Brennan who was supposed to be fishing.

"Maybe some instant coffee then," said Helena closing the bedroom door on waiting suitcases and half-packed clothes. Wire hangers littered the floor. Empty drawers hovered open. The white clam diggers draped a wicker chair. "I'll be going back tonight. Now that the rains have stopped and the sun's out, it's time to go home. Isn't that always the way?"

The kitchen was messy but intact. Helena filled a glass kettle and washed out three plastic cups. She produced a red jar of instant coffee and repeated, "What is your problem with the phone call?"

Asked Walker Thomas, "Would you say you have a happy marriage?"

"I would say my girlfriend Tiki has a happy marriage," said Helena trying to turn on the right burner, "She married a chicken farmer from Woods town. They have three kids, a fourth one in the brooder and live in a house that smells like cow shit. Which is all right I guess if that's what does it for you. Last time I saw Tiki, she was baby sitting some noisy peeps scrambling around in a tin spaceship."

"That would be the brooder," said Walker Thomas emitting a faint smile.

"Whatever," replied Helena, "I settled for a small wedding myself because it was Rodney's second trip around. But I'm sure you already know that. I did get a flashy rock, though. And our honeymoon wasn't all that dull. The pea brain tripped off the excursion boat and fell into the Seine."

186

"I remember that river," said the black man.

"You've been to Paris?" asked Helena.

"I've been to France," said Walker Thomas, "World War I. Were you on La Rive Droite or Rive Gauche?"

"The Left Bank," replied Helen, "Rodney's choice of course I wanted to honeymoon on the north side."

"Molly and me went to Niagara Falls," said Bo Brennan watching Helena's housecoat flap open and close, "We was just about a puddle jump from that bear I got mounted back at the station house."

Walker Thomas nudged Bo Brennan and nodded to Helena Hollister, who went on to confess that while Rodney loved the Orsay Museum and Eiffel Tower, she preferred the clothing stores and nightclubs. She also said their marriage had been over for a long time now, which explained her cool response to Rodney's current woes. Concluded Helena, "Of course we did share the same toothpick occasionally, and that was about the size of it."

"Yes," said the county detective smiling, "That matches your husband's story and I'll take a rain check on the coffee."

"My husband is a very jealous man."

"Yes, Ma'am."

"Insanely jealous."

"Yes, Ma'am."

"What will happen to him?" asked Helena.

Walker Thomas removed his working hat and adjusted the white tie. He picked a pine needle from a shoe lace and looked around for an ashtray. He asked suddenly, "Is there a second bow?"

Helena flinched.

"A backup bow," explained the black man, "I thought your husband might pack a spare in case the wood splits. Bows do that sometimes."

"We both know that Rodney uses a fiberglass bow," said Helena curtly. She moved the kettle to the glowing burner, and gave up a spoon search when Bo Brennan announced his coffee choice was black. She turned back to Walker Thomas and said, "Actually, there is another bow. It's back in Delaware Township. Rodney forgot to bring it. Sometimes he does. This time he didn't. You have to know Rodney. He lives in the dim light zone."

Walker Thomas nodded and asked for a yard-stick.

"A ruler?"

"Yes Ma'am. Or a curtain rod. Maybe a shade stick. It doesn't have to be numbered."

Helena rooted through closets and banged the bedroom storage drawers. She returned with a fresh towel for her wet hair and searched the larger kitchen cabinets. She asked, "Is there any chance that Rodney's lawyers will get him off?"

Walker Thomas shrugged off the question and told Helena the closet broom he spotted would work fine. He balanced his smoldering pipe on a rubber sink mat and briskly entered the tiny hallway. He turned to face Helena and Brennan who stood midway between the kitchen and sitting room. The detective lieutenant held out the broom. His black eyes brightened as he said, "Let's imagine that this broom is a bow and I'm pulling back the string."

"Okay," said Helena pretending interest, "You have captured my attention."

"You must be very courageous."

"I'm trying to be," she said.

Walker Thomas lowered the broom. "Not now. Not here. I meant at the pit. Just prior to Elmer Kane getting shot. You must have been very plucky."

Helena's eyebrows rose. She looked at Brennan who looked at the ceiling.

"It's the direction of that arrow again," said the black man, "Elmer Kane was headed into the pit.

Therefore, the shaft should have pierced his neck from right to left. But the entry point was not on the right side. The arrow came in from the left rear."

"I explained that in my statement," said Helena.

"According to your statement," replied Walker Thomas, "Elmer Kane suffered a sore conscience. He wanted to talk to your husband. When I asked why you would take the boy to a spot where your husband shot bow, you said you didn't want Rodney to find Elmer here in your cabin. I found that strange because you controlled the car. Why didn't you just drive Elmer home,

"You didn't answer," continued the black man locking eyes with Helena Hollister, "Then I asked, why did Abel Johnson say that you and Elmer held hands. You laughed and said, *do I look like Mother Goose.* Then you added that Johnson was just making a saucy story, spicier. I accepted that story because of the topography. From Mister Johnson's pit position, you can only see the head moving along the ridge. So, Mister Johnson could not have seen the boy's hands,

"Then I asked, how did Elmer Kane get turned around so the arrow entered his neck from the rear. You answered, *When I saw my husband turn and fire, I grabbed an arm to pull the boy out of danger.* And that matched up with Mister Johnson's testimony."

"You have quite a recall," said Helena.

"I have a problem."

"Really?"

Walker Thomas raised the broomstick to load another imaginary arrow. He drew back the invisible string and swung the proxy bow toward Helena as he said, "Bo and I reset the murder scene down at the pit. We do that sometimes. Reconstruct events. It helps to see how some thing might happen."

"Ducky," said Helena.

Continued Walker Thomas, "Bo drove a pipe into the path. We pretended the pipe was Elmer Kane. Then Bo went down to the firing line on Lane 14, while I stayed next to the pipe. On command, Bo spun and pretended to fire."

"You pretended that Elmer Kane was a pipe?" laughed Helena dryly, "Your imagination matches your recall. Maybe you should write children's books. Now, I really do have to pack."

Walker Thomas held the phantom bow in his left hand, close to Helena's face. His right hand gripped the imaginary string. Instead of letting go with the right hand, he popped open the fingers on his left hand.

Helena jumped.

The broomstick bounced off the floor.

"I think you can see the problem," said Walker Thomas.

"And I think you almost poked my eye out," cried Helena.

"I too jumped," said the black man looking pleased over a point proven, "I forgot all about Elmer Kane. I saw a figure firing an arrow in my direction and I hit the dirt."

Helena finished roughing up damp hair and dropped the crumpled towel over a kitchen chair back. She spit chewing gum at a brown bag under the sink and lit a cigarette. Blowing smoke through her straight white teeth, she chided, "So you are not my prince in shining armor. Maybe you could audition as the midnight pumpkin and your friend here could be the stage coach."

Bo Brennan subconsciously sucked it in while Walker Thomas acknowledged The Cinderella Story that currently ran at the Elk County Playhouse.

"The answer should be obvious," said Helena, "I tried to pull Elmer out of danger before my husband actually released the arrow. Then as Rodney fired, I dropped to the ground just as you did. . .you wanted to ask me about a phone call?"

"Yes. . the phone call," mused Walker Thomas fingering the subtle mustache beneath his tiny nose. He mentally dismissed the shot that dropped Elmer Kane and again raised the broomstick. He fired one more invisible arrow while explaining, "Your husband shoots Elmer Kane. Comes up the path. Realizes what he's done and starts to call the station house. He panics and hangs up before running. That would account for the first phone call. But, we didn't find any of Mister Hollister's prints on the receiver,

"Or," said the county detective retracing his steps, "Your husband comes up the cliff. He panics. He doesn't go to the phone. He just runs. Now his prints are not on the receiver. But, that doesn't explain the first call."

"I didn't know there was a first phone call," lied Helena.

"Sure as I'm standing here," firmly replied Walker Thomas, "I was at the desk. Bo here was on the john. The call came in minutes before your call. Some one was definitely on the line. There's no question about that. Whoever it was, didn't say anything. They just hung up."

Helena found an aspirin bottle stored in the silverware drawer next to the sink. She trashed the cotton and wiped off a dusty glass. Her head throbbed from a long night on the Island, bouncing over dance floors and taking on free drinks. She washed down the tiny white pills with orange juice and said, "I'm sure lots of people call the police and hang up. You do get wrong numbers and crank call don't you?"

"We do get nuisance calls," admitted the black man re staging the murder scene, "So in that case, Mister Hollister comes up the cliff and doesn't touch the phone. Just runs. We catch up with him and he tries to fib his way out of the killing. He fabricates the phone story. He says he tried to call for help, but couldn't get through. He then claims the phone was out of order as an afterthought."

"Yes, that's probably what happened," agreed Helena.

Walker Thomas fished a paper from his shirt pocket. "But that's not what your husband said. This is a copy of Mister Hollister's statement. Your husband didn't say the phone was out of order. He said the phone was only working one way."

"One way?" laughed Helena eyeing the plastic wall clock, "That sounds like Rodney."

"Yes Ma'am, but it puzzled me that Mister Hollister would word a statement in such a manner.

Why wouldn't he simply say the phone was dead, or that he couldn't get the call through. Maybe the line was busy. But why would he say this?" asked Walker Thomas tapping the wrinkled paper.

Helena handed Bo Brennan coffee that looked like soiled bath water. She set her watch with the wall clock, and opened the sink window to let out steam clouds that now choked the kitchen air. Explained Helena, "Rodney cooks, I don't."

Continued Walker Thomas, "So I figured if the range phone only worked one way, that had to be incoming and not outgoing, because we couldn't hear Mister Hollister. Therefore, he must have heard us, or heard something."

Helena stopped staring at the Grundy twins who gave up emulating Miss America, and now slung mud pies at each other. Helena let the window fall with a bang and peered at the county detective. She said flatly, "You went to the county seat and talked to Rodney."

"We just got back," said Bo Brennan.

"And what did he hear?" asked Helena.

"Your husband heard a Negro accent," replied Walker Thomas, "My accent. I have a black man's voice. Bo here has a white man's voice. I'm sure you can tell the difference between a white man and a black man, even over the telly phone."

"Well, you were at the desk," said Helena, "You took my call."

"But it's not my desk, Missus Hollister. It's not my office. So. .if that wasn't your husband on the line, how did he know I was at the desk? Now we are back to square one. If Mister Hollister did try to call us, who wiped his prints off the phone?"

Helena rubbed her face and said she felt naked without makeup. She tossed the ocean of red hair, now dry and suddenly disheveled. She lit another cigarette and returned the broom to the closet. She cleared some dishes from the table and adjusted the tap water to hot. She rechecked the wall clock and said, "I must have mentioned who was at the desk and Rodney picked up on it. . .

. .now if that's all gentlemen, I really do have to finish packing," she added lightly.

*   *   *   *   *

The two men climbed into the squad car and sat idle. Bo Brennan looked troubled. Walker Thomas looked at Brennan. Each remembered the sequence of events that followed Helena Hollister's phone call of death at Pykes Pit. Walker Thomas summoned the ambulance, and then yelled for Brennan who was upstairs shaving. Ambulance in tow, they reached the state highway as Corvette taillights headed north. Walker went on to the range with the medics while Brennan chased down Hollister. After which, Brennan brought Hollister back to the pit so Brennan could check the crime scene. The black man broke the silence. "By then however, Missus Hollister was at the hospital for shock treatment. And as I recall, we took all three statements at different times, and at no point was she ever alone with her husband."

Bo Brennan pulled the fishing rods from the back seat and grudgingly locked them in the trunk. He fired up the '57 Plymouth and rubbed his pale blue eyes, weary from a nightlong vigil with Bingo who had grass on the tummy. He touched a match to a large stogie and asked, "So what now, pumpkin?"

Walker Thomas grinned and rolled down the window for air. He looked from the Hollister cabin to the phone pole poster that advertised the fore-mentioned Cinderella Story. The smile turned sober as he murmured, "A pumpkin, a stagecoach and a handsome young prince. Well, we now know this much. She's not going to fit the glass slipper. You still got that part-timer guarding the pit?"

"Freddie Kramer? Yeah, he's still camped out down there. And he will be until Willard forgets about closing the range. Or Molly has pups. Whichever comes first," growled Brennan.

"Good," said the black man, "Have Kramer dig around for that second bow. Meanwhile, patch me through to the courthouse. We need to nab Judge Lucas before he leaves for lunch."

*   *   *   *   *

County Sheriff Eugene Baker got to the Hollister cabin within the hour. He waited for a door response in order to hand-deliver the subpoena.

"What this mumbo jumbo means is that you are required to appear before Police Chief William Bo Brennan on September Seventh," said Baker eyeing Helena's bulging sweater, "That would be this coming Sunday, for further questioning in the murder of one Elmer Lewis Kane."

Baker looked at the suitcases stacked on the porch and added, "Understand that we can't legally confine you, Mrs. Hollister. You are free to leave and come back. However, Lieutenant Detective Emmet Thomas requests that you stick around."

After Baker left, Helena braced against the inside of the cabin door, as though shutting out an intruder.

Moving to the picture window, she looked out over the happy waters and cursed the fateful wind that brought the vacationing black man to Hobbs Creek. She dropped the car keys into her handbag and brought in the suitcases.

"Shit," she said.

CHAPTER 19

Dateline: Post 911

"Looks like we are still alive," said Adam Quayle picking up the red phone and shutting down a website that advertised a Florida retirement village. He dropped a shiny putter into an idle golf bag and asked, "What happened that you are still on the case?"

"Somebody pulled the right strings some where," replied Special Agent, Jeremy Wade from halfway around the globe, "Evidently, your Commissioner Lewis has a friend in high places."

"Where are you now?" asked the current Hobbs Creek police chief.

"The Isle Of Capri," replied Jeremy Wade.

"No shit."

"Scouts honor,"

"I'm green with envy," said Adam Quayle, "So what do we have?"

Jeremy Wade stood on the outdoor balcony of the blue and white villa, and peered down at the Marina Grande. Cabin cruisers and flashy rowboats dotted the Port de Capri. To his rear, hillside buildings and green foliage fronted the steep mountains. To the north, a long jetty formed the shape of a rectangle. Jeremy watched a seagull investigate a beer bottle and said, "What I have is a headache from too much wine, and too many singing waiters. Exactly what kind of mate are we looking for?"

"An American," replied Adam Quayle.

"Piece of cake," said Jeremy Wade eyeing the tourists and beach umbrellas that blanketed the white sandy beaches. "Do you have a preference or can I just pick one?"

Adam Quayle smiled and opened the faded folder entitled *The Pandarus File*. He turned to the last page and ran a finger over the final paragraph. He removed a hanky from his dress blues and wiped off his tiny reading glasses. He retraced the paragraph and said, "Before this case went to the back burner, the Hollister's red Corvette turned up deep in the Pine Barrens. However, we never found Helena Hollister. Not a trace. Not so much as a footprint. Of course, there was rain. Natives claim the Jersey Devil got her. The lead detective, Lieutenant Emmet Thomas felt she skipped the country. Thomas maintained that person or persons unknown, assisted Helena Hollister in what Thomas termed as *making a getaway*,"

"There is male clothing in the master bedroom," said Jeremy Wade, "But no paper trail. It's almost like somebody wiped the place clean of identification, which doesn't make sense. This case is forty years cold. We are either chasing a ghost or someone with a gray beard and a walker."

"Get the shoe size and the suit size any way," said Adam Quayle, "Anything else?"

"Knee socks," said rookie Jeremy Wade running a second check through the marble top chests, "Who the hell wears knee socks? And poker chips. Looks like these two like to gamble."

"Monte Carlo?" asked Adam Quayle.

"It's right around the bend by boat," said the special agent, "I'll check it out tonight, but don't get your hopes up. Our file shot of Anna Ward is not a good likeness, and right now all eyes are focused on the Monaco Grande Prix."

"Anything else?" asked Adam Quayle.

"White Ladys."

"Isn't that a cocktail?"

"There's one here in the sink," said Jeremy Wade testing with a pinky, "Gin, lemon juice and dry wine. My live-in makes these at Christmas. Only she uses an egg."

CHAPTER 20

Wednesday Afternoon: September 3, 1958

"So that's what a White Lady tastes like," smiled Walker Thomas from a bar stool at the horseshoe counter. He emptied his hard-bowl into an ashtray stamped *Grogans.* He took another sip from the long stemmed glass and said, "We have a file clerk over at the county who makes these drinks for our Christmas party, but I think she uses an egg."

"Gin, lemon juice and a shot of dry wine," said Henry Porter scratching his ruddy nose wart, "Some barkeeps use an egg, but that requires straining and I don't have the time. Especially when it's busy and I'm on by myself."

"And it was busy that Friday evening of the fracas?" asked Walker Thomas.

"It was."

"And Missus Hollister had four of these?"

"She drank one," said Porter pausing to wrap a fresh apron around his middle age spread.

The black man looked confused.

"I served her four," explained Porter, "Took back three later on when I cleaned up. That was right after I got back from the station house. The drinks were not even touched. Guess she didn't like them. That happens sometimes. Folks pick something off the drink list and don't know what they are ordering."

"But she usually drinks screwdrivers?" asked the county detective seeking confirmation.

Porter nodded. "And her husband drinks milk, which always draws a snicker from this crowd. Most of these locals can brew better whiskey than I buy. I can tell you this much. Hollister is a lousy tipper and his wife has a roving eye, if you know what I mean."

The side street pub was dark but for a neon glow over the pool table, and the kitchen light coming between the swinging doors. The black man struck a match to study the cocktail list printed on a laminated cardboard folder. He rubbed his pencil-thin mustache and asked, "I wonder why she would order three more if she didn't like the first one?"

"You're the detective," shrugged Porter teasing open a window shade to welcome the afternoon sun. He loaded the cash register and set the bar up for business. He then suggested, "Maybe she just wanted to appear to be drinking."

"Maybe she wanted to appear more intoxicated than she really was," mused Walker Thomas loosely repeating the same thought. He studied wall posters from the Big Band era that smiled toward the dance floor. Each picture glistened behind a glass overlay. Every face wore an autograph in the entertainer's own handwriting. Walker Thomas could almost hear the fluid clarinet notes, the throaty trombone wail. He asked, "You want to explain again how that jukebox works?"

"I'll show you after I break up this ice," replied Porter.

The jukebox sat between the pub's two fire places and a side door that opened onto a gray slate patio. The rambling roof was also slate, as were the winding walkways that begged for flower borders and more weeding than Porter was inclined to tackle. A white trellis marked the main entrance. A picture window overlooked the stream that ran through town and eventually emptied into the bay. Another setting, another time frame, the sprawling brick tavern would be a showplace. But this was Hobbs Creek, and Henry Porter was little paint and less putty. Born poor. Twice divorced. Multi support payments to make, Porter worked hard to keep overhead down, rather than appearances up.

"It hasn't been an easy row to hoe," he said while straightening floor tables, "Which is why I'm still pissed over that chair incident. Outsiders can not appreciate this, but I'm the first owner to make this place go."

"But there were some big names in here," said Walker Thomas pointing to the wall posters.

Porter flushed. "Those musicians never really played here. The pictures came from my brother-in-law who mops floors at a Sommers Point night club."

Walker Thomas nodded.

Grogans Bar & Grille began as a ranch house built by a stonemason named Paul Grogan during the Roaring Twenties. After the '29 market crash, Grogan sold the property to an Orville Rivers who remodeled the main house into a restaurant called The River Front. The business gradually went to sea and the endless work hours landed Rivers in sickbay. In 1946, Porter assumed the neglected mortgage, latched onto a liquor license and renamed the place Grogans for luck. Most likely it was the booze rather than chance that turned the business around and brought a smile to the cash drawer.

"You have to smack it just about here to get a record to play," said Porter pointing to a long crack in the jukebox cover, "And if you kick the base at the same time, you will get your money back. The locals all know this. It's the smart-ass city folk who can't make the thing work."

"So that's how you knew it was Missus Hollister who played the stripper song," said Walker Thomas.

"She called me over for assistance as I headed for the kitchen," the bald bartender went on to explain, "Had her coins hung up. Actually, the song is called The Strip Polka. Johnny Mercer. That's him on the wall. He also did the sound track for Song Of The South. I loved that movie. Especially James Baskett as Uncle Remus."

Walker Thomas coughed and stashed his pipe for the moment.

"Anyway," continued Porter, "I keep that song in the jukebox because most all my customers do the Polka."

"And Missus Hollister knew how to Polka?"

Henry Porter snickered. "As a matter of fact, she didn't know anything about Polka's. She's more the Rock & Roll type."

"Is that a fact," said the black man.

'That's a guess Lieutenant," said Porter kicking the jukebox and pocketing the coins, "And while I'm sticking my neck out, here's another conjecture. That strip tease act was not as spontaneous as Mrs. Hollister made it out to be."

"How's that?" asked the black man.

Porter shrugged. "Just a feeling. She hurried into that little skit too fast for something off the cuff. And she went right for Elmer. Not the other way around like she said it happened. At least that's the way it looked. I could be wrong, so don't quote me."

Walker Thomas donned his shiny work fedora and stepped over a runaway cue ball rolling across the dance floor. He asked Henry Porter for a third time, "And there's no chance that Missus Hollister and Abel Johnson ever met here at the bar?"

"No chance," replied the bald bartender.

"But it does get busy in here," noted Walker Thomas, "It must be hard to watch everybody."

Porter ushered two juvenile pool players outside and snapped off the neon light. He tabled the cue ball and setup a beer for Corky Tabor, after collecting the money upfront. He ran a damp towel over the glossy bar top and whispered, "I know my clientele, Lieutenant. Take Corky down there. I never serve him anything stronger than he is. Those two kids that were just at the pool table are driving, but a'int old enough to be. I've never seen the Hollister woman except on Friday nights, and Johnson only frequents here on Mondays. Abel hates crowds."

"It was worth a shot," said the black man.

"Sorry I couldn't be more help, Lieutenant. I always work with the authorities. You can tell Bo Brennan that for me. And you can also tell him that Luke refused to replace my busted chair."

"And Bo's toaster?" ribbed Walker Thomas.

Henry Porter smiled. "No comment."

The county detective collected his duty pipe from a tin ashtray and paused by a door sign that read: *Where The Elite Meet.* He said over his shoulder, "Call me if you think of anything else, even something little. You never can tell."

"There is one thing, Lieutenant!" yelled Porter as Walker Thomas disappeared through the doorway, "You hardly touched your White Lady!"

"You drink it," said the black man with a grin, "I don't want to get tar and feathered."

CHAPTER 21

Walker Thomas found Mildred Sweeny among the chrysanthemums at Ottos Farm Outlet. The black man said *hello*, received no response and opened the leather folder that held his badge.

"It's a crime what they palm off for mums these days," offered the woman.

"I'm working on the Elmer Kane murder," said Walker Thomas.

High noon passed by but humidity hung in there. Mildred Sweeny wiped her wrinkled brow and rolled up a sweater sleeve that drooped below a rumpled elbow. Her heavy heels wobbled on the gravel caked floor. She clutched a weathered bleacher while scrutinizing the flowered rainbow of brilliant colors. She tilted one of the cardboard pots and said, "Can't be too careful around here, don't want to be a carting home any spider mites."

Otto's Farm Market sits just east of Hobbs Creek on Route 91. The open-air stand faces Shore Road to nibble on beach bound traffic, but most of Otto's trade comes from local residents. Endless tilled soil stretches out of sight. Woven between road traffic noise, you can hear the distant chug of a flatbed tractor hauling crop baskets. Ottos grow their own corn, tomatoes, peppers and melons. The apples and peaches come in by truck along with other odds and ends. Two cash registers take in the money, one inside and one outside. Walker Thomas sat on an empty fruit basket and removed his left shoe. He opened a penknife and said, "Your store was closed. Barney Kibble said you might be down here."

"You rode with Barney Kibble?"

Nodding, the black man asked, "Do you own a slow moving cat?"

"Don't like pets," snapped Mildred Sweeny.

"That's good," said Walker Thomas picking a stone from the soft rubber sole. He pocketed the pen knife and then asked, "You close on Wednesday?"

"Close at noon," explained Mildred Sweeny, "Always have. My late husband Jake always closed early on Wednesdays and I keep the same hours. The money a'int worth your health. That's what Jake always said."

The woman felt the leaf bottom of a rather large plant with yellow petals and an orange drop center. "Not that I care how perfect these mums are anyway. Only use them for decoys on mischief night. Gives the little brats something to uproot and they leave my roses alone."

Walker Thomas stood and tested the restored shoe. He peeked under the green leaves and said, "You won't likely find any spider mites here. These are Garden Chrysanthemums. Spider mites are much more common in Florist Chrysanthemums. Also, spider mites are too small to be seen by the naked eye. But they do leave footprints. You have to look for white and yellow dots on the upper leaf surfaces, or a cover webbing, should infestation become heavy."

The white woman stared at the black man. She clutched her handbag and asked, "Is that badge real?"

"Three Forty Three, Homicide Division," said Walker Thomas slowly expanding his arms, "And I got a Confidence with a stem that long."

"That so?"

"Cops can grow roses just like anyone else," said Walker Thomas, "I stay mostly with Hybrid Teas, myself.

"Well, if you want to talk Hybrid Teas," said Mildred Sweeny handing back the silver ID badge, "I got a Beaute' from France that's just about perfect as you can grow them."

"I've got a Chrysler Imperial," said the black man who didn't own a car, but had a rose of the same name.

"And," said Mildred Sweeny proudly, "I put a Kordes Perfecta in our local show last week that really got the judges a whispering."

"A Kordes Perfecta!" exclaimed the county detective, "That's from Germany. It just came out this year!"

"Yes-sir-ree, and it's a beauty."

"And you took first place?"

"I got honorable mention."

A bearded salesman in a battered straw hat and sunglasses showed up. Walker Thomas helped carry the selected pots past birdbaths and doghouses to the outside register. Said the black man, "Missus Sweeny, I need you to verify a case statement for me. Barney Kibble claims that Missus Hollister was in your store the day before the killing."

"The lady in the papers?" whistled the curious salesman.

"The same," replied Walker Thomas giving the man that much and nothing more.

Mildred Sweeny snorted and said Barney was barred from her store because he had fleas. She lifted a puckered chin and peered through bifocals at the photograph held by the black man. She tilted her head and snapped, "Well if you would turn the dang thing right side up. . . yeah. . .that's her. Don't get many calendar girls at my place, but that's her. Rents one of them cabins up on the lake with a husband twice her age. And they got money I hear, but she sure didn't spend any of it."

"Two dollars and seventy five cents," said the salesman.

Mildred Sweeny straightened with a groan and complained that rheumatism makes you old before your time. She took a string purse from her black handbag and sorted change as Walker Thomas held up a hand to ask, "Missus Hollister didn't buy anything ?"

"Not a button," replied Mildred Sweeny.

"Then, what was she doing in your store?" asked the county detective.

"That will be two dollars and seventy five cents, Millie," repeated the salesman.

"She wanted to use the john," said Mildred Sweeny handing the salesman an even two dollars in coins. Quickly, she took back a nickel. "You can't have that one. That's a buffalo. They are going to be worth money someday. And Herman, you can tell Otto that I want the soft drink guy down at my place the next time he shows up."

"Yes ma'am."

Mildred turned toward Walker Thomas and said, "Damn delivery men. They hate doing small stops. Claim it don't pay them. And when they do stop, they jack up prices over what they charge the food chains. And that's against the anti-trust laws, but I suppose that's not your department ...Herman, try to keep the mums on the trunk mat ...Anyway, I really didn't want the Hollister woman to use the john. Told her the sink was out of order. But, she was wiggling and everything, so I gave in and let her...Herman, you are getting mud all over my trunk."

"So Missus Hollister didn't buy anything," mused Walker Thomas, "Just used the toilet."

"She didn't do that either."

The black man stopped while striking a match and stared at Mildred Sweeny. Then he queried, "She didn't use the toilet?"

"I can hear the hopper flush from where I slice meat," explained the owner of Millies Meat Market, "And you know them city folk. Always in a hurry. Well, she weren't any different than the rest of them. The hopper never flushed. And this is the funny part. After she left, I went back to check, and it didn't need flushing. I can't figure what she was doing in there. What with no sink. There a'int no looking glass."

Walker Thomas placed a thumb to cheek and used a forefinger to rub his silver mustache. He looked from Mildred Sweeny to the sky above, then back to Mildred Sweeny. He re-opened his ID folder and said flatly, "I need to see that rest room."

"You want to sniff around my bathroom?"

"Yes Ma'am."

"You know I'm closed for the day."

"I can get a court order."

Mildred Sweeny rubbed sweat off a grotesque neck goiter with a hanky kept in her handbag. She swapped the pink lace cloth for car keys while she eyed the neatly dressed black man. She wormed beneath the clammy steering wheel and rolled down the drivers' window to let out bottled heat. She cracked the door to pull in a caught dress hem and said, "You put out that smelly pipe and promise to help unload these mums, and I'll show you the rest room."

Millies Meat Market sat between First National Bank and a card shop that doubled as the Hobbs Creek Post Office. A pole sign that read *Milli-s Established In 1919* overhung the lumpy pavement. A drop bar inside the solid front door made rear entry a necessity.

"I live in the first house behind the store," said Mildred Sweeny driving around the block, "Makes it real easy to keep an eye on the place, but a problem getting trucks in. The drivers jam up the street when they bring the crates through the front. If they come through the back, they park in my yard. Either way it's a pickle. Bo Brennan writes them a ticket when they block traffic. Or, they use my driveway and bust another section of chain link. Most of the fence is down already."

Walker Thomas looked from the battered property divider to the hunched over woman wrestling with a stubborn back door lock. Asked Thomas, "What was the problem?"

"Damn fools don't know how to back up a truck, that's the problem."

The black man waved off this wrong response and re phrased the question. "But why was the sink out of order?"

Mildred Sweeny stepped over some wooden soda cases and fumbled for the light switch. Millies sold everything from hardware to hat pins. The meat was fresh. Service slow. Half the customers were on the tab, a privilege not given by chain stores cropping up outside town limits. Explained the woman, "They get the new folks, mostly. New folks like new stores. Guess they are too good for my place, which probably explains why the Hollister woman was only in here once before."

"So Missus Hollister has been here before," said Walker Thomas.

"Didn't buy anything then either," recalled Mildred Sweeny, "Just poked around. Anyway, I got to take care of my regulars. And it a'int the mouthy ones I worry about. It's the quiet types that pay up and just don't come back. They are the ones that kill your business, at least that's what Jake always said."

Mildred Sweeny was almost seventy. Her late husband Jake died five years back leaving Millie the market and numerous unpaid bills. She never bore children and her life long friends seemed to vanish like village house lights after the Eleven-0-Clock news. "Got a younger brother somewhere in North Dakota," she said while screwing a fresh bulb into a tired socket, "Never hear from him, though. Might as well be dead for all the good he does me."

Millies' single rest room sat off the sales floor entrance. A wall section behind the sink was torn out. Various pipes cluttered the moldy floor. The towel holder was empty, trash can full. Stale air and other odors stifled the tiny room. Mildred Sweeny pushed a window up and said, "Lawdy knows what's taking so long. Jake would have had that faucet fixed in a jiffy, and without all this mess."

"All this for a bad washer ?" asked the county detective.

"That's how it started," said Mildred Sweeny, "Then one of the intake pipes started to leak. Must have got jarred or something."

Walker Thomas searched the black hole in the wall. He peeked into the toilet tank, and stood on a broken hopper seat to check behind a faded curtain.

"If you find any roaches," said Mildred Sweeny, "They are not roaches. They are water bugs. We do get water bugs down at this end of the county. ..and big ones I might add."

"I'm not looking for roaches," said Walker Thomas climbing down cautiously. He studied the scattered pipes. Some were copper, some galvanized. He picked up a section of one inch round, threaded at each end. Looking puzzled he asked, "What are these doing here?"

"I assume they are part of the job," replied the woman.

"I don't see how they could be," said Walker Thomas, "These are gas pipes. Copper is what they use for water these days. Now take this one here. This one is for gas."

"I'm no plumber," said Mildred Sweeny.

Matching caps lay nearby. The county detective peered through the pipe and screwed on the proper cap. He dropped a length of copper tubing into the opposite end. The gas pipe was big enough to conceal an arrow.

He stared at Mildred Sweeny and asked, "Who did you say was doing this job?"

"We only got one handy man in these parts," replied Mildred Sweeny, "Abel Johnson."

CHAPTER 22

The hounds warned of approaching company. Abel Johnson paused with choppers axe poised high overhead. His muscular arms glistened in the supper time air. Sweat beads dripped from his stubble chin. A grimy tee shirt draped over a nearby wheelbarrow. Johnson's target was a rigid oak log he aimed to split down, to fire up the kitchen stove for chili.

Frowning, he watched the animals pace the dirt runways, and claw at the wire mesh that enclosed their prison home. Johnson once owned four hunting dogs. One beagle refused to heed commands. Thus, the short tempered handyman shot the ill fated animal through the head, a loss Johnson planned to recoup when Billy Thompson propagated pups.

Billy was the local dogcatcher with a bitch in heat. Johnson had a spare Winchester. The two men hunted together and would barter off anything from sterno cans to snake skins. Billy took the rifle in advance, while Abel caught the weak end of the hand shake when the beagle never got pregnant. Later, it became Billy's turn in the barrel. The rifle discharged on a bumpy, back woods ride and blew a hole through Billy's windshield. Luckily for Billy, pride was the only casualty.

Johnson peered toward Route 91 as a distant blue jay chimed in with the yappy dogs. Two rutted tracks led up to Johnson's split log cabin. Once past a smelly outhouse, the sandy trail skirted the barn and ran forever through the somber Pine Barrens. As Johnson made out the high tail fins of the oncoming car, he cursed and spit tobacco juice at a rusty plow carved in the backyard soil. Turning back toward the main road, he watched small dust clouds shoot from churning wheels, and then evaporate as the bouncing police car stopped next to his battered green pickup. He resumed whipping the axe blade downward. The log shuddered but held. He backed off for a longer swing.

"There really wasn't any fire," explained Walker Thomas stopping short of flying wood chips, "Bo just drives that way sometimes. Keeps him sharp to chase down a moonshiner or some hightailing bank robber. Now, if this was a genuine emergency the bubblegum light and the siren would be going."

Johnson stared at the visitor and returned to the task at hand. He took a full swing on the next chop. The axe head locked into the splintered oak. Cursing, he spit more tobacco and looked past the black man. The wedges to free the blade were in a tool shed next to the chicken coop, and a fair walk away. Johnson weighed the choices and re gripped the handle in a sudden tug of war.

More sweat and swear words followed. Abel Johnson's good eye blazed, which made the marble replacement appear sadly silent. He stopped to pick away a splinter that scraped against the green, glass ball. The real eye was lost to a lollypop stick years back, when Abel and twin brother Jason fled an unpaid storekeeper.

It happened on a Saturday night. Bath time. Followed by a rare trip to town. The candies sat in open containers near the cash register. While their father strained to restart the family jalopy with a hand crank, Abel devised what the two boys thought was a pretty clever scam. Jason would tip over a can goods display. During the commotion, Abel would slip out the market door with the sweets. The ploy didn't fool a watchful proprietor who chased the callow shoplifters over a hefty property hedge. Jason made the hurdle cleanly, but the dull footed Abel tripped and came up howling, a taffy stick jutted from his left eye socket.

KYLE KEYES

The accident led to a series of *firsts* for the young yokel: his first encounter with the law; his first ambulance ride; that choking sniff of hospital ether. Also, it was the first time either boy saw toll bridges or city lights. The elder Emil Johnson did not believe in book learning or indoor plumbing. He kept the clan housed in the back woods, where his English bred wife tried to teach the twins basic table manners.

Before local truant officers found the Johnson cabin, Hitler invaded Russia and Emil struggled to dodge the draft. Over the next five years he moved the family from Hobbs Creek to Turners Crossing, then to Piney Hollow and back to Hobbs Creek. The boys spent their studying years hunting, fishing and trapping. They pumped up the dreary winter days by hanging tom cats from a wayside train station, much to the disdain of city bound commuters.

On the family's return to Hobbs Creek in 1946, the elder Johnson found his former home vacant. He staked a claim known as Squatters' Rights. Emil never did get a proper deed to the four room cabin. Nor did he ever pay a penny in real estate taxes. Once, when a nosy assessor tried to peek inside, Emil ran the man off with a shotgun. After which, the elder Johnson taught a young Abel a lesson in politics. Said Emil, "The government is just a bureaucratic body that sizes up what you got, then figures up a tax to git it away from you."

Emil also didn't believe in lawyers, doctors, insurance agents or undertakers. In the winter of '53, Jason suffered a fatal appendicitis attack. A week later, Emil and his wife Edith died from pneumonia. True to his father's creed, Abel buried them in the back woods. Eventually, Bo Brennan dug up the reeking bodies so Doctor Hooper could fill out proper death certificates.

"Glad I caught you in," said the bony black man, "I got a couple more questions concerning the death of Elmer Kane."

More wood chips flew.

Walker Thomas removed a black leather billfold tucked between his yellow dress shirt and green suit trousers. He joked about guarding against pickpockets, as he produced a receipt torn from too many folds. He waved the shabby document like a paper flag and said, "This is what brought me out here. This work order. One of your work orders. You might want to take a look at this."

Johnson stopped wrestling with the splintered oak. He wiped debris from his bronze body and wrapped the grimy tee shirt above his ears - Indian style. He stomped off to return with two wedges and a second axe. The wedges were pie-shaped with a flat top for pounding. Johnson spit just short of the law-man's feet, and leaned the second axe against a large oak that hovered over an empty woodshed. Halfway up the tree trunk loomed a black hole that blue jays and squirrels traded off each fall and spring. Acorns already littered the sandy soil. Thus, squirrels wanted to move in before the birds were ready to leave. One king-size blue jay waged an aerial assault against a papa squirrel that sat on anxious haunches at the tree base. Walker Thomas switched his gaze toward Abel Johnson and said, "I guess you don't plan on being around this winter."

Johnson's good eye wavered.

Walker Thomas motioned toward the empty wood shed. "I just thought you'd have your winter wood by now letting it season."

The squirrel attacked the busy tree hole as Johnson beat a wedge on each side of the jammed axe head. Johnson learned this technique from trial and error - widen the crack and free the object. And it worked. Almost. The axe head popped loose, but one of the wedges stuck. Swearing, Able Johnson swung a frustrated blow downward.

The blue jay screamed.

The squirrel retreated.

The black man's wooden foot clamped onto the axe head.

Johnson flinched.

"Now, you can talk to me here," said Walker Thomas with angry eyes sparking, "Or I can drag your baggy ass over to the Highway Patrol barracks, and you can explain to Captain Moore why you don't have any tags on that pickup truck."

Abel Johnson stopped chewing. And spitting. He glared at the huge silhouette in the nearby police car. Slowly, the Hobbs Creek handyman conceded the axe handle. Bottled air hissed through his rotted teeth. He straightened the kinks from a throbbing back, and fingered his matted hair as he offered the black man some well water.

"I would love some cold well water," said Walker Thomas, "And it's Lieutenant, not Sarge."

The outdoor pump was a iron spout mounted on a tarnished pipe that ran forty foot deep, and some thirty yards from the oblique privy. A tin cup hung from the pump. A priming bucket sat nearby. Johnson poured the stagnant wash into the spout as he worked the swayback handle. The earth rumbled. Fresh water gushed upward. Muttered Johnson, "Lost this eye in

Korea. Shrapnel from a hand grenade. We wuz the first troops there. Twenty fourth, Infantry Division. Started fighting just outside of Osan. That's south of Seoul. I went down like a stuck pig. Then after most of my unit got wiped out, I jumped back up and took the bunker myself. Single-handed. Later on they gave me The Purple Heart, and sent me home with a hand-shake from MacArthur."

"Thee Douglas MacArthur?" asked Walker Thomas with a low whistle.

"Yep, Thee General Douglas MacArthur himself," replied Abel Johnson.

The two men squatted on a sun baked rail road tie. Walker Thomas finished the water and handed the cup to Abel Johnson who was really drafted at the conflict's close. Johnson reached the induction center, flunked the physical, and returned to Hobbs Creek as a 4-F. He picked up the battle details from two battle weary, Army sergeants camped out at Grogans Bar & Grille.

"Well, I had a brother who lost an eye," said the black man, "Clarence Irving Walker. We called him Spider because he was so skinny. Only he lost his eye falling on a lollypop stick."

"No shit?" choked Johnson spitting out water, "That sure is a freaking way to lose an eyeball."

"Yessuh, and it wasn't entirely Spider's fault. We kids were always warned not to run with a taffy in our mouth. So, Spider was hand clutching the thing when the boss man's bulldog broke loose. Spider tripped over a garden hedge running away, and the taffy stick stabbed right through his eye socket. Spent the rest of his life looking like he was winking at somebody."

"No shit," mumbled Abel Johnson.

"Gospel truth. Didn't use marbles in those days, though. Just sewed the eyelid closed and called it done with." A distant rifle shot shattered the meaningless patter. The black man stood up to check his bottom for creosote stains and continued saying, "What I wanted to ask you is this, Mister Johnson. How did you happen to be at the pit when Elmer Kane was killed?"

"Meaning what ?" snapped Johnson.

"It was Sunday," replied Walker Thomas.

The handyman picked lint from his belly button. He watched the head squirrel stakeout the tree hole from beneath a crumpled roof that once shaded the cabin's back steps. The sloping cover fell victim to a recent windstorm, and the corrugated tin now waited in Johnson's bulging job jar. He poured the remaining water over his head and refilled the bucket for the next prime. He used his tee shirt to wipe out the cup and said, "Look Sarge, I a'int no church goer. Never have been. Probably got as many Sunday jobs as weekday work. Some times I hit a snag, granted. Some saintly soul don't want me around on the Lord's Day. But other than that, Sunday morning is just another git up time for me."

"And you always start work that early?" asked Walker Thomas.

"I'm Army remember," said Johnson, "Gitting up at four bells is routine with me."

Walker Thomas gave an understanding nod.

"Besides," growled Johnson, "Mayor Green was on my back to git the job done. Like it was a matter of life and death. Damn politics. Green don't give a shit about that range. It's this upcoming election he's worried about."

"Yessuh, I talked to Mayor Green," said Walker Thomas looking dubious, "But he says you been sitting on that job all summer. Green claims he gave you that job back in July. He says you could have installed that safety chain on any given day."

"That so?"

"That's what the mayor claims."

"And did His Honor tell you I had a cash flow problem back in July," said Johnson stomping out a small brush fire ignited by pipe ashes. He threw water over some scattered leaves and returned the bucket for filling. He then went on to explain that a certain banker was to blame for the cash flow problem.

"John Kane?" asked the black man.

"The same," replied Abel Johnson, "Had me remodel the kitchen pantry, then complained that the door swung the wrong way. The bastard. Like it really matters which way a pantry door swings."

"Plumb was more the problem than direction," said Walker Thomas, "When you open the door, the top hits the pantry ceiling. Also, I believe the mayor got you some special requisition money for the Pykes Pit project."

"That so?"

"His secretary showed me the paperwork," said Walker Thomas striking a fresh match, "It was dated three weeks ago, at which time the mayor thought you would start the job."

Abel Johnson eyed the pipe smoke that drifted skyward and opened a tobacco pouch of his own. He stuffed a brown chaw between his random teeth and spit a path through a weedy vegetable garden. His face looked cocky as he motioned the black man to follow. Said Johnson, "I just might have something here that will clear the air."

They stopped at Johnson's battered green pickup, an early model Studebaker with fender-mount head lights, and two carriage walls topped by wood rails that cried for varnish. Salt air pitted the vertical grille. One taillight hung from a twisted wire. Johnson rummaged through papers and beer cans, and then flipped Walker Thomas a shiny blue notebook. Said Johnson, "Everybody thinks their job should come first in this line of work. Some people want their job done yesterday."

Walker Thomas thumbed through the logbook. The pages were stiff. There was a sticky spot on the cover where the price sticker had been peeled away. He handed the book back to Johnson who waved hungry flies from the cab area and rolled up the driver's window. He grabbed the ignition keys and locked down a rubber hood latch.

"The point is this," said the handyman while slamming closed the passenger door, "I was at the range on that particular Sunday morning, because that was the time slot I had open to do that particular job."

THE PANDARUS FILE

Walker Thomas retook the book. He gave the notes a second look through. Numerous jobs were hastily outlined. Some finished, some not. The work orders ran from June through September. None of the words were misspelled. The penmanship looked more female than male. He handed back the notebook asking, "And that fatal Sunday morning was the first time you remember seeing Helena Hollister?"

Johnson nodded. "I told Johnny Law that back at the station house. And you just saw for yourself, the notes in this here book match up with the completion date you got on that work order, there."

"Oh. . . this is not a work order for the safety chain," said Walker Thomas reopening the rumpled paper, "In fact, this isn't even in that log book. Guess you forgot to enter it."

Abel Johnson looked confused.

"This is your work order for Grundys," explained the black man, "They live at 16 Lakeside Drive. That's right next door to the Hollister cabin. This receipt says you worked for the Grundys back in July. The second and third week of July to be exact. Just about the time Mayor Green gave you the pit job. You screened in the Gundy's back porch and fixed some loose roof shingles."

Abel Johnson gradually shifted from confused to uncomfortable. His spit dried up. He mumbled some thing about an errand he needed to run.

Walker Thomas rested his clubfoot on the truck's running board. He brushed a pine needle from his hat brim and watched the six-o-clock sun glint off a side mirror into the watchful eyes of Bo Brennan. Continued Walker Thomas, "I talked to a real estate agent named Julie who confirms a statement that Mister Hollister made earlier. Julie claims that the Hollisters occupied their cabin those same two weeks in July,

"Then I talked to Missus Grundy, and she tells me that Missus Hollister spends a lot of time out back working on her suntan. In fact, Missus Grundy claims the girl is out there almost every day. Seems like Missus Hollister won't go to the beach looking like a tourist."

The black man's steady stare locked onto Abel Johnson's good eye.

"Anyway Suh. . .I just thought since you and Missus Hollister were right next door to each other, every day for ten days, that you two just might have seen each other."

CHAPTER 23

Today, the Mt. Loyal City Jail is a sober steel and concrete structure, that looms along the muddy banks of South Branch Creek. Cells are crowded, beds a premium. Occasionally, waves of gleeful inmates go free to make room for additional hard cores. The phrase *Lockdown* is a household word. Guards patrol in battle groups. Playgrounds, libraries and workshops give a rehabilitation illusion, but only the backwaters run untroubled. Even the warden wants out.

In 1958, City Jail was the basement of a three story, Georgian Colonial at the corner of Market and Union. Two giant lanterns lit the front entrance to the yellow brick building: the New Jersey Coat Of Arms etched the granite over twin oak doors. A solemn courthouse heard sworn pleas on the middle floor. Administration offices lined the first floor. Little League equipment occupied the attic. Walker Thomas hobbled down six concrete steps of an outside stair well, and through a steel door. A bleak faced guard checked identification before unlocking an inner door.

"Elroy!" exclaimed the black man, "It's me, Emmet!"   "

Orders," replied the stoic guard, "I need your badge number to grant the pass."

T'was common knowledge through city pool rooms and back alleys that Mt Loyal Jail could be knottier to break into than out. There were no electric eyes to be tripped, nor rude spotlights to make you cringe, like darting naked for the phone as the doorbell rings. Not even a hand crank siren was installed. The casement windows were not barred because the 8x8 foot cells lined both sides of a center, cinder block wall. Yet, any of the 22 cage doors could be unlocked by simply removing the hinge pins.

Oddly enough, jailbreaks were few. The leaky basement mostly held street vagrants, and first time offenders awaiting trial - and sometimes a busted heart with a load on. Death row and other serious cases got transferred to a tighter prison. Lower Elk prosecutor, Kelsey Fortes detained Rodney Hollister until Walker Thomas could finish a thorough investigation. Once past the sally port, a rotund police sergeant with a small paycheck and big key ring unlocked another door. Said the sergeant, "Any trouble and he comes out to a pod, it's your call."

"Cell's fine." Walker Thomas pointed a thumb over his shoulder and asked, "What's with Leroy?"

"He's taking the state police exam," replied the inner guard.

"You need sunglasses for that?"

"He wants to look the part."

"I thought maybe he was hiding out from his girlfriend's husband," said a grinning Walker Thomas.

Replied the inner guard, "No, that little affair is finally over. The husband came home early, and we had to rescue Elroy off an upstairs window ledge."

Visiting hours were over. Supper should not have started. Angry inmates raked metal trays across steel bars and chanted, *No mo fish. No mo fish.* Walker Thomas walked past outstretched arms and inquired as to what was the problem. Replied the inner guard, "Hutch got a good buy on flounder. So, we've had fish for seven straight days. Fortunately for Hutch, the county freeholders don't eat here."

Rodney Hollister's cell was next to the end. The last cell in the musty dungeon stood empty. The cell on Rodney's right held a fat man attempting a headstand. The inner guard unlocked Rodney's cage door, which someone painted half black and and stopped. Said the inner guard, "Give a whistle when you are ready to leave."

"I've got a loose denture," said the black man.

"Then give a holler," said the inner guard.

Walker Thomas packed the hard bowl and stared at the gangly figure sprawled over a saggy cot. Gray khaki replaced Rodney's high cuff jeans and checker board shirt. Black oxfords replaced the range boots. A tin cup sat beneath a tarnished corner sink. A brown food tray splattered the dismal concrete floor. Walker Thomas used pipe smoke to ward off body odors and urinal stink as he noticed Rodney didn't care for dinner, either.

"Oh Rodney likes fish," said the fat man trying to headstand, "Rodney likes all seafood. It's the boiled potato he doesn't like. Rodney claims when you boil a potato, you lose the vitamins and minerals and end up with useless mush."

"Yes, that's been all over the radio lately," said Walker Thomas, "And you need to remove your shoes for better balance."

The fat man tumbled backward and rolled to his feet. He stuck a warm hand through cold bars. His busy eyes sparkled. "I'm Charlie, Rodney's best friend. I own that pie-shaped car lot downtown."

"The one with the big rubber chicken hanging out front?" asked Walker Thomas.

"I even did a TV ad once," crowed the fat man withdrawing the un permitted handshake, "Maybe you saw it? I'm dressed up like Chicken Little, amid car prices falling like stars."

"I must have missed that," confessed Walker Thomas.

"Fortunately, there was no dialogue. I tend to forget my lines when the camera zooms in and the mike comes on."

"Good thing you're not in politics," said Walker Thomas.

Charlie was Gerald Charles Hawkins, a high-school dropout who made a buck by bending the truth. His pie shaped lot was deeded Hawkins Cool Wheels, located on a mid-city strip dubbed Shysters row. The rubber chicken was a helium balloon that began as a chicken hawk. Charlie's wife said the hawk idea might give customers the wrong image, and repainted the high flying, eye catcher to show a smaller beak and a crimson comb. Explained Charlie, "My wife's a fine artist but it wasn't really necessary. Actually, I have a pretty good reputation in this town."

Actually, Charlie had a lousy reputation. Turn back the clock and the chubby 40 year old would sell a horse with no teeth, or a six-gun with a bent barrel.

Most of his cars had the mileage reduced. Leaky brake lines were merely pinched closed. His engine knock remedy was a good dose of sawdust down the crank case.

"Rodney was my first customer," said Charlie, "He loves antique cars and I sold him a cream puff Model T, purchased from an out-of-state auction. That piece was a real page out of history."

The car stocked a planetary transmission with two speeds forward and one reverse. There were three pedals: the right one worked a transmission brake; the middle one was reverse and brake; the left pedal provided low, neutral and high. Rodney got his feet mixed up and backed the Tin Lizzie off an elevated show stand. He crushed the spoke wheels and dragged down massive overhead, light strings. The two men got into a shouting match that ended when Everett Hollister paid damages, and Charlie Hawkins bought the first round of drinks.

"Strange way to become friends," said the black man.

Charlie Hawkins nodded. "And a friend in need is a friend indeed as they say. Never dreamed I would wind up here, though."

"Yes, they filled me in upstairs on how you come to be here," said Walker Thomas.

"Actually, I started with a pretty good plan," explained Rodney's best friend, "But I couldn't get the dynamite. Did you know you need a permit to get dynamite in this county?"

"Yes I know that," said Walker Thomas.

"So, I switched to Plan B," continued Charlie Hawkins, "I tied a rope between my car bumper and a casement window. I saw that done in a movie using a horse. But you can see my problem there. These cells don't back up to the windows."

"And that's when you decided to sneak in a file hidden in a cake?"

Charlie Hawkins flushed. "It was the best I could come up with on short notice. And I had to do some thing. I am partly responsible for what happened. It was my influence as a club officer that got Rodney into bow shooting."

"I thought maybe it was the family name that got Mister Hollister into bow shooting," suggested Walker Thomas politely, "I thought maybe Mister Hollister looked like a possible cornerstone for the new club building."

The Belly Snake treasurer went from red to purple. He pressed his double chin between the rigid bars and whispered, "And now they are gonna gas him. I guess you know that. They are going to gas him, aren't they?"

"They are not going to gas me, Charlie and I wish you would stop saying that," cried Rodney swinging feet to floor. He stifled a yawn and rubbed weary eyes, red from worry. He turned to the black man and said, "I don't think my bank account is any of your freaking business."

"They are going to gas you Rodney," said Charlie.

"They are not going to gas me, Charlie!"

"Are too,"

"Are not!"

"Are too!"

"For chris'sake Charlie, they don't even have the gas chamber in this state. They use an electric chair."

The fat man removed shoes and rolled onto his palms. Puffing, he pushed with heavy legs in a renewed attempt to get lively feet over an idle head. Crashing, he conceded that since the state used an electric chair, the judge would probably fry Rodney. After which, the hyper millionaire hurled a metal tray against the resounding bars that separated the two cells.

The inner guard scurried back.

"I'll handle this, Kelly," said Walker Thomas holding up a hand.

The inner guard left checking over a dubious shoulder. Walker Thomas stared Rodney back to the cot, placed the tray on a stack of stale magazines and asked, "Do you know what Goofballs are, Mister Hollister?"

"Yes, I know what goof balls are," replied Rodney glaring at Charlie Hawkins.

"Are you on any kind of barbiturates?" asked Walker Thomas.

"Rodney would not be on barbiturates," said the fat man, "Rodney doesn't even use aspirin. And when he has an upset stomach, he takes nutmeg in water. He won't even drink hot tea."

"Barbiturates can be antispasmodics," said Walker Thomas, "Sedatives. Like sleeping pills. Do you take sleeping pills?"

"I know what barbiturates are," snapped Rodney yanking off his shoes. He threw the laced oxfords at the floor, one at a time. He rolled up a brown blanket that made the body sweat and the skin itch. He threw the blanket at the oxfords and stared at the black man to say, "I don't take sleeping pills. I do not use cold tablets, or tooth ache drops. And Charlie, I don't put nutmeg in water to cure gastroenteritis, also known as Stomach Grip. I use ginger in water for an upset stomach. Now, allow me ask to you something Lieutenant whoever you are. Why are you here? I mean right here. Right now. Talking about Goof Balls and barbiturates."

"He's trying to help," said Charlie cheerfully.

"Actually, I work here," said the black man staring flatly at the Delaware Township tycoon, "This is my headquarters. But for me, your white ass would be on its way to Trenton City right now."

Rodney Hollister bit his tongue and turned toward the blank inner wall. He stood with hands on hips and looked away as the county detective went on to explain that he and Police Chief Brennan became suspicious over the milk.

"We stopped by your cabin yesterday morning, just in time to see Missus Hollister empty out some milk," said Walker Thomas, "When chance allowed, I sniffed around the sink. But nothing smelled sour. Frankly, I was puzzled. Why would anybody waste a good container of milk?"

"It was probably goats milk," said Charlie.

"It was goats milk," muttered Rodney, "Helena doesn't like goats milk. Helena doesn't like any kind of milk, except for cooking, which she's not fond of either. In fact, I'm not sure now just what Helena does like."

"So you drink the goats milk?" asked Walker Thomas for clarification.

"It's good for my allergies," said Rodney.

"That's true," confirmed Charlie Hawkins rolling into the cell bars with a thud. He let out a yelp and went on to explain that his best friend had a long list of allergies. Rodney couldn't go near grass or feathers without sneezing. Sweet potatoes made Rodney break out in big purple blotches. Onions brought on migraine headaches. An allergist tried shots but Rodney would not hold still for the needle. Then, a second opinion came up with goats milk.

"I am not afraid of needles, " said Rodney.

"So, Missus Hollister doesn't use milk," said the black man thoughtfully, "Not even when she drinks coffee."

"Helena drinks White Ladys and Screwdrivers," said Charlie struggling to regain balance. He wiped gravy from his britches and paused to catch a breath, "I can vouch for that. She doesn't even drink water. Sometimes the four of us dine out, and Helena always orders Screwdrivers and White Ladys."

"Yes we know about the White Ladys now," replied Walker Thomas moving on, "Anyway, I asked Chief Brennan to collar the old guy who roots through everybody's trash before the garbage truck shows up. He calls himself The Colonel. Wears a Confederate cap. Has a combat boot on one foot, a sneaker on the other. Mister Hollister here might have seen him around ?"

"Guess not," continued the black man, "But we did give the Hollister's cabin number to the Colonel, and a box of cigars. And he did come back with the bottle. Then, we checked out the bottle here in the lab."

"And?" asked Rodney showing some first time interest.

"The lab boys found traces of barbiturate," replied Walker Thomas.

"In the goats milk?"

"Coated on the inside of the bottle."

"Helena put barbiturates in my goats milk!"

"Pentobarbital," said the black man studying the surprise on Rodney Hollister's face, "Pentobarbital is a sedative commonly used in sleeping pills."

"I'll kill the bitch!"

Charlie Hawkins chuckled. "I don't think Rodney was on a sedative, Lieutenant. If he was, it wasn't working."

"Knock it off Charlie," snapped Rodney.

"I'm only trying to help," said Charlie Hawkins coming up a foot short of touching his toes.

"They also found something else," said Walker Thomas, "Traces of an amphetamine that can be used to excite the central nervous system. An amphetamine that can be purchased over the drugstore counter. Everybody can buy it. Even kids. And this is the interesting part, and I didn't know this myself until I talked to Harold Robbins."

"I don't know any Harold Robbins," snapped Rodney, "Could we get to the point."

"Harold is our lab chemist," explained the county detective, "Wears a small, red bow tie and kinda keeps to himself. Anyway, Harold says when you mix the amphetamine with the barbiturate, the sedative has a paradoxical effect. Instead of calming down a person, it beefs them up. Creates excitement. Confusion. Irrational behavior. City kids mix them together to make Goof Balls. A large dose can cause temporary madness. A small dose can make an upset person fly off the handle at the smallest irritation."

Cursing, Rodney kicked over the magazine stack. Paper covers flew all directions.

"Did the milk ever have a slightly bitter taste?" asked Walker Thomas, "A large dose would leave a bitter taste.   A small dose might not be detectable."

"I don't think Rodney needs any kind of Goof Ball," suggested Charlie Hawkins.

"Charlie, will you shut the hell up," cried Rodney.

"A small dose is my guess," said the black man watching Rodney Hollister pace the cage like an angry rooster, "Missus Hollister probably gave you small doses of barbiturates and amphetamines from time to time. Maybe to experiment. Establish a pattern. Set a scene. And if that's the case, well. .that would shed some light on your behavior that Friday night at Grogans. And, it would explain the station house out-burst that followed. Both of which seemed a bit over done."

Walker Thomas paused to pack his hard bowl and wait for Rodney Hollister to rundown. Then the county detective went on to explain that the Goofball break through did not unravel the mystery of who shot Elmer Kane.

"What did happen at the shooting range?" asked Charlie Hawkins, "The papers weren't too clear. They called this an unprovoked homicide and Rodney won't talk about it."

THE PANDARUS FILE

"The newspapers don't have all the facts," said Walker Thomas, "There were death threats made that we didn't release pending further investigation."

"But now we have new evidence," snapped Rodney glaring at the county detective, "Now it turns out that I was crazy on Goof Balls when I threatened to kill that retard, and you are killing my lungs with that stinking pipe!"

Walker Thomas emptied the hard bowl into a coffee can designated for cigarette butts as he relayed to Charlie Hawkins, that the late Elmer Kane was not a retard. The papers had that wrong. Also, the lab results on the milk bottle were not public record. The county detective swung a steady gaze to Rodney and said, "The lab results could have been made public, Mister Hollister. But they were not. Nor will they make tomorrow's headlines, unless the leak comes from your own lawyers."

Rodney gave up digging at the angry cyst that grew under his knotty red hair. He stopped glaring at Walker Thomas and watched a butterfly bang against a casement window. Helena had covered all angles, he muttered bitterly. She had touched all bases. He flopped face down on the cot. He rolled over and sighed like a Dear John recipient on an afternoon soapie. Eventually he mumbled, "Just what is it you want to know?"

"I asked you this before and never got an answer," said the black man, "On that morning Elmer Kane was killed, how long was Abel Johnson ever out of your sight?"

"I don't know," said Rodney, "Not exactly."

"How 'bout a guess?"

"Maybe 30 seconds."

"Even on that last shot?" asked Walker Thomas, "The shot that Johnson baited you into taking."

"Johnson didn't bait me into anything! I wanted to try that shot. And I didn't miss by all that much, either."

"Yes," said Walker Thomas, "But was there ever a time long enough for Mister Johnson to do and undo a breakdown bow?"

"No."

"You seem very sure."

"I should be," said Rodney, "I have been over this a hundred times in my mind. Right before the shooting, I kept turning around. There was no second bow. Not a breakdown. Not a homemade job. Not any kind. There was never anything in sight but Johnson, a sledge hammer and wide-open spaces. And I wasn't strung out on Goof Balls."

"The D.A. is just going to love you,"   said Walker Thomas rapping on cell bars to signal the guard,   "This Justin Pierce, your probate attorney. You told me to talk to him, and he sent me back to talk to you. He said this was client privileged information. So be it, Suh. But before I leave here today, maybe you better tell me something about your father's will."

"I can tell you about the will," volunteered Charlie Hawkins.

"You know what's in the will?" asked Walker Thomas.

Suddenly, Rodney Hollister jumped from the cot to the steel divider that separated the two cages. He shook gelid bars that refused to quiver and screamed, "I'm warning you for the last time Charlie, shut the fuck up!"

*   *   *   *   *

Lights were out and radios off as Rodney rolled from under the fuzzy brown blanket. He peered into the next cell and said, "Charlie."

"Yeah?"

"You asleep?"

"Yeah."

"Look I'm sorry okay." mumbled Rodney, "I didn't mean to curse at you."

"No it's not okay."

"It's not okay?"

"No it's not okay," repeated Charlie.

"Okay then."

An hour later Charlie Hawkins stood at the steel divider and whispered, "Rodney?"

"Yeah."

"You asleep?"

"Yeah."

"How come you told me what was in the will and you wouldn't tell the lieutenant?"

"Because you are my best friend."

Charlie nodded and then said hesitantly, "I thought maybe it was because your father referred to Helena as that *little tramp gold digger.*"

"My father didn't hate Helena," said Rodney moving to the corner sink. He splashed cold water on his face. He lit a cigarette. Cursing, he flicked it into the toilet. The smoking cylinder hit the water with a fizz. He interlocked his bony fingers and bit by bit, he confided to Charlie that Everett and Helena had an affair that went sour. Then, after saying that out loud for the first time ever, he removed the gold band from his left hand.

He slumped on the cot edge and watched by moon light, as a blurry bug followed a floor crack that ran between his feet.

"Did they really think I didn't know," he said bitterly.

CHAPTER 24

Dateline: Post 911

"Where are you?" asked Adam Quayle.

"I'm in this bedroom high rise over a perfume store," said the rookie agent via satellite, "And judging by these wall posters, our target appears to be into bull fighting."

"Player or watcher?" asked the current police chief of Hobbs Creek from the squeaky desk chair.

"Watcher," said Jeremy Wade, "Unless he keeps all work paraphernalia at the arena."

"I've been to Spain but never Madrid," said Adam Quayle.

"Think trees," said Jeremy Wade, "This city has more trees than dogs to go around."

"And Monaco was a dead end ?"

"I couldn't come up with one hit," replied Jeremy Wade.

Adam Quayle put the red phone on speaker and refit his hearing aid. He folded hands behind head and watched a noisy meat wagon exit the new firehouse that now sits at the corner of Elm and Main. Said

Quayle thoughtfully as sirens subsided, "So it appears we have a guy in knee socks who fancies himself a bull fighter, and a high stakes, lady gambler whom nobody remembers."

"It could be visa-versa," suggested the special agent assigned to local authorities, "Maybe it's the lady who watches the fights, and the guy who bets the odds. The stadium's not far from here. I'll try showing- ."

Suddenly, Jeremy Wade's voice dropped to a whisper. Adam Quayle slapped at the hearing aid and raised the speaker volume as he sought an answer to lost communication.

"Sir," murmured Wade, "There's somebody in here."

A second noise came from the kitchen. Jeremy Wade pocketed the two-way and drew a 9mm from a shoulder holster. He spun through the doorway and lowered the weapon at an intruder wearing a red poplin jacket and black knit cap.

"Right there," barked Wade, "Freeze!"

The intruder carried a leather knapsack and a pair of quick hands. He levered the gun upward and punched the rookie agent windless all in one motion.

"Which way did he go?" Jeremy asked a door-man who pointed past a curbside dumpster filled with demolition debris. The special agent skirted the blue container in time to see a red poplin jacket mount a motorbike and head toward Plaza de Toros.

Jeremy Wade grabbed an idle bike from a cafe patron and gave chase. Traffic on Calle de Alcala was heavy and he all but lost the red jacket among tour buses. He ditched the motorbike between medium trees that ease Domingo traffic onto Alcala. He leapfrogged over four lanes of car horns. He hurried across the massive courtyard, and followed the red jacket through the grand entrance, of the renowned Madrid stadium for bullfighting.

CHAPTER 25

Friday, September 5, 1958.

He made it look nonchalant enough, gazing at the sea and sky while walking barefoot and backward through the sand, as though picking a touchdown point meant little more than a change in wind.

T'was a gloomy postseason day at the Jersey shore; windy and cloud studded; the jagged coastline no longer a smorgasbord of bright umbrellas and near naked bodies. Plenty of open spots existed between the weedy dunes and lappy waters' edge, yet he chose to drop his fiery red towel next to Helena Hollister.

"Hi, I'm Lance Wainwright," he said smoothing out the lumpy bedding.

Helena gave him a welcome stare and reached for an envelope concealed in a magazine entitled Red book.

He muttered something about soaking up rays, but his blue steamy eyes looked like a sailor seeking shore leave pleasures. He brushed sand from his hairy blond legs, and rubbed creamy lotion over muscular shoulders as he said, "Certainly is a dark postseason day here at the shore. It's times like this when you have to beware of cloud burn."

"Cloud burn?" echoed Helena pretending to be a tourist who thought sun poisoning could only occur on a sunny day.

"That's not really true," he explained, "Skin can blister without a bright spot in the sky. That's why meteorologists call it cloud burn. I once suffered a bad case of Photo dermatitis on a day just like today."

Smiling, Helena continued to pick the legs off a frightened bug she found in her beach umbrella.

Lance Wainwright claimed to be a 27 year old, CIA agent who traveled worldwide posing as an Olympic figure skater. He lived from a suitcase and would awake each morning with a call from The Director. After which, he would skate off on the thin ice of a new day, never knowing which highball might be his last.

"How exciting," bubbled Helena.

His real name was Bernie Swartz, age nineteen. He sold vacuum cleaners door to door in South Philly for straight commission against no draw. He was on vacation with a hundred and seventy-five dollars begged from his father, on a payback promise before last quarter taxes were due.

"I like your wide neck," said Helena.

"Thank you," beamed Bernie Swartz.

He was supposed to be the courier. Helena had agreed to pay Abel Johnson ten thousand dollars to drop Elmer Kane. And that was a higher figure than the Hobbs Creek handyman could fathom, as she knew it would be. The fattest bankroll Abel ever flashed was one dollar bills, sandwiched between two fives.

They had swapped wisecracks for days as Helena sunbathed behind the cabin, while Abel tacked up Grundy's screening. The barbs were on a school yard level. *I've seen better shapes on a beer bottle. I think you've got the screen inside out.* Then on the afternoon Johnson finished the porch, she tossed out the offer - a payoff that would send the handyman to the moon and places beyond. Johnson could only whistle as Helena outlined the plan.

The money was to be in cash. No checks, and no bills higher than a twenty. Thus, Helena created a luggage problem. She needed to transport a hefty pot of gold from First Savings Bank to Johnson's doorstep without arousing suspicion. *This is your fetish* reminded Johnson while packing up tools. Then eyeballing Helena's healthy bikini the handyman added, "I'm sure your twisted mind will come up with something."

She did.

They would use a commercial toolbox and a random car in one of the county's numerous junkyards. At pay time, she would pack the money in the tool drawers and relay to Johnson which car and which junkyard she selected. They would use a courier to safeguard against police surveillance and possible phone taps. She would spend afternoons at the beach. Johnson would send an envoy between the hours of two and three. The envoy would be someone Johnson trusted. Male. Blond. An outdoors type. She would say *I like your wide neck*. After which, the messenger would reply *Likewise.* Helena checked her watch. It was 2:55pm. And a faded beach marker told her for the umpteenth time that this was the Sixth Street entrance. She repeated, "I like your wide neck."

"My neck?" said Bernie Swartz.

"Neck," cried Helena, "Your neck."

"Well, I'm rather fond of it, myself," said the puzzled nineteen-year old.

Helena groaned and rolled face down in the sand.

"Are you alright?" he asked.

"I think I just busted a fingernail."

Bernie Swartz frowned, and then broke into a wide grin to show off straight white teeth, high lighted between deep dimples. "Before signing on with Uncle Sam, I was a Hollywood stunt man."

"Really," muttered Helena.

He propped on a sandy elbow while expanding the lie. "I was the double for James Dean in Rebel Without A Cause. I rolled free from the car just before it went over the cliff."

"That's too bad," said Helena dryly, "Maybe you should go back to Hollywood and try it again."

"Actually, road racing was my first love," said Bernie Swartz as a skinny shadow drew near, "I had a '39 Plymouth with a souped up jimmy engine, and a high speed rear that would just about outrun anything. Talk about living on the edge. It still gives me the chills just thinking about it."

It was Helena who froze.

The approaching shadow wore street clothes and a dress hat. The legs moved with a hitch. Pipe smoke filtered the heavy salt air. Tightly, she clutched the envelope that contained Abel Johnson's payoff instructions.

The shadow drew closer.

She was on her belly, the magazine a good arm's reach away. She faked a noisy yawn and buried the envelope beneath her blanket. She rolled over to greet the steady eyes of Emmet Walker Thomas. She upset her soda bottle and cursed softly as volka and orange juice gurgled onto warm sand.

"It's good I'm not on beach patrol," kidded the county detective. Then eyeing a Charles Atlas ad inside the magazine, he added, "I hope I didn't kick sand in your face."

"I think the beach for colored folk is farther on down," said Helena politely.

Bernie Swartz jumped to his feet, flexing all muscles simultaneously. He sized up the skinny new comer and growled, "This might be a public beach, but the party is private. You might want to move on before you get hurt."

An awkward stillness followed, broken by late summer thunder and two hungry seagulls fighting for a discarded fish head. Walker Thomas let go of a buoyant hat brim long enough to produce his homicide badge. After which, Bernie Swartz chose to move on. He gave the three ring Ballantine sign as he backed onto a broken bottleneck and yelped. Between curse words, he named an Island pub where for the price of a beer, you could hear a piccolo and organ play hits of the day. Hopping around on one leg he added, "Sometime around eight."

"I'll make a note," said Helena, "Here in the sand."

Walker Thomas eased onto Bernie Swartz's flame red towel and struggled with a knotty shoelace. The county detective winced. His dress sock came off with the shoe to reveal a bloody toenail. He emptied sand from the black oxford and said, 'Your neighbor Missus Grundy told me where to find you. She saw you leave the cabin in your swimsuit. . .this sure is a long beach."

"I had to get away from the four walls," said Helena," "And I think your toenail is ingrown. I had one of those growing up. Hurt like a bastard."

Wind spasms kicked up sand sprays. A toppled radio sang a muffled version of Jailhouse Rock. The county detective removed his sweaty suit jacket to let salt air whip through a canary yellow shirt with cut-a-way sleeves. Smiling, he pressed a clamshell to one ear and said, "As a boy growing up in Macon, my brother Jesse and me would take two tin cans and a string ball. We'd punch a hole through each can bottom, knot the string through each hole. Then we'd stretch out the line to see just how far we could get our voices to carry."

"Fascinating," said Helena.

The black man chuckled. "One time we made it from the barn, clear to the chicken coop. The secret as I recall is to keep the string taunt."

"Is this a magic trick?" asked Helena.

"Making the string tight help the vibrations carry the voice," explained Walker Thomas still reminiscing. He buried the shell and went on to say, "I enjoy looking back sometimes. I think we all do. Sorta takes the edge off this scary age we live in."

Helena peered over the white sunglasses. She chided, "A fluorescent green tie might go nicely with that shirt and I'm sure you're not here to tell me how you and brother Jesse invented the first telephone."

A pimple-faced vendor under a cardboard hat stood between entrance dunes and rang a bell.

"I'm buying," offered Walker Thomas.

Helena snapped the magazine closed and said, "Lieutenant, you don't look like a swimmer or a beach comber, and I have no fetish to revisit my child hood. Somehow, I think you have already done that."

The black man returned with two ice cream sandwiches and no change. He scratched the frozen wrapper from cookie-coated sides, and stuffed paper shreds into his shirt pocket. Between bites he stared at the lusty redhead and said, "I'm having trouble with your story."

"You mean my statement," said Helena licking cream from the other sandwich.

"Missus Hollister, I spoke with Elmer Kane's aunt. Nice lady. Makes a great cup of tea. She baby sat Elmer on that day of the killing." Walker Thomas slapped through pockets to produce an auburn object about five inches long. "Before I forget, let me ask you about this."

Helena's eyebrows flinched.

"This is a doggie bone," said the black man.

"Yes I can see that."

"A rubber doggie bone," pointed out Walker Thomas.

"I've heard they are good for your teeth," said Helena.

"I found this bone embedded in the sand down by the water."

"So you are a beach comber," said Helena.

"Oh no," replied Walker Thomas, "Not here on the Island. I found this by the water behind your cabin. Just about the spot where you might have landed when your husband shoved you down the embankment. I found this rubber dog bone close to the property line where the heavy underbrush grows."

Helena pretended to study the artificial bone purchased from the Five & Dime back in Delaware Township. Silently, she cursed. She had dumped the gunnysack on the way to the hospital. She ditched the plastic tablecloth on the return trip. The rubber mouth piece had been overlooked. A stupid blunder. She finished the ice cream and lit a cigarette. Blowing smoke through her straight white teeth she said, "I did not actually crash on the beach. I ended up in the water. But then you already have that information in my affidavit."

Walker Thomas opened a small notebook and read aloud a portion of Helena's statement, "Rodney punched me in the solar plexus, pushed me down the property line and into the lake. After which, he used the *f* word to call me a bitch."

"I think he screamed slut," said Helena, "And it's nice to know you can read and write. I'll buy you a copy of Gone With The Wind if chance permits."

"Margaret Mitchell," replied the black man, "Did you like Gone With The Wind?"

"I don't read," said Helena.

Walker Thomas wiped ice cream spots from the red blanket and sat back down. He fingered his trim mustache thoughtfully and listened to the relentless breakers slap against a nearby jetty. His steady stare locked onto Helena as he said, "Clinic records don't mention your clothes being wet, Missus Hollister. And when I talked to Doc Hooper, he 'members you being more dirty than muddy. So, I thought maybe you never actually landed in the water."

"The answer is quite simple, Lieutenant. I was wet coming out of the lake, but only damp later on. The doctor just didn't notice," explained Helena handing the rubber dog bone back to Walker Thomas. Then switching from testy to sarcastic she asked, "Is this an important clue?"

"I would say puzzling," replied the county detective, "I know you don't own a dog. The Grundy's own a dog, but don't bring the dog down here because of ticks. Of course the bone could belong to a stray or maybe some other neighbor's dog."

"There are dogs on the far side of the lake," agreed Helena quickly, "Rodney often complains that he can't sleep for their barking."

"But I don't think this was dropped off by a neighborhood dog," said Walker Thomas holding the bone high in the hazy sunlight, "See this line of indentations? They are very minute. Almost invisible to the naked eye. The lab boys thought human teeth made them. So, they took a saliva test. Unfortunately, they came up dry because of recent wet weather. But, we are still convinced these are human teeth marks."

The black man smacked a fist into an open hand and went on to say, "I just can't figure why a human bean would run around with a doggie bone in his mouth . . .or her mouth as the case may be. Well, it's not important let's get back to John Kane's sister."

A runaway breaker washed the area. Walker Thomas snatched his suit jacket from floating away, and then continued saying, "Aunt Sarah claims Elmer left the house that Sunday morning at eight-o-clock. She remembers the time because the hall clock counted off eight chimes as the front door closed. She thought that odd since Elmer's church service doesn't begin until nine-thirty. Also, he left without breakfast and Elmer never skips breakfast. Aunt Sarah claims he eats his weight every morning for breakfast."

"You want me to hold your badge, Lieutenant" asked Helena.

"Thank you but I can probably manage," said Walker Thomas wringing out coat sleeves and dumping shoe water, "Now we get to your statement. You claim Elmer showed up on your cabin porch at eight-fifteen."

"Sometime around eight-fifteen. It could have been eight-o-clock. It could have been eight-thirty."

"But, I logged your call in at eight-forty," said Walker Thomas, "Giving you ten minutes at the pit, five minutes to talk Elmer out of your cabin, and another ten minutes driving time, that would put the time closer to eight-fifteen."

"So, make it exactly eight-fifteen," conceded the lusty redhead, "If you're going somewhere with this Lieutenant, I wish you'd get there."

"I guess the point is this," said the black man snatching his airborne hat from a sudden wind gust, "I don't know how Elmer Kane got from his doorstep to your porch in fifteen minutes. Can you help me out with that?"

"No, I can't."

"Can't think of anything?"

"No," snapped Helena.

"Well, it's a good five mile hike," said Walker Thomas, "Elmer didn't drive out to your place. No license. His bike is still in the garage. I checked on that. He didn't take a taxi. I looked into that, too. I even checked the cabs out of Carson City, and as far away as Manahawkin. Fact is Missus Hollister, I can't find anyone who even saw Elmer Kane on that particular Sunday morning."

Helena rolled tummy down and rivaled the wind to open a second magazine - this one entitled, Clothes And Todays Woman. She studied a page of unfitted shifts copied from a Paris creation called a chemise. Cupping hands to light a cigarette she said, "Well in that case, he must have hitchhiked. Have a nice day, Lieutenant."

CHAPTER 26

Dateline: Post 911

Some twenty five thousand spectators gasped when the red jacket and black hat streaked across the bullfight arena. The gasps turned to cheers as Jeremy Wade entered the ring in hot pursuit of the red jacket. Then, real pandemonium erupted when El Toro forgot the matador to chase after Wade.

The three figures reached the far side of the Las Ventas arena just as the bull closed in on the special agent. The bull lunged. Jeremy hurdled the barrier wall to safety. The crowd became one body in a standing ovation.

The red jacket disappeared.

"Tracker 2-8," cried the rookie agent now outside the stadium, "This is Tracker Six."

"This is Two-Eight," replied a distant voice somewhat garbled.

"Josh, I need satellite coverage," requested Jeremy Wade scanning Calle de Alcala for the target.

"Josh called in sick, Jeremy. This is Frank. What's your Ten-Twenty?"

"Forty, Twenty-Five, Fifty-Six north by Three, Thirty-Nine, Forty-Eight west," replied Jeremy Wade.

"Target description?" asked the distant voice.

"Caucasian, medium height, black knitted cap and wearing a red poplin jacket," replied the rookie agent.

"Holy shit," exclaimed the distant voice after a short pause, "You just gave me the co ordinates for the Plaza de Toros de Las Ventas, Jeremy. Are you telling me that you chased a red jacket across a bull fight ring?"

"It's not funny, Frank. I lost my wallet and almost lost my prostate."

"I'll notify the director, Jeremy," said the distant voice, "You are either under paid or over paid. I'm not sure which."

"Yo ho, just find me the red jacket, Frank."

"Stay put," said the distant voice turning serious, "I'll bring the area up on the big screen, and we will begin the scan. Two-Eight out."

"Tracker Six out."

CHAPTER 27

Saturday, September 6, 1958: another duty day at the shore; this time a bit more sunny. Again, Helena had to conceal Abel Johnson's payoff instructions. She sighed as she spoke to the black man sitting on a suit coat in the sand, "You missed the ice cream trunk, and that's too bad. I thought maybe we could try the fudge pops today."

"I don't think Elmer Kane hitchhiked," said Walker Thomas keeping a wary eye out for runaway breakers, "I talked to Martha Kane this morning. That be Elmer's mother. She's still pretty upset, but she did tell me that Elmer never dared hitchhike. Missus Kane claims her son was real scary about climbing into strange cars. Seems that Elmer was kidnapped once by two crazies looking for a big ransom."

"Really," said Helena, "I hope they brought their own block and tackle."

"Which means that whoever drove Elmer to your cabin that fateful Sunday morning, would have to be someone Elmer knew," said Walker Thomas thoughtfully, "Or at least someone who didn't frighten him.

Also, I find it strange that the boy would pick that early hour to apologize over some thing that happened two nights previous."

Helena shrugged. "It was Elmer's decision. It just wasn't his day."

Laughter pulled their eyes seaward. Two teen-agers used the waters' cover and some horseplay to explore body secrets. As each breaker died, the boy and girl moved out deeper. Off to their right, a pot-bellied man wearing earplugs added more string to a diving box kite. And beyond, a misty ship stole along the brink where sea and sky become one. Said Walker Thomas, "Then there's this business with Barney Kibble."

"You rode with Barney Kibble?"

"Yes Ma'am."

"Bravo."

Walker Thomas smiled. He opened his tattered notebook. His bony black fingers traced over scribble as he mixed text with ad lib, "Mister Kibble picked you up last Saturday in driving rain. That was the day before the killing. You carried a black umbrella under your arm. A man's umbrella. That's what caught his eye. Mister Kibble thought it funny that a lady like you would carry a man's umbrella. Now, when he dropped you off, you ran through rain with the umbrella closed. Yet, you left the market with the umbrella open. But by that time, the heavy rain had subsided."

"A lady like me?"

"That's what he said," replied the black man.

Helena coughed and then forced a small laugh saying, "Just for the record, it was a black umbrella. I'm sure you noticed it when you poked through my cabin. It belongs to Rodney. I don't pack an umbrella for down here. Rodney on the other hand is afraid of meltdown."

"But it was a gentlemen umbrella," said Walker Thomas.

"It was a man's umbrella," confirmed Helena.

"And a man's umbrella is longer than a lady's umbrella," said the county detective.

Helena wiped sand from her red toenails and slipped on beige sandals. The envelope that contained Abel Johnson's payoff instructions now lay safely in her handbag. She rolled beach belongings into Bernie Swartz's forgotten towel and returned the black man's polite smile. She purred, "You think I hid an arrow in an umbrella. How clever of me."

"The thought did cross my mind," said Walker Thomas.

Helena examined her red forearms and rubbed her heated shoulders growing warmer. Frowning she said, "I think I'll call it a day before I get sore. And as I recall, I had the umbrella up when I entered the meat market, and down when I came out. Of course it's Barney Kibble's word against mine."

Walker Thomas called through cupped hands as the woman departed, "Why didn't he take it with him?"

"Take what?" yelled back Helena.

"The umbrella! Since it was raining that day, why didn't Mister Hollister take the umbrella with him?"

"He was going to. He just forgot it, pure and simple!"   "

And the seating arrangement?" asked the black man, "I wanted to ask you about the seating arrangement that night at Grogans!"

Helena stopped between dunes. She sighed. Scattered heads gawked. She dropped paraphernalia on a faded entrance bench and plowed back to where Walker Thomas stood. She relit the cigarette that hung from her lips and blew smoke at a passing seagull.

"According to your statement," said the black man, "You and Mister Hollister sat down first. Then, Elmer Kane came in and took the adjoining table. Yet, when I talked to Henry Porter about the bar floor incident, he claims you and Mister Hollister showed up at 9:05pm and sat down next to Elmer Kane. Porter remembers the time because the kitchen normally closes at nine-o-clock. But on that particular night, Porter kept the kitchen open fifteen extra minutes because your husband made a big scene over getting a bowl of shrimp. And Mister Porter said that Elmer Kane was already there. Elmer came in at his usual time which is eight-o-clock. Mister Porter will testify to that. Elmer always came in at eight-o-clock because he had to be home by ten."

"He was a good boy wasn't he."

"That's the way I understand it," said Walker Thomas trailing Helena Hollister back to the beach entrance. He tucked his head into a nearby trash can to light the hard bowl against gusty wind. Then he cried, "Isn't that your magazine? I think you threw away your magazine."

Helena flicked her cigarette toward the Sixth Street curb, and tossed Bernie Swartz's towel into the trashcan to keep the discarded magazine company. It was obvious now that the courier could not get through. She would have to shift to Plan B, the progressive code. She cursed softly and fished for car keys.

"I might have misstated myself earlier," she said turning to the black man, "Actually, after we sat down,

Elmer got up from his table and took the table next to ours. . .I would offer you a ride Lieutenant, but we don't seem to be going in the same direction."

CHAPTER 28

"There, I hope that satisfies you Lieutenant," snapped the leggy owner of Edna's Luncheonette. She snatched the first drinking glass and handed Bo Brennan the plastic serving tray to hold. She tied a loose apron about a tight waistline and suggested, "It was probably just dishwasher spots anyway."

"Yes Ma'am, but that second trip was not really necessary," replied Walker Thomas as Edna Whipple bustled off. The county detective peeked up from his morning paper and through the coffee steam at Bo Brennan. "I didn't mean to make her upset. It was probably just dishwasher spots. I shouldn't have said anything."

"Edna's not upset over the dirty glass," said the burly police chief, "Edna's upset because you didn't order her world famous flap jacks."

"I don't like pancakes," said Walker Thomas. Breakfast cluttered the checkered table cloth, which forced the county detective to read from his lap. He studied the local classified section. He circled an obscure advertisement under Help Wanted and pushed the paper at Bo Brennan. Then referring to flapjacks the black man said, "Flour batter sticks to my throat."

"Flapjacks aren't pancakes," said Edna Whipple sashaying by, "Try one."

Scowling, Brennan eyeballed the platter that sat across the table. The bacon was crisp, the home fries golden brown, the eggs round and yellow and perfect. He shoved the paper aside and went on to explain that Edna Whipple was just shy of forty. Still. Yet unmarried. Her life fetishes were the front room luncheonette, an over weight poodle named Duchess, and her reputation for flapjacks. Edna made the best flapjacks in Lower Elk County. When you dined at Edna's, you ate flapjacks. If you did not order flap jacks, Edna put them out as a side dish to hopefully generate future sales.

"They taste like oatmeal," whispered Walker Thomas retaking the newspaper. He made another mark on the classified ad and casually pushed the paper back under Brennan's nose. Then noticing the table quiver, the black man produced a camping knife that doubled as a screwdriver.

"Edna's from Vermont," explained the police chief, "Up there they mix oatmeal with wheat flour, eggs and corn syrup. The cakes take longer to rise, but Edna says the taste is worth the wait."

"I don't use corn syrup," said Edna Whipple leaning over Bo Brennan with ice water, "I use maple syrup and what's your friend doing under my table?"

"One of these legs come loose," called out the black man, "I have this same table. There's a recess in this cross piece that keeps the nut from turning, but the stove bolt worked loose anyway. It just needs to be tightened."

"So, maybe you would like some flapjacks Mr. Chief Of Police," purred Edna Whipple.

"Griddle cakes are not on my diet," said Bo Brennan peeking at the woman's ample cleavage. He gave the circled ad a bored look, folded the paper and pushed it back across the table saying, "Damn but I'm thirsty this morning."

"Beer does that," chirped Walker Thomas now topside again. He re opened the classifieds, made another notation and pushed the paper back toward Brennan.

"Well, one of these days Bo honey," said Edna Whipple leaning deeper over the table to refill a sugar bowl that didn't need refilling, "Anyway, it's always a pleasure having you stop in."

Molly's sister Betty Jane came down with severe flu symptoms late Saturday afternoon, and wound up in County General. Betty Jane had no husband. Her wedlock children were now married and lived out of state. Thus, Molly spent the night on a hospital sofa, which left Brennan to shift for himself. After an evening of suds and TV, Brennan awoke with an empty stomach and gassy butt. He took Bingo for morning business and then decided to eat out. His fishing buddy came along for company.

"I have a third cousin in Camden City who was doctored for Hepatitis," said Walker Thomas making another notation on the news paper, "Dinah Dallas Dee Dudley Dorothy Thomas. Later, they discovered she merely had the flu."

Bo Brennan stared at Walker Thomas.

"My uncle got the name off a tombstone," said the black man, "And I wish you'd look at this ad, Bo. You might find it interesting."

Brennan munched on dry toast and studied the modern art splashed over a lavender chair rail before looking downward. Burping, he shoved the newspaper back across the table and growled, "You know I don't like puzzles, Emmet. Molly solves the puzzles in our family. I have trouble with a door key."

"You'll like this puzzle," said the county detective producing a pencil with sharper lead.

"I will huh?"

"You know what a progressive code is?" asked Walker Thomas.

"No, but I'm sure you're gonna tell me," mumbled Brennan, "And we don't need to whisper, Emmet. No one's in here but Edna, and she's not overly interested either."

A grinning Walker Thomas used the pencil as a pointer to explain how the progressive code works. The decipher takes the first letter of the first word, the second letter of the second word, the third letter of the third word, etc. Then the decipher sections the letters into words. Concluded Walker Thomas, "Try it on this help-wanted advertisement I circled. This ad caught my eye because it's too long and worded funny."

"Emmet, you don't really believe that Helena Hollister and Abel Johnson are sending messages to each other."

"I do."

"And do you think that jackass Johnson could decipher a progressive code?" asked Brennan.

"I don't think he has to," replied the black man, "I think it's Abel Johnson's code. I think he taught it to

Missus Hollister."

Mockingly, Bo Brennan sniffed the black man's coffee cup and said, "Johnson can't even fill out his own tax forms, Emmet. Old Man Mayo does it for him down at the filling station. That was after Johnson sent his paperwork to Trenton and his money to Newark."

"Everybody has a side we don't see," said Walker Thomas changing course on the flap jacks. He washed the last bite down with water and wiped his mouth with a real napkin. He paused to light the hard-bowl and then continued saying, "I think what we got here is a cryptographer. We know Johnson is a war buff. So, maybe he's a nut on decipherment. There's a page marked red, and a page marked purple in the back of his log. The words that follow make no sense. But, Red and Purple were Japanese codes during Pearl Harbor times. Purple was 97-shiki O-bun Injiki, devised by Captain Jinsaburo Ito of the Imperial Navy who thought the code unbreakable."

"Emmet, before you get too far into this story," said Brennan, "I would like to get out of here before I go out on pension."

Walker Thomas flipped a paper place mat face down and handed the burly police chief a pencil. The black man told Brennan to decipher just the circled part of the inquiry. Thomas told Brennan to omit the heading and sign-off words. Reluctantly, Bo Brennan wiped up some spilled water and doodled away. He dropped the pencil suddenly. Decoded, the want-ad read: *Handyman - Payoff delayed -Contact later - Cash Customer.*

"Son of a bitch," exclaimed Bo Brennan shaking noisy ice in a sweaty drinking glass. He watched Edna Whipple saunter through a door that opened to the kitchen. A service counter ran the inside wall that divided the cook station from the dining area. A wall hole served as a pass-through. Edna would place the orders on the counter from the kitchen side, and then walk them from the counter to the tables. As Edna bent to wait on some newcomers the watchful police chief said, "I suppose Abel and the woman could prearrange something like this. For sure Abel knows that Smitty reads everybody's letters before he delivers them. So, Mrs. Hollister wouldn't trust the mail. And Abel doesn't have a phone."

"Which means Mister Johnson could call her from an outside booth, but she would have no way to contact him."

"Not to mention that her phone could be tapped," mused Bo Brennan.

"If there wasn't so much red tape tied to a phone tap," said Walker Thomas.

"But they wouldn't know that," agreed Brennan standing to leave.

The black man flipped a coin over the check. He clucked as it came up heads, and peeked through cigar fog to ask, "So will you ever try any of Edna's flap jacks?"

"Just keep moving Emmet and one of these days I'm gonna check out that coin of yours," growled Brennan as the church crowd pushed through the front door. He ignored a parting look from Edna Whipple and grabbed a toothpick stored near the cash register. Climbing into the police cruiser Brennan added, "Besides, I don't like little dogs that sniff at my socks."

"But she did give us the meal free," said Walker Thomas.

"Yes Emmet, she did give us a free meal," replied Brennan.

"It's probably the uniform," said Walker Thomas, "I wonder why she never married. She turns a nice ankle."

"She's looking for the perfect ten," explained Bo Brennan, "And it doesn't always have to be the uniform, Emmet."

THE PANDARUS FILE

The two lawmen entered the station house to find Adam Quayle behind the duty desk.

"Where's Jeeter ? asked Walker Thomas

"Out to lunch, Sir," replied Quayle.

"Lunch!" boomed Brennan, "He comes in late for oversleeping and he's out to lunch already!"

Jeeter and wife Betsy Sue now shared the same mattress again, their trial separation over. There were conditions. Jeeter would give up Friday night shuffle-board at Grogans Bar & Grille. Jeeter would wipe down bathroom walls after showering. Jeeter would elevate their living standard to match Betsy's expectations. The latter meaning: wall-to-wall rugs; brand name silver ware; dishes other than plastic; and real furniture for the front room. In return, Betsy would come back to bed.

Jeeter agreed.

They sealed the deal with a night between the sheets, and now the fragile desk clerk dwell at Fishers Pond, designing a car engine that would run without pistons. This was an idea that Jeeter believed would revolutionize the automobile industry - also fatten the Potts' skimpy bank account. T'was one of those moonbeam schemes that seemed to fade in raw day light. Thus, Jeeter now sat on a muddy water bank, with an empty coffee cup, scratching his head.

"Just ducky," muttered Brennan tossing his cowboy hat toward a wall peg. He retook the swivel chair and picked up a ringing phone. He wiped dirt clumps from the ink blotter and barked, "Well Quayle you can just hike it on over to Fishers Pond and tell that nitwit that Lieutenant Thomas wants him back here."

"Yes Sir," replied the rookie officer.

"No I wasn't talking to you Edna and yes I can hold," Brennan said into the phone. He palmed the receiver and asked of the black man, "Do you think this plan of yours is going to work?"

"No promises," replied Walker Thomas jotting down the County Times' phone number, "I gotta check out something with Jeeter first."

Brennan hung up the phone and buried his cigar in the big green ashtray as he grunted, "Well Emmet, when you get done checking out whatever it is you're checking out, you can tell Potts to take his toolbox over to Edna's place. She's got a table that just collapsed."

CHAPTER 29

Dateline: Post 911

Jeremy Wade rested on a bench facing Plaza de Toro. Two large pine trees loomed to his front. Traffic reflections played off a Toyoto window sign to his rear. He was just ready to move on when his two-way went off: "Tracker Six, this is Tracker Two-Eight, ova."

"This is Tracker Six," responded Jeremy now alert and foot ready.

"We've got the big board up and running," said the distant voice, "Target is on bus at stadium gate."

Jeremy flipped-closed the cell phone. He ran between cars on Calla de Julio Camba and back onto Plaza de Toro ground. He stopped under the sign that read ANO 1929 and whipped out the two-way. "Two-Eight, this is Six. There's three buses out here. Two red and a blue."

"It's red bus number one four six," replied the distant voice.

"Roger that," said Jeremy talking over traffic horns. He pushed through the gate-bound crowd and zigzagged past the giant statue of matador and bull. As he reached curbside, the traffic light at Alcala and Camba changed.

The bus left.

"Shit," muttered Jeremy, "Two-Eight this is Six, I need the next stop for that bus to Molinos."

"Two-Eight to Six," said the distant voice, "We have contact with dispatch. Route override in place. Bus will be stopped at Manuel Becerra."

"Roger that," cried Jeremy grabbing a nearby motorbike.

"And Jeremy."

"Yeah Frank?"

"Don't storm the bus. This guy might be armed and he might take hostages."

"Roger that."

"And Jeremy."

"Yeah Frank?"

"There's sidewalk construction at Cardenal Belluga," said the distant voice, "Use the cafe side of the street, and don't run over any pedestrians. This a'int the movies. We're already on the hook for two motorbikes."

CHAPTER 30

Sunday Afternoon, September 7, 1958

Helena Hollister emerged from the cabin bedroom carrying a brown leather quiver and a fistful of aluminum arrows. She was shoeless, wearing a frown and no lipstick. She sat the shooting gear on peanut butter and jelly smeared over the kitchen table. She fastened the peek-a-boo housecoat and said, "I do hope we get this over with before the witching hour."

The black man smiled politely.

"I didn't hear you pull up," said Helena.

"I'm not surprised," replied Thomas covering his ears in a mocking gesture that caused his prime suspect to disappear. She lowered the bedroom radio and returned to the kitchen as a familiar voice said, "your contact station."

"WINS out of New York," Helena explained, "We get the Philly sounds in Delaware Township, but here I get my home station... if conditions are right. Rodney says it depends on the moon or tide if you can believe that. Whatever, at least it's rock and roll and not that twang these pineys listen to."

"Your reception probably follows the coastline and did you know that Richard Penniman hails from my home state?" asked Walker Thomas. Getting no answer the black man from Bibb County went on to elaborate, "Little Richard from Macon, Georgia."

"It's nice you keep in tune with the times," said Helena pulling and throwing hair curlers into the sink. She spit stale gum into a fresh trash bag and searched a counter drawer for cigarettes that weren't there. Still frowning she parted the side curtains and said, "I don't see any car."

"Hiked in from the highway," fibbed the black man wanting the woman to think he was alone, "Have to keep this leg in shape."

"Commendable I suppose," said Helena, "But you need to consider wheels. Those high speed chases must be hell with the bad guys in cars and you on foot."

There was a time when Walker Thomas could outrun most cars. Brother Jesse swore that Emmet once ran the hundred meters in ten seconds, and broke the four-minute mile back in 1913 - officially broke in 1952 and 1964. Then came Walker's wooden leg and the blinding speed screeched to a halt. Added the county detective, "After that it was calisthenics and gymnastics. Leg weights. On my back with knees up, doing what you white folk call bicycles. I didn't like that form of travel though. Never felt like I was gittin' anywhere."

Helena gave the black man a frozen look. She spread loose arrows over the tabletop and fingered the heads while explaining, "These are hunting shafts. The points are triangular and much wider than target heads. You can see that, Lieutenant."

"I look for running to make a big come back," said Walker Thomas still stalling for time, "Maybe some President will start up a physical fitness program. May be jogging."

"Not that I'm an archer of course," continued Helena, "But Rodney did waste my time with the finer points of playing Robin Hood. And the magazines he subscribes to: Bowsight; Hunters World; Field and Pheasant or something like that. Beats me why grown men shoot at defenseless creatures. If you wanna fight, take a subway ride."

"Physical fitness fads run in cycles," said the black man talking a bit louder, "Some date back to Biblical times and even before then."

"Thinking back," said Helena, "Incompatibility was maybe the key problem with our marriage. That, and of course the age barrier. You never know these things until it's too late."

"And most folks don't know this," said the black man, "But hieroglyphics found in primitive caves show that certain forms of exercise actually predate Greek culture. Greece of course being the first civilization to embrace calisthenics on a large scale."

"Are we on the same page?" asked the woman.

"Ma'am?"

"The real point is this," said Helena Hollister putting the subject matter back on track, "At the time of the shooting, Rodney possessed all the arrows that matched the death arrow. There were no other arrows. Feel free to look around."

Walker Thomas leaned over the tarnished sink to watch Angela Grundy cram twin girls, and perishable food into a seam-busting station wagon. He sipped on Helena's instant coffee and slid his black fedora beneath a chair. Struggling to get comfortable he said, "The sooner we wrap this thing up, the sooner we can all go home."

"Your coat's hung up on your suspenders and I can't wait to get out of this flea trap," muttered Helena, "Which will be first thing in the morning unless Police Chief William Bo Brennan invents another delaying tactic."

"The subpoena?"

"Yes the damn subpoena," said Helena.

"We expected you to come in this morning," said Walker Thomas.

"I called first," replied Helena, "You weren't there. Some kid answered, clucking about three grown men fixing one broken table leg."

"That would be Patrolman Adam Quayle," said the black man coughing lightly, "And we do have more questions."

"So ask," said Helena.

Walker Thomas pressed open a folded paper. The city police lab found more than just blood on the death arrow. They also found water stains, clay and traces of plaster.

"Plaster," echoed Helena Hollister.

"Wallboard dust," said Walker Thomas, "We found minute traces of plasterboard dust laced through the feathers of the death arrow. We also found matching dust on the bathroom floor down at Millies Market."

"Plaster dust is plaster dust, Lieutenant. Anything else?"

"Did you know that Mister Johnson plans to take a trip?" asked Walker Thomas

"I hardly know Abel Johnson so I could not know if he's going bye bye," said Helena curtly.

"Oh he has a trip planned, alright. I called City Airport. Turns out Johnson has a cousin just outside of St Louie. Clayton, Missouri to be exact." The black man donned readers and opened his pocket notebook. "I got it here that Johnson made flight reservations to Lambert Municipal Airport for Sept 4. Lay over two days. On to Vegas and later Honolulu. He canceled the flight, reset the plans for the sixth and postponed again."

Helena rubbed her mouth. Her oval lips burned from too much sun. She mumbled something about being more brown than Walker Thomas and left in search of lip ointment. She returned with the large white handbag and emptied the contents onto a messy counter top. She lit a cigarette and said through a hazy smoke ring, "So maybe the man's afraid to fly."

"I think the man expects to come into money," said the county detective, "I think Mister Johnson is waiting for money that keeps getting delayed."

"Would you like something stronger than coffee," offered Helena gesturing toward an open bottle next to a tall glass, "It is past noon. Maybe a shot of Volka?"

THE PANDARUS FILE

Walker Thomas arose from the breakfast table and washed out his cup, still almost full. He wanted yet another peek out the kitchen window. People named Henshaw summered in the cabin directly across the lake. They were close friends of Bo and Molly. All four dated back to schoolyard pledges and songs of *All For One And One For All*. Though, there was that day when Bo Brennan bumped heads with Buck Henshaw over Molly McGuire, Brennan's wife by her maiden name.

Henshaw quarterbacked the high school football team. Brennan played a lackluster center. In their senior year turkey game, Henshaw cursed out Brennan over a bad exchange. On the next play an angry Brennan blew Henshaw into the backfield with the hike. Henshaw came up with the loose ball, got confused and ran through the wrong goalposts. After which, Brennan told Molly that Henshaw was a guy who went both ways. The hatchet long buried, the burly police chief now carried the door key when the Henshaw cabin went off-season.

"If you wish to wash dishes," said Helena, "The soap powder's under the sink."

Walker Thomas emptied his hard bowl into an empty soup can and added water. He poured the wet ash down the sink drain and washed his hands as

Brennan's '57 Plymouth pulled into Henshaw's driveway. Once Brennan was inside, the black man returned to the table saying, "Let's get back to these arrows. These feathers match the feathers on the arrows we pulled from Mister Hollister's range target."

"All my husband's arrows have blue and white feathers," Helena quickly pointed out, "Which are not his true colors by any means."

"Yes, but they also match in another way," said Walker Thomas.

"I hope this isn't another puzzle," said Helena, "I'm not very good at puzzles. Vinnie always solved the tricky stuff back on the city block. That was before he blew himself up with a pipe bomb."

"Yes.. well. . I'll try to be explicit," said Walker Thomas, "All these arrows have clean, dry feathers. The arrows we pulled from the range target had clean, dry feathers. But the death arrow had soiled feathers. In fact, the death arrow looks like it spent the night out in the rain. And that got me to thinking. Maybe it did. Maybe it spent the night in one of those scattered pipes, Johnson utilized for the safety chain. He didn't bring those pipes that morning like he said. We know that now. He dropped those pipes off late the night before."

"Really," said Helena.

"I have a witness," said Walker Thomas, "Little Timmy Harper."

"A child ?"

Walker Thomas nodded. Timothy Harper was the eldest son of Thomas Harper who owned Harpers Garage, a Hobbs Creek gossip hangout. On the eve of the murder, Timmy and sidekick, Jodie Herman played big-game hunter in the woods near Pykes Pit. It was a last camp-out before school started. The boys hoped to get a bead on the Jersey Devil.

"Of course," said Helena, "The Jersey Devil."

"That's what they said, Ma'am."

Walker Thomas paused to ambush a table fly feasting happily on the peanut butter and jelly stains. He missed and sent his coffee spoon to the floor. He wiped mud from his white shoe tip and sat back up saying, "Timmy never saw the devil, but the boy did see the green pickup at the pit. And the boy did see Mister Johnson unload the pipes for the safety chain."

"And this Timmy whats-his-name saw Abel Johnson with a target arrow?" asked Helena.

"No Ma'am. Timmy Harper did not see Abel Johnson with an arrow in his possession."

"And the other boy?"

"Jodie Herman didn't see anything because he left his glasses home."

A laughing Helena said, "So now you're cross-examining children. You must be single, Lieutenant. Trust me. Never believe anything a child says. I was a child once. They lie a lot."

"Of course if Abel Johnson did take that arrow to the range," mused Walker Thomas, "And if he did conceal the shaft in a pipe. . .well. . .that would account for the soiled feathers."

The black man looked impatiently toward the silent wall phone. He unzipped his tobacco pouch and leisurely repacked the hard bowl. He struck a match. Then another. Stalling for more time he said, "Maybe Mister Hollister meant to kill you. Maybe it was a missed shot that struck Mister Elmer. Maybe Mister Hollister is a Pandarus."

"A what?" asked Helena.

"Pandarus, the infamous archer."

"Lieutenant, I don't know any Pandarus," said Helena, "But I'm sure you would love to tell me."

A delighted Emmet Walker Thomas explained that Pandarus earned fame as the Trojan War soldier who ignited pandemonium with a bow and arrow. The gods ordered the Greek myth hero to kill Menelaus, king of ancient Sparta. The kill shot missed and only wounded Menelaus below the belly.

"You mean he got shot in the balls?"

"No Ma'am," said Walker Thomas, "But that miscue did rekindle the war, and also prevent the peaceful return of Helen Of Troy - which was the will of the gods or so the Iliad goes."

"It does tug at your heart string doesn't it," said Helena locking eyes with the black man, "Lieutenant, I had no motive to kill Elmer Kane."

"It must be tough sittin' on a pot of gold with a locked lid," said Walker Thomas, "I couldn't get any where with this Justin Pierce, but Judge Lucas did subpoena me a copy of the Hollister will. We know about that clause now. The one that Everett Hollister inserted before he died."

"I'm listening," said Helena dryly.

"According to the will," said Walker Thomas, "Your husband is the only legal heir to the Hollister fortune. Should Mister Rodney die from anything but natural causes, the entire estate goes to a boy's school in Nebraska. However, there is a clause in the will that pertains to Missus Hollister."

Helena blew one last smoke ring through her straight white teeth. She snuffed the cigarette and said,

"You can spare me the fine print."

Continued Walker Thomas, "This clause that cuts you off, could possibly be negated. But it would take some doing. Also, it would draw non-stop media glare and round the clock scrutiny - had your husband been killed. However, the way this thing played out, you now stand to get everything. Your husband has no grounds for divorce. He can't throw you out of the house. And while you can't touch the assets, he can't deny you support from the dividends, which come to a very hefty sum."

"Bingo Lieutenant," said Helena, "You now have a motive, anything else?"

The county detective waved the Help-Wanted clipping at Helena. "I called the news paper, Missus Hollister. It took a while but I finally reached the girl who handled this ad for a handyman. She said a female placed the ad over the phone, and the billing went to Betty Grimes in Delaware Township. This Missus Grimes it turns out, lives one block from where you live. The name and address are valid. But, when I called Missus Grimes, she didn't know anything about this ad. So, I have to figure you plan to reimburse her when you get home."

THE PANDARUS FILE

Helena picked up the wall phone. She repeated *hello* a few times and hung up.

"Who was on the phone?" asked the county detective.

"It must have been a wrong number," said the young woman.

"It was not a wrong number, Missus Hollister."

Helena looked puzzled.

The phone rang again. Walker Thomas arose to free a walkie-talkie from an inside pocket. He pulled a shiny antenna up through a scruffy leather case and said, "Bo, can you hear Missus Hollister?"

Walker Thomas looked at Helena. "He can't hear you."

"Who can't hear me," asked Helena.

"Chief Brennan," bubbled the black man, 'He's in a cottage across the lake. He's on the phone with you and he's on the walkie-talkie with me. He can't hear you, but you can hear him. Isn't that right, Missus Hollister?"

Helena's eyes showed genuine alarm for the first time since the investigation began.

"Jeeter Potts worked for the phone company," said Walker Thomas unscrewing the plastic mouth piece from the handset, "He showed me a little trick. This phone and the range phone are both the same type, a non-coin 500. The caps just screw off. That's because this phone is a billing phone, and the range phone is an emergency phone that only connects to the station house."

The black man fished an aluminum disc from a breast pocket and continued, "This is the transmitter disc. No wires. No solder joints. The disc just rests on two contact points. Now, the diaphragm in the top cap is wired. But this transmitter is not wired. This thing just slips in and out."

Walker Thomas dropped the perforated plate into the handset and replaced the cap. He exchanged words with Bo Brennan and then said to Helena, "Bo can hear me now. And I can hear him. We can both hear each other. But without the transmitter in place, this phone only works one way. You can hear a message coming in, but you can't get a message out."

The county detective gathered his jacket and walkie-talkie. He stood by the door and said, "When you left the room to get the hunting arrows, I tinkered with the receiver. I wanted to show how a phone could be out of order and suddenly work again. Now, the other disc - the one from the range phone - I sent that over to the county for fingerprints,"

THE PANDARUS FILE

The black man's steady eyes stared at Helena Hollister as he said, "I know you remembered to wipe your husband's prints from the receiver, Missus Hollister. But. . . did you 'member to wipe your prints off the disc?"

CHAPTER 31

"Maybe she's not gonna spook," grumbled Bo Brennan staring out the windshield of the 1957 police cruiser.

"Perhaps," replied Walker Thomas, "But she can't know we came up dry on the finger prints. She's just waiting for the harborage of darkness."

"The what !" cried Bo Brennan.

"Cover of darkness," explained Walker Thomas, "Harborage means shelter or cover."

"Emmet, where the hell did you go to school !"

The two lawmen sat parked behind a large billboard that overlooked the Route 92 and Lost Trail intersection. Post supper traffic swelled as weekend tourists headed home. The black man peered between flying cars and down the rutted entrance road to Abel Johnson's lonesome cabin. An inside light went on as the porch light flickered off. Asked the black man, "Are you sure he doesn't have a phone? She might be desperate enough to chance a phone call."

"Well, I'm almost sure," replied Brennan.

"Almost sure? I thought were sure."

"I didn't say for sure, Emmet. I said mostly for sure. I don't recall a phone the last time I was in Abel's place."

Walker Thomas winced saying, "I thought you checked the cross reference just to be double sure."

"Emmet, I don't keep records on hunting shacks," muttered the burly police chief pulling crackers from the glove compartment. T'was week three of counting calories and Brennan now weighed a tad under 400 pounds - if you could trust Molly Brennan's bathroom scale, often jimmied to the light side. He stared sourly at the soda wafers before handing the wax container to the county detective. Mumbled Brennan, "Mrs. Rodney Hollister is most likely halfway back to Delaware Township by now, and don't get crumbs on my clean seat covers."

"So when was the last time you actually saw inside Johnson's cabin?" asked Walker Thomas.

"Exactly or approximately?"

"Try to keep it within a century," replied the black man.

"Couple a months back," said Brennan, "Got a stolen property complaint with a description that matched Johnson. Turned out to be Abel. Earlier, I had sent Billy Thompson on a dog call. Only when Billy got to the call site, the dog wasn't a dog. It was a coon. And Billy's a little squeamish about raccoons. So he calls in Johnson who's supposed to be able to trap almost any thing. Johnson sets out a wire cage and winds up with Henry Dooley's pet rabbit. By the time I got out here, Abel had the rabbit in a pot making stew."

Walker Thomas stared at Bo Brennan. Asked the black man, "Is this where you tell me there's a hair in your stew?"

"It's a better line than most of your jokes," said Brennan tuning in the car radio, "And I can tell you for sure that Abel Johnson doesn't have a phone."

"How's that?" asked Walker Thomas as a red Corvette sailed by in the passing lane.

"Our mark?" inquired the burly police chief.

"Wrong year," replied Walker Thomas.

Brennan used a shirted forearm to wipe away windshield condensation. He reset the rear view mirror and wrestled off the new boots. His toes said thank you as he pointed upward. "Look at those line poles. No phone wire, Emmet. At least not on the poles that lead to Johnson's cabin. Which means that Abel still uses Mayo's phone booth for a must call."

"Excellent observation," said Walker Thomas, "We could use a man like you over at the county seat.

Of course, you would have to scrap the cowboy hat."

Brennan pointed to the tree line behind Abel Johnson's cabin and explained, "Our lady can't get in from the rear, either. Once around Johnson's privy, the road turns into a skinny trail that goes nowhere. Folks disappear in them woods and never show up again. Hence the name, Lost Trail."

"Like in the Bermuda Triangle?"

"Or the Boston subways."

"Or maybe that ten spot I gave you to hold for me," said Walker Thomas scratching to open the cracker package, "Anyway, I don't think Missus Hollister will skip out. She's a smart lady. If she walks, Abel talks. She has to know that."

"You want me to help you with that ?" asked Bo Brennan.

"No, I just want the package opened," replied the black man, "I don't want the crackers pulverized and while I'm thinking about it, how did you make out down at the pit?"

Brennan stopped yawning long enough to push a hand through his sandy hair. He closed the Sunday sports section and squelched down the police band to answer the black man's inquiry. "You had to be there, Emmet. Quayle wouldn't play the part of Johnson because Quayle didn't want to get muddy. So, I had Potts pretend to be Johnson, and Quayle pretend to be Hollister. Then I had to send Kramer for more water to duplicate the crime scene because Potts stumbled over the buckets. We had to bury the bow in the mud to keep it submerged. The arrow got stuck up the pipe, which threw our time table off. As Quayle took a shot downrange and turned around, Potts didn't even have the second bow loaded yet,

"You really had to be there," snickered the burly police chief, "But I can tell you this much. Abel didn't have any bow hidden in a mud puddle."

"And the range guard never turned up any thing ?" asked Walker Thomas.

"Not a clue," replied Brennan, "No foxholes or trap doors in the basin floor. No hidden caches any where. Nothing unusual topside. Kramer did come up with a theory, however."

"Good," said Walker Thomas polishing off the soda crackers, "We need some input on this case."

"Freddie thinks the Jersey Devil did it."

"You want to hand me my tobacco," said the black man.

"It's just a thought," mumbled Brennan.

"Looks like you are sitting on it," said Walker

Thomas.

Brennan tossed over the leather pouch and said that Quayle and Potts also came up with theories. Quayle believed that Elmer and Rodney Hollister were past their ill feelings. Quayle suggested that Helena Hollister lured Elmer to the pit on a promise to learn archery. Thus, they would have brought a second bow with them.

Walker Thomas opened the car door to pack his hard bowl. He banged dead ash against a nearby tree and said, "I'm listening."

"Once Elmer and the woman reached the ridge top," said Brennan, "Quayle thinks Mrs. Hollister threw the bow down to Johnson who made the death shot, and then threw the bow back up. After which, Mrs. Hollister hid the bow in the nearby underbrush until Rodney Hollister left the area. Then, Mrs. Hollister stowed the bow in Abel Johnson's pickup, far from the crime scene, "Quayle points out that if Helena Hollister and Abel Johnson did in fact kill Elmer Kane, then Mrs. Hollister could have delayed screaming until they set the stage they wanted Rodney Hollister to witness," concluded Brennan.

"And Potts' theory?" asked the black man.

"Jeeter thinks Johnson had a tiny cross bow hidden up his underwear," said Brennan sniffing the night air, "Emmet, I hope you're not setting the woods on fire with that pipe ash."

The county detective fingered his tiny mustache, thoughtfully. "I like Quayle's thinking but it's contrary to the footprints. Also, Missus Hollister and Johnson could not toss a bow in and out of the pit without tipping off Elmer Kane."

On that September Sunday in 1958, Cincinnati swept a double header from the Phillies, 6 to 4, and 9 to 2. Growling, Brennan snapped off the dashboard radio. He mentioned the possibility of a major sports complex coming to Delaware Township, and tossed the news paper into the back seat. He studied the north bound traffic now reduced to clusters, and listened as a waking hoot owl sounded bedtime.

"I hear you," said Walker Thomas, "But as long as we come this far, we need to sit it out."

Stillness filled the night air, but for rustling leaves and a few million noisy crickets. The two men stared at the star-studded system we call the Milky Way. Walker Thomas identified the Big Dipper and the North Star. He was about to expound on black hole theories when Bo Brennan began to snore, and the Red Corvette rolled into sight, simultaneously.

"It's the fourth car in line!" cried the black man

"And she's got her right-hand signal on," said Bo Brennan waking up fast, "She's going to make the turn into Lost Trail."

Walker Thomas grabbed a flash camera from the rear seat and said, "We let her drive down to the cabin. We wait until she's inside. Then we move in. No head lights, and kill the engine early. With a little luck, we can catch them exchanging money."

"Just like that?" snorted Brennan.

"I said with some good fortune."

Luck was with the lady. Before Helena Hollister could reach the intersection, the lead car braked for a deer that picked that moment to cross Route 92. The second car in line slid into the lead car. The third car slammed into the second car.

"Shit," said Bo Brennan switching on the siren and bubblegum light. He grabbed for the two-way, "Potts!. ..we got an accident out here. .we're gonna need the ambulance!"

As the police cruiser pulled onto the high way, Helena Hollister turned off the direction signal and continued on down the road.

"Damn," said the two lawmen in unison

. CHAPTER 32

Dateline: Post 911

"Damn," said agent Jeremy Wade as the red jacket and black hat failed to step off the bus marked Los Molinos.

"Tracker Two-Eight, this is Tracker Six," cried Wade making phone contact.

"Board the bus, Jeremy," instructed the distant voice.

The driver didn't speak English, but understood the badge and kept the bus docked. Jeremy studied the remaining passengers. One thin man wearing an orange shirt clung to a little boy. A suit and tie studied an open newspaper. The remaining male was bald with a potbelly.

"Somebody forgot their wraps," called out a female voice from the rear.

"Damn," said Jeremy.

The red poplin jacket and black knit cap were jammed under the last row of seats. Jeremy renewed phone contact and then returned to the medium strip at Manuel Becerra. He picked up the stolen bike from beneath the evergreens as sirens drew closer. He stared up at the Optica Roma sign on a nearby high rise as he muttered into the two-way, "Frank, we have another problem."

"This is Tracker Two-Eight come back."

"I'm surrounded by cops."

CHAPTER 33

Monday, September 8, 1958

Helena Hollister again packed for the return trip to Delaware Township. Abel Johnson sat in his cabin with a morning coffee and stewed over the newspaper ad that promised him money, but at a later date. The two Elk County lawmen were one chore away from Pirates Cove, a fresh water oasis just south of Hobbs Creek.

"So why is we papering the ceiling?" asked the black man trying to push the refrigerator aside.

"Because this is our ticket to go fishing," said Bo Brennan, "And don't worry about that ice box. If we don't move it, we don't have to paper behind it."

Toby Gillis returned from the cove earlier with a trunk load of catfish. Toby was the local postmaster and parttime fire chief. Toby also knew about Bo Brennan's *top secret* fishing hole.

"I just hope that idiot don't fish it dry," said the burly police chief, "And we're papering the ceiling cause Molly wants it papered. This is supposed to be the new look"

"Papering three walls and painting over one is considered today's look," said Walker Thomas, "And for what it's worth, Captain Lewis pulled our guard off the pit sometime last night, which means your man will git no shift relief."

Wasted cut-offs and spent razor blades littered the green linoleum floor. A teeming trashcan set near by. Bingo stretched across a hairy doormat, head nestled between forepaws, eyes alert, daring someone to spill paste. A warm water bucket leaned against a cast iron radiator. The next strip in line draped the kitchen table. Said Bo Brennan from a shaky step ladder, "Hand it up to me, Emmet and don't fret about Freddie. The mayor already sent him home for budget reasons."

"I hope you're giving the paper time to relax," called in Molly from the hallway.

"The paper can relax when I relax," growled Bo Brennan.

"Did you say something, dear?"

"No I didn't," called back Brennan pushing the maverick strip across the ceiling, with a stiff brush strapped to a broomstick. The paper end over the stove drooped. He gave the wanton flap a coax. It drooped again and he gave it a whack. Growling, he wrapped fresh tape around the double handles as he went on to explain to Walker Thomas, "Seems your county man grabbed all the daylight hours, so Freddie hit the department up for bonus time, which didn't sit well with His Honor. The good news is that now we get our range back."

Walker Thomas combed white paste from his silver hair and washed up at the sink. He toweled off and stared out the side window. A schoolboy sat on the tailgate to a melon truck. Two angry pedestrians pushed the curbside button on Hobbs Creek's moody traffic light. As the melon driver worked a frustrated U turn over a wayward shopping cart, the agile youngster jumped free and disappeared. Said the black man, "And now for the bad news, Bo. This thing's gittin' away from us fast. I talked to John Kane. He stays in contact with colleagues from other banks. Kane told me that Missus Hollister deposited ten thousand dollars back into a branch account at First Savings early this morning."

"Well, sometimes justice takes a holiday," said Brennan inching up the ladder. He used a straight edge and fresh blade to trim the final strip. He wiped away excess paste and stepped down to survey the job. "How's it look?"

The first strip had went up slightly crooked which caused each additional piece to gap at one end and overlay the other. Seams only butted here and there. One strip was on backwards.

"It looks good," said Walker Thomas as Hobbs Creek's newest law officer appeared in the doorway. The rookie paused for air. His eager eyes looked troubled.

"What is it, Quayle?" asked Brennan.

"Sir," said a young Adam Quayle, "Bertha Curdy has a bat in her bedroom and I think that last strip just came down."

"Bertha Curdy could use the company," said Bo Brennan pulling Bingo out of the trash basket. He wiped flour paste from the dog's nose, and grabbed a yardstick to coax the fallen strip from behind the radiator. He yelled for Molly to call the dog. "Before he throws up!"

"What should I do, Sir?" asked Quayle.

"Send Potts over there," replied Brennan. "Have him close the windows and open the door. The bat will fly out."

The rookie officer shifted uncomfortably, "Sir, Corporal Potts is not here."

Overnight, Nikita Khrushchev rudely demanded President Eisenhower pull the 7th Fleet out of the Quenoy Islands. This headline news rattled cold war sabers, and sent Jeeter Potts back to Pastor Rodgers for another Armageddon talk. *Especially now with the A-Bomb being a world, play toy.* Potts also told Rodgers that Russia might arm a Sputnik with an A Bomb. Rodgers told Jeeter to give up Rock And Roll music and attend church on Sundays. Jeeter Potts was now back at Fishers Pond waiting for the sky to fall.

Bo Brennan opened his mouth, closed his mouth and then shook his head in disbelief. He handed Adam Quayle the car keys and said, "Stop at Mayos and put the gas on our tab. Then round up Jeeter and get him back here. I'll tend the desk. And Quayle, don't be peeling tires."

Sometime later, Brennan returned with two cups of station house coffee, plus a candy bar behind a pocket flap. He put fresh water down for Bingo and stared at the detective lieutenant. A nearby paint can remained closed. An open newspaper covered the floor. Said Brennan, "I can't believe that woman would run through the house with a bucket on her head. Bats don't attack your hair. That's just an old wives tale. And Emmet, I thought you were gonna paint the window, you being so good with detail and all."

"Bo, look at this," said Walker Thomas studying a newspaper ad for Reynolds Shooting Supplies, "Here's a bow identical to the one Mister Hollister owns. I think they call this a re curve."

"It is a re curve, Emmet," said Bo Brennan, "But that's not a local shop."

Walker Thomas pushed Bingo off the wrinkled paper and motioned for Brennan to look closer, Said the black man, "Tell me what you see."

"I see a bow," replied Bo Brennan.

"Yes, but look just over the grip, right where my finger is pointed."

"I see a paw print and some dry mud, Emmet. What do you see?"

Replied the black man, "There's a small clip here that looks like a steel strip. Wish I knew what that was."

*   *   *   *   *

"That is an Audio Release Gauge," said Harry Reynolds tapping the metal strip mounted on a bow held by Walker Thomas, "I'm sorry I hung up on you guys. I didn't know you were police officers. I had lane trouble when the phone rang, and I'm on today by myself."

"I didn't know anything like this existed," said Bo Brennan.

The three men faced downrange in Reynolds' shooting gallery, located just south of Camden City. Six narrow lanes spanned the cinder block building entitled Archers Alley. Paper covered, straw stood as targets. Motors and chain pulleys brought the bales up to the firing line.

"My ad reads Shooting Supplies because indoor archery has not really caught on yet," explained Harry Reynolds.

Originally the flat roof structure was a bowling alley operated by pin boys, and then a warehouse for surplus furniture. An influx of houses with automatic pinsetters closed the bowling lanes. Sudden tax increases sent the sofas and settees to South Carolina. Harry Reynolds took over the lease from a car dealer who wanted to sell Edsels.

"Have you ever used an Audio Release Gauge before?" asked Harry Reynolds.

"Emmet's not into shooting bow," said Brennan.

"I didn't think so," said Reynolds easing the bow from the black man loading an arrow, "Anyway, I believe indoor bow shooting will be the next big craze. That's why I keep up on the latest methods and equipment."

"And this Audio Release Gauge is some thing new?" asked Walker Thomas.

"It's new for this area," said the fidgety forty year old, "Don't know for sure where it started."

"I like the no-walking part," said Bo Brennan pulling house arrows from a punctured bulls eye.

Reynolds pushed the bottom button on a nearby electric box and the straw bale creaked back down range. He picked a cigarette butt off the floor as he pointed to a wide red line that crossed the building. Explained Reynolds, "This is the firing line. The shooter never steps beyond this point. It's a safety feature that keeps my insurance rates down. I work a lot with beginners and it's hard to watch everybody all the time, especially when the weather turns cold and I get busy."

A gold tooth showed as Reynolds again tapped the Audio Release Gauge and said, "Now this little gimmick, I sell these year around. They work good for the novice who can't achieve a consistent bow pull."

"And Mister Hollister shot bow here?" asked Walker Thomas.

"He was one of my first customers."

"And he had one of these ARG clips?"

"Put it on myself," said Harry Reynolds as the entrance buzzer sounded, "The ARG clip doesn't come with the bow. It's an accessory. Like buying a car. Everything's optional. I sell bows that don't have a sight. You have to pick your own. I sell arrows without heads. You can choose your own feathers. Wide. Narrow. Any color."

Brennan pulled Helena Hollister's picture from his vest pocket. "Did she ever come in here?"

Harry Reynolds studied the photograph and whistled. He lowered bushy eyebrows and shook his head no.

"Are you sure?"

"Trust me," replied Reynolds running for the phone, "I haven't seen anything like that since I stood door at The Ritz. Most the women who come in here have hairy forearms and leg muscle knots."

Reynolds hung up from the call and paused over the water cooler. He waited on a customer peeking into a glass display case stocked with finger gloves, arm guards and bow straps. He returned to find the black man sorting through bows stored in wire containers that headed each shooting lane. Reynolds asked, "Is there something else, Lieutenant?"

"I notice these bows don't have an ARG clip," said Walker Thomas.

Harry Reynolds smiled patiently and stacked the house arrows points down, feathers up. "Notice the length on these arrows, Lieutenant. They are all different sizes. And this laminated bow is a house bow. That's why it doesn't have an Audio Release clip. This equipment is for folks who come in with no gear. They also don't have the same arm span. Therefore, an ARG clip would be useless."

Seeing the question mark on the black man's face, Reynolds went on to explain that custom arrows get sized down. "We have a little machine out back that matches the shaft to the shooter's arm length."

"He cuts the arrows!" cried Walker Thomas swapping looks with Bo Brennan.

"That's what I'm trying to tell you," said Harry Reynolds, "An ARG clip won't work unless the shafts are custom cut."

Walker Thomas shoved on his black dress hat and shortened a parting handshake. He stuffed the hard bowl into a shirt pocket and stopped at two busy phone booths just outside the building. He shouted over traffic noise to the burly police chief, "Will that two-way of yours work up here?"

"I can try a patch-through," said Bo Brennan emerging into the sunlight.

Seeing the impatient black man, a teenage caller held up his middle finger. Walker Thomas motioned to Bo Brennan who immediately pulled the bearded youth from the glass doors and sat him on top of the phone booth.

"Bo," barked Walker Thomas, "Radio Quayle first. Have him detain Helena Hollister. I don't care how he does it, but don't let her leave the county. Then contact Bucky Harris. Tell him we need a crack shot marksman with a bow. Have the bowman meet us at Pykes Pit. We'll pick up Johnson on our way in."

The black man fished for pocket change and phone numbers.

"After I call headquarters I need to verify some thing with Reynolds," he added trying to out yell the livid youth perched on the phone booth.

The four letter words stopped abruptly when Bo Brennan tossed the boy's motorcycle into a passing garbage truck.

CHAPTER 34

The strapping ex military man stepped up to a rickety card table hastily assembled near Lane 14. He wore a crew cut and an olive drab uniform. A missing patch imprint said he retired as sergeant. A swagger told the world he once gave orders for a living.

"This is John J. Streaker," announced Walker Thomas emptying pipe ash onto the basin floor. Overhead, tree tops swayed in an afternoon wind gust. Dead leaves swirled in growing numbers. The single phone line that spanned Pykes Pit took off spinning like a schoolgirl's jump rope. Unhurried, the black man re-packed the hard bowl and hand-cupped a match for lighting. He turned back to the group and said, "Thank you for your patience. We can now wrap up this case with everybody's cooperation."

"His name is Stryker," said Bo Brennan trying to whisper upwind, "John J Stryker. Like in striking out."

Duplicates of Rodney Hollister's shooting gear lined the folding table: one bow with an ARG clip; one black quiver almost new; one finger glove; one arm guard; and ten arrows minus the death arrow that Walker Thomas held aside. The black man explained the restrictions on trial exhibits, and why Judge Lucas had to appoint a courier to match bow and shaft sizes. Thus, the shooting gear arrived last amid some grumbles now subsiding.

"At least the sun won't be a factor," muttered Stryker eying angry clouds off to the south. He used a foot and some knee leverage to slip the string onto the bow. Then he said, "If we're gonna do this we better get it on."

Walker Thomas leaned toward Bo Brennan to ask, "Who is this John J. Stryker?"

"Williams isn't home from work," whispered back Brennan referring to ace archer, Mark Williams. "Bucky then called this guy who's also an expert bowman. And, he's experienced with the audio clip."

"Does he have the right arm span?" asked the black man.

"He does," said Bo Brennan.

Walker Thomas signaled for silence and said, "Now folks...John Jay here has volunteered to help us out. He has the same arm span as Mister Hollister, and matching arm spans is vital to this demonstration."

Helena Hollister lit a cigarette while checking her white tennis shorts for dirt marks. A nearby Abel Johnson stood quietly with hands on hips and stared at the blue uniforms posted about. His real eye looked jumpy. Said Helena, "I hope this little side show doesn't waste every one's time."

Walker Thomas looked to the path where two county detectives erected a cardboard figure shaped like a man. Pointing upward the black man said, "That is the spot where Elmer Kane was shot. The distance from this firing line to that silhouette is 75 ft. And, the distance from this firing line to the bulls eye on Lane Fourteen, also measures 75 feet."

"That means both distances are equal," said Adam Quayle stepping up to join the black man. Then catching a look from Bo Brennan, the eager rookie re took his position next to the fragile desk clerk.

"And you Jeeter," said Brennan quietly, "Either turn off that noise you call music, or hop it back to the station house and relieve Kramer."

"I would really like to get started before the rain hits and feathers get wet," said Stryker.

"I thought Jeeter had the day off," whispered Walker Thomas handing the marksman an arrow.

"He does," whispered Brennan, "But he got wind of this demonstration and forgot about working on his time machine, or whatever that contraption is in my garage."

"So that's why the cruiser's outside," whispered Adam Quayle.

"It's in the genes," growled Brennan, "Jeeter's grandfather was an inventor of sorts. Came up with an electric car that used a patchwork of extension cords."

"You can't be serious," said Adam Quayle .

"Gospel truth," replied Bo Brennan, "All his neighbors kept tripping over electric wires."

"We're underway," barked John J. Stryker from the firing line. He readied an arrow. He locked onto a sight picture and hit the bulls eye on Lane 14. The shot made Bo Brennan whistle and the black man smile.

"I talked to a Mr Harry Reynolds at a Camden County indoor target range," said Walker Thomas addressing the group, "Mister Hollister practiced bow there. He bought equipment there. Also, this Harry Reynolds verified that Mister Hollister liked to experiment with new techniques. In short, anything that might better his inadequate skills."

An impatient John J. Stryker whirled and fired at the cardboard silhouette that stood halfway up the walkway. Feathers whistled. The silver shaft gleamed. The arrowhead pierced the dummy's cardboard neck.

"Sergeant Miller," called out the black man, "Would you stand that silhouette back up and fix the bracing better, thank you."

Flying sand and a stubborn tripod leg made for minor headaches above. Eventually the card board cut-out stood back in place. Meanwhile, another arrow hit the bulls eye downrange.

"Harry Reynolds fitted Rodney Hollister's bow with an Audio Release Gauge on August 30th," said Walker Thomas waving a yellow receipt for all to see, "I don't think you knew that, Missus Hollister. I don't think you knew your husband bettered his bow with an ARG clip. That was the Saturday you duped Mister Hollister into returning home for the so-called forgotten shooting gear. I have the receipt right here. You didn't know he visited Reynolds Shooting Supplies before he made the return trip."

Helena lit a cigarette and blew a smoke ring skyward. She said coolly, "I'm listening."

Walker Thomas turned toward John J. Stryker to ask, ""Would you show everybody what an Audio Release Gauge looks like?"

The marksman pointed to the steel spring clip mounted just above the bow grip.

"The purpose of the ARG clip is to gauge the target shooter's draw," continued the county detective, "You load the bow with the arrow running through the clip. Should you release the arrow prematurely, the feathers will snag causing an errant shot. You have to pull the shaft completely through the Audio Release Gauge to make the clip snap shut."

John J. Stryker made a dry run with an arrow while explaining, "Listen closely and you will hear the clip snap shut. It's that snapping noise that tells the shooter when to release the bow string."

"I've done a fair amount of game hunting and I never needed no dime store gadgets," said Abel Johnson spitting tobacco juice into a coffee container left behind by Freddie Kramer.

"The ARG clip is not for game hunting," said Adam Quayle, "The ARG clip is for *known distance* shooting."

"Quayle, Lieutenant Thomas has the floor," growled Brennan, "And Potts I'm not telling you again about that radio."

"If my hair gets wet," said Helena checking for raindrops, "I'm going to be pissed."

Walker Thomas held up a hand for silence and then echoing the marksman, the black man said, "It's that snapping noise that tells the shooter when to release the bow string."

THE PANDARUS FILE

John J. Stryker continued to alternate arrows into the targets. Feathers wedged between feathers as steel points pounded the perspective bull eyes. The swirling wind suddenly softened making the task easier. Stryker's sixth shot went down range, his seventh was earmarked for the dummy that waited on the path. Walker Thomas handed the arrow to Stryker who aimed, fired and then blinked as the howling missile flew high over the target.

A hush fell over the basin, then a buzz.

"That!" cried Walker Thomas, "Was the death arrow. . . . . Sergeant Miller !"

"Yes Lieutenant?"

"Did you see where that arrow went?"

"Yes Lieutenant."

"Please fetch it down here," said the black man "And bring the arrows from the dummy."

While Sergeant Miller worked topside, Adam Quayle retrieved the lane target arrows. When all shafts were back on the table, Walker Thomas waved another paper slip and said, "This is a second receipt from Reynolds Supplies. Mister Hollister had six arrows custom cut on that same day he bought the ARG clip. It's right here on this receipt. Six shafts sized to exactly twenty-nine and one-quarter inches."

"Lieutenant, this is old ground," said Helena, "Shaft count means nothing. You can't prove how many arrows Rodney actually took to the range."

"We're not concerned with arrow count," said Walker Thomas stacking the silver shafts nocks down, points up. One tip stood above the rest. Said the black man, "That's the death arrow. That arrow is three quarter inch longer than the custom cut shafts. It's that extra length that made John J's last shot miss high. Which brings us to our point. You can't use an ARG clip effectively if the shaft length doesn't match the shooter's arm span."

Walker Thomas challenged the wind to relight the hard bowl. He turned back to face Helena Hollister and Abel Johnson and said, "I don't think Rodney Hollister used a longer arrow on that fateful Sunday morning. It would negate the ARG clip. He was practicing with the shorter arrows. I think you two brought the death arrow down here."

A low whistle sounded from the crowd. Jeeter Potts turned the radio off completely as the basin fell silent, a hush broken only by the hungry hawk that patrolled Pykes Pit. The scavenger's piercing scream echoed through the basin, freezing the squirrel that lived on the overhead phone line.

THE PANDARUS FILE

"I don't see how Mister Hollister could have made that shot," said Walker Thomas staring at the Hobbs Creek handyman, "Not under the light of this new evidence. What do you think, Suh?"

Abel Johnson shifted feet. Sweat beads formed on his forehead. He stopped spitting and looked toward Helena Hollister.

"Not with the two shooting distances being so identical," continued the black man, "Not using the same sight picture but with a longer draw to clear the clicker. I don't think anybody could make that shot."

Helena frowned. She flashed Abel Johnson a *keep quiet* look. She lit a fresh cigarette. She blew a defiant smoke ring at Walker Thomas and muttered, "We'll take this up with my lawyer."

"It is ironic Missus Hollister," said the gimpy black man from Macon Ga., "You designed identical shooting distances to add credibility to your story, and to Mister Johnson's story. That's why the one rail post was raised. That was a distance marker. It was your job to make sure Elmer Kane stopped at that point. You needed to show that Mister Hollister could make that shot despite his ineptness with the bow and arrow. And it's these equal distances that will establish his innocence."

CHAPTER 35

On September 23, 1963 a Mt Loyal jury found Rodney Rowand Hollister guilty of killing one Elmer Lewis Kane.

The media-covered trial took an unusual turn when District Attorney, Kelsey Fortes filed the jury into Pykes Pit for a second ARG demonstration. Again, John J. Stryker fired a death arrow replica. This time the 30-inch shaft hit dead center because Stryker did not load the arrow through the clicker. The point was to show how easily the ARG clip could be neutralized. After which, Judge Lucas struck ARG demonstrations and arrow lengths from the record.

Eventually, the Hollister lawyer team won out over the John Kane charisma, and the murder charge dropped to manslaughter. Sometime later, Rodney Hollister died fighting an inmate over a chicken leg that rolled onto the damp prison floor. The knife was tagged contraband, and changed the prison's search & seize procedures.

On September 9, 1958, one day after the first ARG demonstration, Abel Johnson died from smoke inhalation when his cedar log cabin caught fire. Body bruises revealed that the Hobbs Creek handyman had been kicked unconscious and then gagged and bound.

Shortly thereafter, a forest ranger spotted the Venetian Red Corvette deep in the South Jersey, Pine Barrens behind Johnson's cabin

Helena Hollister was not with the car. The red headed temptress vanished, holding the missing piece to the Pykes Pit puzzle.

CHAPTER 36

Dateline: Post 911

Jacquas Paul Bardeau took a window seat that overlooked the Capri Harbour. He ordered a bottle of Amarone, and studied his rugged looks in the polished table top. He needed some sleep and a good shave. He waved off a singing waiter and was halfway down a crinkled menu when the old man entered the cafe.

"Jocko?" queried the newcomer.

"Monsieur, we are not acquainted," said Bardeau with a wave off of the arm, "This table is taken."

The old man toted a black leather satchel. He walked too steady for a cripple with a cane. His gray beard looked pasted on. He whispered to the waiter and then joined Bardeau at the table.

"Monsieur, you must leave," cried the French man nodding toward two gay men across the room, "Mademoiselle will join me shortly. She will think I am one of them."

The old man dropped the cane and peeled off the beard. He pulled the red jacket and black cap from the satchel. "You left these on the bus, Sir."

THE PANDARUS FILE

Jacquas Paul Bardeau arose to run. Jeremy Wade flashed the 9mm and the Frenchman sat back down. He filled a second wine glass and sighed, "How did you find me?"

"One of the passengers heard you mention you needed sea legs to ride that bus," said the rookie agent pushing aside the offer, "Then it hit me that you might have a boat."

Jeremy Wade pointed toward the Grande Marina. "I found the boat. I saw the name Helena painted across the stern. That's when I knew you would be back."

Jacquas Paul Bardeau sliced a thick slab of house cheese. He drank both glasses of wine, made the sign of the cross and said, "I wish for that the bull had got you, what is it you want, Monsieur?"

"I want a name," said Jeremy Wade.

*   *   *   *   *

"Holy shit!" cried Adam Quayle into the red phone sometime later, "It's the lawyer! That's how she did it. That's how she broke the will and laundried the money out of the country. She ran off with the freaking probate lawyer. . .Jeremy, have your people check data banks. I'll call Mt Loyal on this end. Maybe we can come up with something."

CHAPTER 37

The ominous jumbo jet dropped through lightning and bounced onto a Nassau International runway. Once inside the Lynden Pindling terminal, Jeremy Wade found the rendezvous sign that read *Baggage Weight Allowances.* Sometime later, he boarded a return trip with a prisoner in tow. There was a brief altercation over tight handcuffs as they took their seats.

"Sorry sir," said Jeremy unlocking the cuffs, "I don't know why the transfer officer used these things. Miss-communication, probably. My orders said *escort only.* You did waive your extradition rights and we tried to be discrete as possible."

The prisoner was Attorney Justin Pierce, his once sharp eyes now glassy, his trim mustache now mousy gray. He stared silently at his polished oxfords and the black knee socks that became his trademark wherever he went. He grimaced as Jeremy Wade relayed the accident details that took Helena Hollister's life.

"I'd like to see the body," Pierce said in a next day face-down with Adam Quayle, "You are bringing the body back?"

"I can't promise that," replied the Hobbs Creek police chief rocking back in the squeaky swivel chair, "You know the red tape tied to an overseas body. Who is Jacquas Paul Bardeau?"

"Our boat captain," said the one time probate lawyer for Everett Hollister, "Jocko called me when Helena went missing. Suddenly, every thing turned hush hush and I knew you were after me. Jocko's job was to clean up the paper trail. Unfortunately, he bumped into your man in Madrid."

"And Abel Johnson?"

"He wasn't stable," said Justin Pierce, "He had to be neutralized. Funny, now thinking back... Johnson tried to rape Helena... which was a joke. She took his eyes out with her bare feet. Stalked him around that cabin like a hungry cat, and literally beat the shit out of him. Then we dumped the car."

"Who set the fire?" asked Adam Quayle.

Justin Pierce looked away as he owned up to burning out the remote log cabin. He found gasoline in Johnson's tool shed. He got the match from Helena. What they didn't count on was the fire company being that alert at 2am in the morning. Said Pierce, "Lucky for us the bastard died before he came to."

Adam Quayle took a crank call and hung up. He rose slowly from the desk. He turned his back to Justin Pierce and stared out the window that overlooks Elm & Main. The bank is still there, but the card shop and Millies Meat Market are long gone.

"I remember when I first saw Helena," continued Justin Pierce, "She came bouncing into our Camden office seeking a divorce. I don't think she even knew we worked for old man Hollister. I listened to her tale of woe and told her to forget it. As it turned out, it was me who couldn't forget her."

"Justin," said Adam Quayle quietly, "There's no statue of limitations on murder."

"Adam, don't quote me the law!" snapped Justin Pierce, "I closed the case for you. Let it go at that."

The current Hobbs Creek Police chief nodded to Jeeter Potts who hit a computer key on his laptop. The signal woke up a sleepy printer two doors down the hall. Potts then brought the paperwork back from the computer room, and dropped the confession in front of Justin Pierce for signature.

EPIALOGUE

Maggie the matron watched Jeeter Potts and Bo Brennan steal down the west wing of the Shady Rest Nursing Home, and head toward the exit sign. The stocky woman smirked and pulled a red cord that ran throughout the one story building. Other blue clad attendants came running.

Brennan and Potts set off a second alarm going out the door.

Maggie blew into a shiny yellow whistle.

Brennan and Potts failed to halt.

"Code four at door five !" Maggie screeched, "Code four at door five!"

Noisy pursuit stopped abruptly when Brennan blocked the door with a giant marble statue that set just outside the parking lot exit. The former police chief brushed off his hands, straightened somewhat slowly and muttered, "One of these days I'm gonna stick that whistle up that woman's ass."

"I can't believe you still have it in you, Sir," said Jeeter Potts looking back at Willard J. Green carved in stone.

"And I can't believe somebody made a statue of that idiot," said Bo Brennan.

Light rain began falling as the two men pulled into County Memorial Cemetery. Jeeter Potts stayed with the car. Brennan trudged between grave markers. He pulled his faded bomber jacket higher as rain fell heavier. He stopped at a stone that read Emmet Walker Thomas.

Brennan bowed his head. After a long moment he said, "It was a trick, Emmet. An illusion. There never was a second bow. That whistling sound Hollister heard was not an arrow. It was a blow dart. Helena Hollister and Abel Johnson killed Elmer Kane with two fence pipes, a concealed arrow and a blow gun."

The two adversaries had hid the blowgun in a pipe that Johnson used for the firing line barrier. They stowed the arrow in the pathway pipe that Walker Thomas alluded to as the *shiny marker.* Once Johnson brought Elmer Kane down with the tranquilizer shot, Helena finished him off with the arrow. Concluded Bo Brennan, "And she gets credit for this, she used the same hole the dart made in case we ran an autopsy, which of course we didn't."

Brennan smacked his heavy hands together, fist into palm as he had seen Walker Thomas do so very often. "Anyway Emmet, I just thought you would want to know."

"Closure?" asked Jeeter Potts as the former police chief climbed back into the squad car.

"Closure," confirmed Bo Brennan, "Is Grogans' still open?"

"New owners but same draft on tap," said Jeeter Potts.

"And maybe a good cigar ?"

"Now you're talking, Chief."

"Now we're talking, Jeeter."

KYLE KEYES